DEAD TUNES

A Dakota Mystery

M.K. COKER

The Dakota Mystery Series:
Dead White
Dead Dreams
Dead Wrong
Dead Quiet
Dead News
Dead Hot
Dead Poor
Dead Head
Dead Tunes

*Dedicated to my mother, who gave us the gift of music,
and to my brothers, whose musical gifts continue to delight.*

CHAPTER 1

THE SINGER WAS A NATURAL.

The high notes pierced the heavy July air with the confident ease of long practice. Clear, exuberant, with a sexy lilt, his song was projected outward by a bandshell of junipers and cottonwoods and carried far by a wide-open amphitheater of prairie. Dipping and twitching, he sang his heart out, despite the mostly oblivious audience. But one man took note—and marveled. Leaning forward from his higher vantage point, the man tried to catch a better look, wondering if his ears or his eyes deceived him.

With a crack and boom, the song ended abruptly. All nature held its breath. The silence was so profound that even the wind ceased, an almost unheard-of oddity in the Dakotas.

Twenty minutes later, Sheriff Karen Okerlund Mehaffey stood over what was left of the body strewn over gravel and grass, leaving a gaping hole in the ground. She hated the waste of life, any life, but *this*?

Smoke still rose from the rended earth, and clumps of moist clay splayed over the road and even beyond the barbed-wire fence into a flourishing cornfield. The stench of river bottom, no matter the Big Jammer River was miles distant, mixed with the distinctive sharp, stinging smell of explosives. Blood streaked the newly laid gravel like ketchup on fries. But far less appetizing.

Standing at the edge of the destruction, Karen held the back of her hand to her mouth. A large shadow fell over her. Marek Okerlund, her part-time detective and half-uncle, blocked her from the view of the two men behind them. She got in a breath then pressed her hand to her mouth again.

"I can't—" Her voice wavered alarmingly.

"You want me to do this?" he asked in his low, nearly subsonic voice that tickled her ears.

No, she couldn't think of tickles. Take deep breaths, she reminded herself. She ran her sleeve down her face then looked up at him. Unlike her own bland blond so common in the Dakotas, his hair glowed a deep chestnut in the hard glancing light of an evening sun. His goatee edged toward a full beard, giving him a solemn Byzantine air that betrayed his Slavic heritage. Somehow, some way, he was holding it together. Four years her uncle's elder, she should be setting the example. She ran her hands down her brown uniform pants, which felt sticky in the heat. "No, I've got this."

Karen turned on her booted heel to confront the two men who stood on either side of what had once been a pretty, winding road of gleaming white gravel that led up to a Spartan home on a slight—very slight—hill near the Ivy Dordt Nature Preserve, which was mostly prairie. The deck that faced that way was almost as big as the house and held a number of tripods.

She went over to the homeowner first. The ponytailed man in a Grateful Dead T-shirt looked shell-shocked. It wasn't the first time she'd seen him that way. Not long ago, it had been because she'd jailed him on suspicion of murder. But he was that rare man who didn't hold a grudge. "Mr. Aspin, I'm sorry."

His dazed eyes rose to hers. "I don't understand why anyone would do something like this."

No, she supposed he didn't, coming from the Twin Cities as he had, though she had to admit that the recycling center manager had stuck it out when bets had been that he'd flee within a month. Most of his colleagues considered the gulags of Siberia preferable to eastern South Dakota.

She turned to look at the other man, one who'd been born and bred Dakotan.

Karl Fike was the uncle of her night jailer, Jordan Fike. The Fikes were a large German Catholic family in a largely German Lutheran and Scandinavian county. While the Fikes were from Fink to the southeast in her sprawling rural county of Eda, Karl had snapped up some of the fertile bottomlands near the now-defunct town of Dutch Corners, which had been flooded a couple years back. He'd gotten the land for a song, rumor went, from a speculator who'd panicked.

Karen cleared her throat and somehow managed to sound professional, a skill picked up when she'd been a dispatcher in Sioux Falls. Unfortunately, her training hadn't included keeping her expression equally neutral, but she tried. "Mr. Fike, can you tell me why, exactly, you decided to blow up Mr. Aspin's new gravel road?"

Tipping his head back to look up at her, the farmer adjusted his grimy seed cap to keep the glancing sun out of his eyes. While her constituents tended toward giants on the earth, Karl Fike could only be called squat, a good half foot under her six-one. Marek's six-nine positively dwarfed him.

"Can blow up my own land if I want."

That brought Jack Aspin out of his daze. "It isn't your land."

"It is too. Or at least it's the public's, including mine."

Aspin stared at the farmer. "The right of way says—"

"There's nothing right about it."

"You gave me permission for the new road."

"Not on my land. You went over. Land grabbers, carpetbaggers, you city people are all the same—swindling a man, taking a mile when I say an inch."

"What are you talking about? We had it surveyed."

Fike picked up a splintered stake and brandished it in

Aspin's face. "This was the boundary line. If it hadn't been on my land, it wouldn't've blowed, now would it?"

"Well, I suppose the road might have a bit of a curve in it, but that's only artistic license—"

"License? License! I don't give no license to artists or nobody else. That's my land. You've no business calling the law on me. It's me who should be calling it on *you*."

"If you had a problem with the road, why didn't you just say something?"

His brow furrowing, Fike glanced at the hole. "Did."

Karen almost lost it then. But Dakotans tended to act, not speak, unless they were like Karen, who'd inherited the gregarious tongue of her Halvorsen kin. "Gentlemen," she broke in before it came to blows. "You are forgetting the dead."

With a start, they both looked at her then down at the mangled body. Unlike the combatants, the flies hadn't forgotten. Having gained their attention—the men not the flies—Karen said, "I take it there's some question about the ID of the body?"

"I told you on the phone." Aspin's eyes welled. "Kirtland's."

For the first time, caution, even fear, rose in the farmer's eyes, but his chin jutted. "Wilson's."

"We'll let the experts make a determination." She kept herself stiffly erect with the discipline she'd learned in the Army. "Marek, see that the proper procedures are taken, won't you?" She simply couldn't hold back her emotions any longer. "I'll wait for you in the Sub."

Minutes later, Marek got into the passenger seat of the old Suburban that served as her official vehicle. He held a box in his lap. "You left me in the lurch."

"I'm the boss." Well, technically, the county commissioners were his boss, to avoid accusations of nepotism in the chain of command. Still, being sheriff did give her some rights. She put the Sub in drive. To her relief, it responded immediately and got her down the section line road in a cloud of dust. That should cover her. She finally let it all out. "My God,

4

Marek... you didn't so much as twitch. How? Are you a robot?"

Then she heard it, the rumble of laughter that crescendoed until it shook the inside of the Suburban over the rumble of the engine. Joining him, she could barely keep the Sub on the lonesome road, grateful that no one was watching, or they might have taken her for a drunk. After they made it back to the courthouse on Main Street in the county seat of Reunion, Karen and Marek lurched into the office.

Deputy Walter Russell, known to all as Walrus for his bald head and windsock of a mustache, stared at them. But predictably, the important question came first. "Is that food in that box, Okerlund?"

As Marek was still mutely shaking, Karen forced out words. "No...no, it's a...a body."

And she doubled over, hands on thighs.

"Of what, a leprechaun?" Walrus tugged at his mustache, as if unsure whether he was getting his leg pulled. "Geez, what have you two been drinking? Never seen the pair of you laughing like loons."

In the midst of straightening, Karen caught Marek's eye, and that was it. She was running out of air, and no doubt turning blue, when Walter jerked the box from Marek's hands.

Her dayshift deputy, who'd lingered to finish up an accident report, set the box on his desk in the open bullpen and lifted the top. His nostrils flared, and he stepped back in a hurry as he got a blast of the rotting smell. Then, cautiously, he peered back in. "It's a... bird?"

"What's left of it," Karen got out. "Don't touch. It's evidence."

Walrus started to chuckle. "What, did some cat burglar swipe Fanny Kostlan's prize parakeet?"

Karen held up a shaking hand. "Stop. I need to breathe."

"Geez, you're killing me. Spit it out. What's the story behind the bird?"

"Mmm. I'd like to hear it."

Karen turned to see that her two swing shift deputies had come out of the breakroom. Sandy-haired Travis Bjorkland, aka Bork, was the one who'd spoken. He stood with his thumbs hooked in his belt, looking at Karen and Marek as if scaling the heights of their sanity. A Minnesotan from just across the state border, he'd been born in the wrong terrain, as climbing was his passion.

To Bork's right, and always a man apart, was Two Fingers. His high cheekbones and coppery skin belied that he was half—an unwanted and unacknowledged half—white, which had kept him from being enrolled into his mother's tribe at the Flandreau Reservation. His lips pursed, his dark eyes hooded, he looked at her as if trying to size her up for a straightjacket for transport to the looney bin. She got her legs back under her and her lungs filled with air, then she straightened enough to sit on top of an eviction notice on her desk.

"I got a call from Jack Aspin." Her voice wavered until she took another breath. "In a very grim, very distraught tone, he told me, 'You need to come out to my place ASAP. We have a body.'"

Two Fingers's head tilted, his eyes on the box. His lips twitched—slightly. "Aspin's a birder, right?"

Bork's fingers danced on his belt as he smiled. "Someone take a potshot at one of the birds that flew from the nature preserve onto Aspin's property?"

"It's not a crime to kill birds," Walrus grumbled.

Karen tucked her tongue in her cheek. Walrus was well acquainted with killing birds, as he took pride in bagging pheasants—and in eating what he bagged. "Actually, that's the crux of it. Aspin claims that the bird's a Kirtland's warbler. Farmer Fike insists it's just a common Wilson's warbler."

Walrus tugged on his mustache. "What's the difference?"

Karen tested her ribs to make sure she hadn't cracked any. "Oh, only a fifty-thousand-dollar fine and a year in jail. Max penalty, but still."

Walrus's bushy eyebrows shot up. "What the..."

Two Fingers whistled. "Endangered Species Act."

Bork held up hands nicked from bouldering in the Palisades near Sioux Falls. "Wait. Farmer Fike, you said? This just gets better. Jordan's father?"

"No, his uncle. Karl."

Walrus still looked disgruntled. "What was Karl doing shooting at birds? The man's not into recreational anything. All work, no play."

"Collateral damage." Karen didn't look at Marek. "He blew up Aspin's new gravel road because it deviated from the straight and true."

While Bork, and even Two Fingers, started to whoop, Walrus's jaw dropped. "Geez, I thought only Kurt got that uptight."

The oldest and straightest arrow in her quiver, Karen's senior deputy was out on personal leave, taking care of his phobia-prone sister, Eva. If he'd been there, he likely would not have found anything amusing about the situation. The law was the law. Period.

The door down to the jail slapped open, and Tammy Nylander hefted her bulk up the last step and entered. "We have a body."

Hysterical laughter filled the room.

The jailer glared, her rounded face grim. "What's wrong with you people? We have a body. Foul play..."

"Fowl." Walrus gasped. "F-O-W-L."

And the peanut gallery howled.

Karen lifted a shaking finger toward the box.

Tammy stalked over, looked down, and wrinkled her nose, but didn't so much as crack a smile. "I'm dead serious." Hands on hips, she shook her head, an adult among unruly children. "Seoul called it in from the Big Jam."

"The what?" Two Fingers asked.

"The Big Jammer River Music Festival at Grove Park." She crossed her arms across her ample chest. "Someone garroted the frontrunner of the Jam Off contest."

CHAPTER 2

S TEPPING OUT OF THE SUB at the top of a rare hill in Eda County, Marek walked straight into a blizzard. In July, that meant only one thing. Beside him, Karen swatted at the fluff of white that floated down from a blue sky going pale and pastel.

"I thought this park was bur oak, not cottonwood," she grumbled.

Both of them had grown up with the sound of cottonwoods rustling—and tree fluff floating—on the Big Jammer that wound its way through the county. The river snaked below the bluff where they'd grown up across the street from each other—a gulf far larger than the short distance would imply and only recently breached.

"Could've come from anywhere," he commented.

The ever-present wind made sure of that—and it had kicked up again after the brief lull at the nature preserve. But as they walked up the hill from the lower parking lot, their deputies trailing behind, Marek could see a few cottonwoods edging the large open area where lawn chairs grew like happy dandelions in stark contrast to the grim faces. The only music he could hear was from the birds. An undertone of murmurs underlay it, a frisson of unease.

Their newest deputy, Seoul Durr, awaited them at the open-air stage. She'd strung up crime scene tape to one side where a trail led around back. She barely looked legal, much less a force to be reckoned with, with her mop of Irish-setter-colored hair and five-foot-nothing height. That she wore a floaty bit of dress in rainbow hues and silver sandals laced up to a more-than-bronzed midcalf didn't help. But if you looked hard enough, you could see the cop in the tawny eyes: flat, focused, banked and dammed of emotion.

She came by it naturally. Like Karen, Seoul was the daughter of a county sheriff, though in Seoul's case, her father was a current sheriff in Iowa. One who'd wanted his daughter to stay far, far away from a badge, even though he'd trained her in some Korean martial art to take care of herself. She'd earned her spot on the roster by taking down not only Karen but one of the previously all-male roster.

The thought that Seoul was closer in age to his eight-year-old daughter than to himself made Marek feel old. He wasn't quite sure how to take Seoul yet, other than to treat her like a live hand grenade. With respect and distance.

Karen didn't have his reserve and reached out to take the floaty fabric between her fingers. "Pretty." She glanced over the crowd clad mostly in T-shirts, shorts, jeans, and a smattering of overalls from the older folk. "You always dress fancy on weekends, Deputy Durr, or were you on a date?"

A flush arose behind the new-copper-penny skin of her face. "I participated in the Jam Off."

Karen's fjord-blue eyes widened. "Just what's the prize for winning the Jam Off? Tammy said our victim was the frontrunner."

A sound of dissent issued out from a little huddle of men nearby. The deputy's flush deepened. "My opinion—and the crowd's. The Jam Off is for anybody to enter. The winner gets to open the main show on Monday night."

"And gets a record contract," said a sulky-looking young woman covered in body piercings and leather. Her face sported massive amounts of paint that rivaled KISS in their day, with jagged yellow lightning bolts.

Seoul ignored her, other than to say, "The chance of *talking* to the head of a label. Hardly a sure thing."

"If you were good enough, which you weren't with your downer blues, you'd get a contract."

Using what Marek considered heroic willpower, Seoul ignored that jibe. As did the three older men in front of a small tent where a fan whirred. Marek decided they must be the judges of the Jam Off.

With a curt order, Karen sent the rest of her deputies off to start taking statements. Then she sucked in a deep breath, as if to expel the rocker from her orbit, but caught herself. Instead, she fastened on Seoul. "Take us to the scene, Deputy."

Seoul did so with alacrity, passing the scowling KISS wannabe and ducking under the crime scene tape. She led them behind the stage to a large white tent and pulled aside the flap with a gloved hand.

"This is where the contestants kept their instruments and waited for their turn to perform," Seoul explained as she sidestepped a moisture-dripping paper cup just outside the tent. "And where the equipment for tonight's concert is kept."

Marek waited for his eyes to adjust to the dim interior. When they did, he saw large speakers, amps, keyboards, and various musical paraphernalia. The tent must have been put up before the sun and heat had evaporated the dew and rain from the previous night, as the grass was still damp underfoot with a few small puddles.

In the middle of the tent, a beefy, bald man lay sprawled facedown on the beaten-down grass, an electric guitar underneath him as if he'd been playing it when death came to tango. Unlike Seoul, he hadn't dressed up for his performance but down: rumpled knee-length khaki shorts and a worn red T-shirt that said *Music On, World Off* on the back. His feet were bare, a pair of flip-flops flung carelessly nearby.

While they had to await the coroner's final determination, Marek could see the cause of death for himself. Someone had garroted the man from behind with what looked like a thin wire attached loosely to two metal triangles. Percussion triangles, that is. One was larger than the other, probably to make a different sound when struck. But the killer must have used them as handles to gain more leverage, not to mention protecting his or her hands. Had the triangles been brought to the scene already strung with the wire, making it a premeditated killing? Taking a look around, Marek saw a stand with two hooks near a drum set. So it looked like the killer had taken what was at hand. What about the wire? Had it come from the electric guitar, perhaps?

"Who is he?" Karen asked into the hush.

Turning his attention back to the victim, Marek got down on his haunches so he could see the face better. Bearded, round, maybe late fifties or well-aged sixties. A faint memory of another July, another performance, another place. "I know him. Or of him. Hal Birchard." Marek tipped an imaginary straw hat. "He's part of a barbershop quartet."

"A cappella group," Seoul corrected. "With the—"

"Bolvins," Marek completed, getting back to his feet. His boyhood best friend, Nick Bolvin, had grown up in a family with two passions: music and wrestling. Nick and his three older brothers had formed a barbershop quartet that had only been broken up when the eldest had become a wrestling coach in Iowa. From what Nick had said, they'd had a revolving door for the fourth member, until finding the perfect bass several years ago in the man who now lay at his feet. Marek had once talked to Birchard on the phone to verify an alibi but had never actually met him.

"Are the Bolvins here?" Karen looked around as if expecting to see the brothers pop out from behind the looming speakers.

Seoul nodded. "Yes, they're some of the people I've got waiting to be interviewed. But they weren't here as contestants. They're going to open the concert tonight. Or they were. I guess that's not happening now." Seoul's stoic mask slipped. "Mr. Birchard did the Jam Off on his own and nailed it. I've never heard a finer fiddle. Man, he played with majors, minors, riffs, reels, and even used the thing as a percussion instrument. He had the crowd spellbound and foot stomping—and that's Dakotans!"

Karen gave her a long stare and the Iowan deputy gulped dramatically. "They even gave him a standing ovation. Of course, Ms. Heavy Metal Rip-off out there will say it's just because he was the last contestant. But the judges must be tone deaf. They should've declared him the winner on the spot."

Karen bit her lip, her eyes still intent on the body. "Do you happen to know if Mr. Birchard had a family or next of kin that I need to contact?"

"The Bolvins told me he's not married, no kids, and no family that they're aware of."

That was a relief. Notifications were the worst part of the job. Marek frowned down at the body. "That's an electric guitar, not a fiddle."

Seoul stuck out her tongue at Marek before swallowing it, as if recalling her job and the man who lay dead. "I don't think it was his." She nodded toward a fiddle on top of the amp nearby. "That's his instrument."

Keeping his distance to preserve the scene, Marek stepped sideways and over, as did Karen. It was indeed a fiddle, but there was something strange about it, though Marek couldn't quite say what. It wasn't just that the fiddle was unusually decorative, with extensive mother of pearl inlay. Or that above the tuning knobs, similar to a prow to a ship, it sported a carved figure. If Marek wasn't mistaken, the horned figure was a devil. Whimsical in intent, perhaps, it nonetheless cast a sinister gaze down the length of the instrument.

Where one metal string was missing.

CHAPTER 3

SOMEHOW, SOME WAY, THE LONG-BED-PICKUP-SLASH-HEARSE darted through the crowd like a buzzing mosquito through a herd of cattle without earning a manslaughter charge for its driver. At least, if the driver *had* hit someone, he could have given the heirs a nice deal on a funeral.

Their coroner and local mortician, Norm Tisher, braked just inches from Karen's kneecap as she stood awaiting him in the upper parking lot. The night's entertainment had just been canceled, and the crowd had surged toward the parking lots, though a fair number of people were still milling about: gawkers, musicians, organizers, and judges.

Trying to corral and interview almost a thousand people just hadn't been practical. But she had announced that she wanted to hear from witnesses who had seen anyone enter or leave the instrument tent after the last contestant had finished. Or if they had seen Hal Birchard at any point in the day other than his performance. Unfortunately, after the Jam Off was finished, most of the crowd had gone to the concession stands or the johns or were talking amongst themselves as they waited for the judges to select the winner. Even the judges, according to Seoul, had taken a break from their labors when they couldn't come to an agreement.

Karen shielded her eyes from the glare of the sun as Tish uncurled like a spring from the cab, his tall, thin body encased in funereal black. He must have come directly from his work, which was often conducted on evenings and weekends.

"Sheriff." The normal laugh wrinkles around Tish's eyes had lengthened into solemn smoothness. "We have a body?"

Though beside her, a silent Marek twitched, Karen wasn't even tempted to laugh. "We do." She nodded at her detective. "Marek can show you. The cause of death's pretty obvious."

"And foul?"

This time, Karen bit the inside of her cheek to keep her expression in check. Sometimes a little gallows humor helped her make it through the blues of the job. "See for yourself. I'm waiting for DCI."

The South Dakota Department of Criminal Investigation out of their branch office in Sioux Falls was set to arrive at any minute, per the text she'd just gotten.

"Ah..." Now the laugh lines wrinkled back into existence. "Awaiting a certain DCI agent, I expect."

She'd been awaiting that agent for quite some time now—their relationship had stalled. Again. Due to understandable, if frustrating, reasons. As Marek led Tish back to the tent, Karen saw the DCI van's driver—far more controlled than Tish's wild abandon—pick his way through the parking lot stragglers with the practiced precision of a former city cop.

Karen waited as the van came to a stop. Jessica Bakke emerged first, a camera slung over one arm and a shoulder bag over the other.

"Hey, Karen, we've got to stop meeting like this." The young trainee's broad smile tugged at the scar she'd never hidden—or the violent rape that had given it to her. "It's been, like, two months, if that." Jessica looked around with a pout. "And this one's just a repeat. We've been here before."

"Sorry to disappoint," Karen drawled. "But at least this body's not in the john."

Weighed down with several bulging bags of equipment,

Agent Dirk Larson, with his dishwater-blond hair and bullet-gray eyes, scowled at her. "Not diving in sewage again. Ever."

"Won't be a problem. The county commissioners coughed up the money to replace that old vault toilet." Karen felt her lips twitch as Larson continued to scowl at her, frustration furrowing lines into his forehead. That gave her perverse pleasure. "Do I have to produce a body to see you these days, Larson?"

He blew out a breath. "Kids. Move. Grandmother."

Typical bullet-style conversation for Larson.

The DCI agent had been a cop in Chicago before his ex-wife cut him off from his two children, turned them against him, and took his money for their—but mostly her—upkeep. That same ex had abruptly dropped Larson's now-teenage kids in his lap a couple months ago, when she found a better sugar daddy. And Larson had reunited with a grandmother he'd never met before and was in the process of moving from Sioux Falls to Reunion, where his kids were already living with their great-grandmother. His tiny studio apartment couldn't hold much more than a teacup poodle, though it would have starved to death with as little time as Larson spent there.

Larson eyed the crime scene tape under the banners for the Big Jam. "Jelly convention?"

Seoul blew him a raspberry then led the agent back to the scene, with Karen bringing up the tail end. When they got to the tent, Jessica handed out hazmat suits.

Marek's was a special order for his large size, and Jessica eyed Seoul doubtfully. "We might have to special order for you, as well. Kids don't usually work for law enforcement."

Seoul stuck out her tongue but took the smallest of the lot. As she looked up after fastening her own suit, Karen pursed her lips. "You look like Casper the Ghost, Deputy." As Seoul scowled, pushing up the too-long sleeves and stumbling over the too-big booties, Karen fought a laugh. "Special order, it is."

Jessica didn't bother to hide her amusement as she made a note on her phone. "One midget..." Getting the evil eye from Seoul, she backtracked. "Mini-ninja suit on order."

"The taller they are, the harder they fall," Seoul muttered.

Tish came out of the tent, his long face longer than Karen thought possible. "Cause of death is, as you said, obvious. Homicide. A terrible thing to happen at such a festive event." He walked away from them with a flagging step, which was almost frightening for a man normally described as a live wire.

In single file, the rest of them marched in silently to start the crime scene survey. Jessica began setting up the camera lights in the dimming interior of the tent. Larson stood still just inside, only his eyes moving across the landscape as if he were a member of Lewis and Clark's expedition—a corpse of discovery instead of a corps.

"You doing okay?" she asked him in an undertone. "Kids?"

"Busy," he replied, and she wasn't sure if he meant he was busy *now* and not to bug him, or if he and the kids were busy, and he didn't have time to think about anything else.

"Wire?" he asked. Well, that answered where his mind was. He was in work mode.

Marek nodded toward the amp. "Think it came from his fiddle there."

Larson reached down into his bag of tricks and pulled out a fingerprint kit.

Karen watched him do his business, his strokes sure and quick. She sighed when the fiddle turned up as clean as a whistle.

Seoul threw up her ghost arms. "We've got nothing."

"Nothing tells you something," Larson countered, giving the new deputy a hard look. He didn't tolerate fools on his crime scene, something Karen had learned the hard way on her first homicide when she'd compromised the scene.

"Oh." Seoul frowned. "Okay. Clean. Wiped?" The frown

disappeared. "So it's telling us what we already suspected—that the missing wire from the fiddle *is* our murder weapon."

Jessica lowered her camera from photographing the body, which the rest of them were ignoring, including Karen. She didn't want to think too much about a life cut short, a talented one at that. It would drive her mad—or make her mad.

"Or maybe Birchard was just obsessive-compulsive about his instrument," Jessica offered.

"But then why leave it out like that?" Karen asked. "Seems an OCD would put it back in its case to keep it in its pristine state."

"And where's the case?" Marek asked.

Smiling faintly, Larson turned away from the fiddle. "Points to the Okerlunds."

Jessica gave them a mock glower. "Teacher's pets."

With his gloved hands, Larson made a time-out gesture. "Time to turn the body. Detective?"

While Jessica began filming, Karen stepped back out of the way, glad to let Marek use his brawn. With his characteristic gentleness, he turned the heavy body while Larson eased over the guitar strapped to the torso. In the glare of the lights, the ruddy face looked almost sunburned, or perhaps he really was, though the full salt-and-pepper beard made it difficult to tell.

Seoul swallowed hard at the congealed blood around the neck and beard. Her skin greened like verdigris on copper. Karen gave her a sharp look, ready to tell her to take it outside, but with a deep breath, the young deputy pulled herself together.

"That's odd." Marek rose to his feet.

Karen looked back at the body. Blocking out the obvious, she slowly looked from the top of the bald head, down the length of the beefy body, then back up—halfway. "His hands."

"Another point," Larson murmured. "Improving."

"Thanks, Teach," she said.

Seoul bit her lip. "What's wrong with his hands? They're clutching the guitar. He must have been playing it when someone came up behind him and—"

Karen hooked her deputy around the neck and almost got herself thrown over the mini-ninja's head.

"Oh," Seoul said in a small voice as she gripped Karen's arm. "Gotcha. Someone tries to garrote you, you raise your hands to your neck. So... maybe the fiddle string cut him so badly that death was instantaneous? Bled out?"

"Let the pathologist determine." Larson went to work on the nearby amp. "Done with the body."

With that, Karen let in the EMT guys. They'd been waiting patiently, their heads bobbing to some silent beat from their earbuds, to transport the body to Sioux Falls.

CHAPTER 4

KAREN WATCHED THE AMBULANCE MEANDER its way down the hill as the last rays died in the skies, hitting the white vehicle with a ball of fire. The remaining festivalgoers lined the road, hats doffed, silent and respectful. There was something almost holy about it—and just as she thought that, a voice floated over the meadow from behind her.

Day is dying in the west.

And as if released from the unnatural silence, voices, high and low, melody and harmony, burst out with pent-up emotion in an amazing wall of sound that washed over the new night.

Heaven is touching earth with rest,
Wait and worship while the night
Sets her evening lamps alight
Through all the sky.

Beside her, Seoul joined the chorus of "Holy, Holy, Holy" in a surprisingly powerful soprano that soared over the meadow. And she thought Marek was humming, as well, somewhere in the lowest ranges, but Karen felt that more than heard it. Lights started to appear, one by one, like ghostly souls alight. They swayed, a visual concert of phones and flashlights.

While the deepening shadows fall,
Heart of love, enfolding all,
Through the glory and the grace
Of the stars that veil Thy face,
Our hearts ascend.

Karen had a hard time finding her voice after the last chord died. She wasn't a singer. Oh, she could carry a tune. She'd sung hymns at church all her life, but this was... well, holy. She could find no other word for it. It was a tribute, a blessing, and an ushering in of that good night—except it wasn't. Not for Hal Birchard. Not natural. Not gentle.

And Karen's job was to find out why. Around her in the meadow, as if awakening from a magical thrall, murmurs arose, and the moment was gone—if not to ever be forgotten.

"Reminds me of 9/11," Jessica said in a low voice, startling Karen, who hadn't realized the trainee had come out of the tent. "You know, when the politicians broke out singing 'God Bless America' on the steps of Capitol Hill."

Larson materialized out of the darkness. "Last and only time they were in tune."

Snorts of agreement echoed nearby. Karen turned to Larson. "Anything we should know about before we start the interviews?"

"Phone bagged. Guitar not plugged in. Amp dead. Mic damaged."

Karen puzzled over that then shrugged. "Maybe he pulled out the plug when he fell and took down the mic on the way." She turned to her detective. "Let's get started on interviews, Marek. We need to—" As she turned, Karen nearly ran into Ms. Heavy Metal Rip-off, Seoul's Jam Off nemesis.

"Let's roll," the young woman snapped.

"Pardon?"

The rocker's nostrils flared, and the silver ring piercing glinted as a full moon filtered through the rustling cottonwoods and hunchbacked bur oaks. "You've put me off long enough. I'm ready to roll."

Seoul scowled at her. "I told you to wait until we got to you."

"Like I'm going to listen to some pipsqueak with a voice to match."

That did it. Karen went toe-to-toe with the nose-ringed rocker. "You *will* listen to my deputy. And you *will* wait until I get to you. Unless you want to spend the night in the tank." For a minute, Karen thought she'd have to follow through with her threat, then the young woman slunk off. Karen turned on her heel to face Seoul. "Who's she?"

Seoul smirked. "Don't know her name. But I'm betting she's the killer. She was sneaking around the competition—and around the judges' tent."

Interesting. "Who found the body?"

The smirk disappeared as the question registered. "Ah... Danielle."

"Danielle who?" Karen stopped as Seoul's eyes dropped. "*My* Danielle? Mehaffey?"

Her late husband's much younger half-sibling had recently surfaced in the tiny town of Fink. Danielle was a runaway with a nose stud, but without the attitude of the rocker. Karen was working with the courts to get Danielle emancipated as a minor, as she'd turned sixteen back in May. Though she'd also offered Danielle a home, the girl had turned her down, preferring her independence. Karen got that. Danielle had earned her small room over the Filler-Up gas station and diner in Fink where she worked as a waitress.

"Where is Danielle?" Marek asked.

Seoul pointed to a dingy old pickup. Karen recognized it as belonging to one of Danielle's geriatric admirers at the diner. As she started toward the pickup, her phone warbled.

She'd finally changed the dispatcher-inspired ringtone from the theme song of the old cop show *Adam-12* after she'd been officially elected sheriff and was unlikely to fall back to her previous occupation. But unable to decide what her new ringtone should be, she'd settled for the default.

After reading the caller ID, she let out a hiss. But her voice was perfectly polite as she answered. "Mr. Nelson, I'm a bit busy at the moment."

"I got the gist," the amateur low-power-FM newshound grumbled. The disabled Vietnam vet was the only source of news in Eda County, and while she'd had her run-ins with him, they'd put that behind them. Mostly. "Hal Birchard gives the performance of his life then ends up with a wire instead of a ribbon around his neck. Any comment?"

Karen took a breath, knowing by the click that she was being recorded. "The coroner has declared the death a homicide."

A pause. "You're not waiting for the medical examiner to make that determination?"

As she'd pretty much always waited for that despite Nails's pressing for more, his question was a wee bit ironic. "Let's just say that there wasn't any doubt, Mr. Nelson. The coroner was comfortable making the determination, and I am relaying it to you."

So if somehow the wire had accidentally wrapped around the man's neck, she was covered.

"All right. Do you have any suspects?"

Now he was just playing with her. Nails knew the answer. "Not at this time. We are in the very earliest stages of the investigation. DCI is processing the scene." Or had. She'd lost sight of Larson, so she wasn't sure if he'd gone back to the tent or was finished. "We are about to conduct our interviews." If only she could get off the dang phone. Marek had already gone over to the pickup and was talking to its driver through the open window.

Nails, however, was in no hurry. "From what I hear, there

were about a thousand people there for the Jam Off. People who called in said that it must be another contestant. Someone even said that some jerk was messing with the competition using a laser pointer. Care to comment?"

Karen knew better than to be drawn into commenting on something she knew nothing about. "As I said, Mr. Nelson, we are in the initial stages of this investigation. And I need to get back to it, so we can find out who ended Mr. Birchard's life. I'm sure you'll understand that time is of the essence."

She ended the call rather than let Nails press on with more questions she couldn't answer. That was his job. But hers took priority. Nails had known he wouldn't get anything juicy from her, just a soundbite for his hourly updates, so mission accomplished.

Pocketing her phone, she joined Marek. He was talking to Harlan Pederson, a widower in his nineties who was still spry enough to live independently, and even drive. At least Karen hadn't received any reports that he was a danger to himself or others on the road.

In the passenger seat, Danielle had her hands wrapped around a Dr. Pepper and looked like she wanted to drown herself in it. Despite the still-cloying heat inside the un-air-conditioned pickup, fine tremors shook her body. Harlan had draped an old horse blanket over her shoulders.

Karen walked around and pulled open the passenger door. "Let's take a walk, Danielle. It'll get the blood flowing again." As the girl blanched, Karen mentally kicked herself. "Sorry. Bad wording. Come on, let's get this done, so you and Harlan can get back to Fink."

Danielle slid out, and the blanket fell off her shoulders. She didn't seem to notice. Karen caught it and handed it back to Harlan. "Don't worry, I'll take care of her."

"Know it. You've done right by her."

Danielle's nose stud glinted ruby red as the girl tried to smile. "Almost free to be me."

It had been a delicate balancing act contacting the right

people to set up the emancipation hearing, as technically, Danielle's guardian was the state of Nebraska. Like Karen's husband, Patrick, Danielle had never had a chance to be adopted, as their drug-addict mother had never relinquished her parental rights and the courts had never seen fit to terminate them because she'd gotten clean just often enough.

However, Karen had managed to keep Lianne Mehaffey in the dark and the bureaucracy at bay when she submitted the petition on Danielle's behalf. The judge was holding a hearing on Monday to make his final decision. As much as Karen would like to think it was a slam dunk, she'd learned never to make any assumptions about Judge Rudibaugh's rulings.

With Marek a silent shadow behind them, Karen led Danielle down a trail, the earthy smell rising to fill her nostrils. Rather than the gentle rustling of the cottonwoods, the bur oaks, twisted and squat, made faintly sinister creaks and groaned in the wind. Overhead, stars winked into being as sounds from the campground drifted over. Likely full up tonight.

"I'm surprised Cookie let you out of the diner," Karen commented after they'd emerged into a small opening in the trees with a picnic table, where they settled. "Did Harlan kidnap you?"

That drew at least an attempt at a laugh, even though kidnapping was perhaps not the best thing to bring up. "As if. No, he was just my chauffeur. You know I can't get a driver's license until I'm emancipated. I came because Hal..." Her voice hitched. "Because... Mr. Birchard... asked me to come."

Asked her? That was very unwelcome news. Was Karen going to have to lock the girl up before she could free her? "You were... involved?"

"No!" Now the laugh was real, if rueful, as she got a good look at Karen's face. "Not like you're thinking. Eww. I mean, he was even older than you... that is... I mean..."

"Approaching geezer-dom. Gotcha." To be that young, to think the forties were ancient. "Okay, then, what was your relationship?"

"Hal started coming to the diner after... well, after everything."

Danielle and several other girls had been kidnapped back in May. That made Karen's investigative antenna quiver, not to mention stir her maternal instincts, what she had of them. "That didn't make you suspicious? That maybe he thought you were fair game?"

"It wasn't like that. He and Harlan hit it off. Talked about folk music, old-timey stuff. Big band. Swing. Polka. Hal talked to all the old-timers at the diner. Recorded some of the songs. Asked to see instruments, music, old LPs, whatever. It was actually kinda neat."

"When did he usually come?" Marek asked. "What time of day, I mean."

Danielle looked at him with caution, which was more than most did. Because of his size, Marek was often able to get people to underestimate his intelligence.

"Breakfast, usually, but sometimes, he'd stay for a couple hours and have lunch, too."

Karen didn't like what she was hearing. "He didn't work?"

"Yeah, but for himself. Computers, I think. I'm not sure if it had to do with music or if that was just his hobby."

"So you never talked about anything except his diner order? Maybe the weather?"

Danielle squirmed. "Well... he was nice. He knew what happened to me. Everybody did. And that I was related to you, so he said he knew he'd better watch his step. He wanted to know how I was doing, if I was going to go back to school, what my plans were. Just talk. Not like there's anything else to do in Fink. And he asked me if I'd like to come to the Jam Off, because he'd decided to compete. It seemed like... well, like a big deal to him. Like he could use the support. I told him I couldn't take off the time and couldn't drive anyway, but Harlan said he'd take care of it. I don't know how, because Cookie doesn't believe in any days off but Sunday, but he did."

Karen smiled. "He must've threatened Cookie with closing the diner."

"Closing... how?"

"Harlan owns the building."

The girl's voice squeaked. "What? When?"

It had been one of the many avenues they'd looked into when Danielle disappeared. "Forever, as far as I can tell. Cookie rents the place from him at a nominal fee. They both get what they want out of the deal, I'd say."

As an owl hooted and an acoustic guitar strummed in the campground, Karen eased into the dicey part. "So, you and Harlan came to the Jam Off together? When was that?"

"About three fifteen. Hal said he was playing early, like third or something, and we thought we'd missed him as it had already started when we found a spot to sit. But Hal found us and said he'd switched with someone else and would be dead last."

At those last words, her skin blanched into ghost territory in the light of the moon. "I can't believe he's dead. He was so... *amazing*. Just awesome. I was sure he'd win the Jam Off. I don't know why it was taking so long for the judges. It must've been killing him."

"Is that why you went to find him?" Marek asked gently.

Danielle nodded. "Yeah, that and to tell him we were leaving. I figured he might want some support. I got some pop for him. He liked Mountain Dew, even for breakfast. Weird, but whatever. I was also... well, curious... why he hadn't come back out. Most of the contestants, if they had instruments, they'd go back there then come back out with the cases or whatever. But he didn't."

Karen shared a look with Marek. If she'd been watching for Birchard, then Danielle might well be the one to crack the case. "You kept watch?"

"Well, no, not really. Harlan started talking about some old music stars back in his heyday, and I lost track of time until he looked at his watch and said it was almost seven and the judges were still on break. It was getting late, and Harlan wanted to go home." She rolled her eyes. "Not even dark, and it was late?"

So much for a slam dunk. At least from Danielle. But Karen smiled at the city girl. "You should know by now that for farmers, especially old-timers, it's early to bed, early to rise."

"Yeah, yeah." Danielle ran her hands down her face. "I bet I don't sleep a wink tonight."

"Did you go into the tent?" Marek asked.

"No... at least... no, I don't think so. The flap was down. I had to set down one of the pops on the ground... guess it's still there?" When she got a nod, Danielle sighed. "I pulled open the flap, just to peek in, and... it took my eyes a minute to adjust. But I called out for him. Hal didn't answer, so I thought maybe he was gone. That is, gone somewhere else. Then I saw him. I started to go in, thinking he was hurt, but then..."

She gulped. "I saw the blood. And... I think I screamed. I don't remember. I stumbled back and fell on my butt, lost my drink, and next thing I know, Deputy Durr was there and making everyone stay back. I didn't even recognize her, you know, when she sang in the Jam Off. She was pretty good, too. But as soon as she started issuing orders, I knew."

A small package with a punch.

Marek leaned forward. "Did you see anyone, at any time, come out from the tent after Mr. Birchard went in?"

Danielle wrinkled her nose, the ruby stud winking blood red. "Well, yeah, I guess. Earlier. That boy who everyone was talking about, the one who was going to do the concert tonight? Josh Bolvin. He seemed pretty steamed, too."

Beside her, Karen heard Marek mutter, "Oh, hell. Not again."

CHAPTER 5

A COLEMAN LANTERN CREATED AN INTIMATE little ship that floated on the risers on the dark stage. Like the devil finial, Josh Bolvin rode the prow. The skinny nineteen-year-old had dreamboat hazel eyes and a fall of wayward blond hair. Like his youngest uncle, the boy had an aw-shucks face guaranteed to draw the heartstrings of ladies young and old. His grandmother, Patty Bolvin, sat midship behind him with her hands on his shoulders, the bulwark never failing. On the final row of risers, the rudder and the rowers, were her three sons: Ned, Nate, and Nick.

As Marek had only recently patched up his friendship with Nick, the last thing he wanted to do was start accusing another member of the family of murder. Last time, it had been the much-beloved matriarch. His own daughter was best friends with Nick Bolvin's daughter, Emily, so if he messed this up, he'd be in deep doodoo.

Marek had met Josh Bolvin before but only in passing, and he had even less of an acquaintance with the boy's father, Nate Bolvin, who was an accountant in Reunion. Unlike his son and the brothers who bracketed him, the accountant was built like a tank, the only son to take after the matriarch.

Ned, the eldest, was wiry, and Nick was lanky. But they'd all, along with the long-deceased Norm and the coach Noel, been champion wrestlers—and perennial All-State Choir members. That they'd done the first had kept them from being hassled for the second.

Marek had experienced something similar, though not at Reunion High. Only his size and his place on the football team in Valeska, where his mother had moved before he'd begun high school, had saved him. But it had been football, ironically, that had led him to music.

He'd been singing in the communal shower after a sweaty, hard-fought scrimmage at the beginning of the school year. With the rest of his teammates, he'd bellowed out their team's theme song for the year, "Another One Bites the Dust." Then in stalked Coach Bousker, his face red, his jowls quivering. He'd gone straight for Marek, who'd desperately tried to recall just what he'd done to screw up. Coach had thrown a towel at him and, his face one big scowl, yanked Marek out of the shower room—which had gone completely silent except for the driving force of the water on dented tile.

Right inside the locker room was a petite woman in a frilly blouse and skirt, her toe tapping, which stopped abruptly as he came in wearing nothing but the towel.

She looked him up and down then nodded. "I want you."

As hoots sounded from inside the shower room, Marek turned a bright red and looked helplessly over her head at Coach Bousker, whose scowl just grew. "Can't have him. Finally found a use for him, keeping my quarterback vertical."

The tapping began again on the tile. "Surely he can multitask."

"Can't. Dyslexic."

Marek hunched his shoulders, though at least by then he knew why he had so much trouble in school.

The sharply angled eyebrows arched. "I can work around that. And I only need him before school. You can have him after school."

Coach shook his head. "Burn him at both ends, he'll fail at both."

"No, he won't." Her smile had plenty of teeth. "I won't let him."

Was he being put in some kind of remedial class? Not his idea of a good time, especially in the morning. "Uh, I don't..."

She lifted a hand. "I want you at my office at seven tomorrow morning. We need time to evaluate. Don't look so scared. It's painless. And we usually start at seven thirty."

He knew he was going to sound stupid. Because he was. "Start what? And who are you?"

"Oh. Didn't I say?" She laughed, a surprisingly full-bodied sound in such a petite woman. "Naegeli Bauer. I'm the new music teacher. I want you for my choir. You're a natural. A true bass. I couldn't believe it when I walked by, so I snuck in and got caught. But all's well that ends well. Remember, tomorrow at seven sharp. I'll be waiting."

Before Marek could get his jaw back up, she'd gone, leaving him with the hooting calls of his teammates.

"If you can't say no," the coach grumbled, "at least be smart and don't go."

But the novelty of being praised by a teacher was greater than Marek's desire to grab every last minute of sleep. His mother, who always left early as the English teacher at the high school, hadn't known about his extracurricular activity. Not until he'd not only made the choir but also excelled, finding the music satisfied something in him that he hadn't known he was missing.

Ms. Bauer had worked with him so he could learn his parts by ear, not sight-read, and even went to bat for him at All-State Honor Choir auditions, insisting that his voice, not his sight-reading skills, should be the measure, given his dyslexia. Though, for some odd reason, he was better at reading music than reading books.

And with Ms. Bauer's help, he'd made the cut at All-State, joining Nick there for all four years of their respective high school careers. For the first time in his life, he'd done something that he'd been sought out for, too late for his father to know. But not too late for his mother, who'd been bemused but happy for him, she having, as she often said, a tin ear and a raspy voice. For the first time, she'd been able to play the proud mother, going to his concerts and to a parent-teacher conference where a glowing report was given instead of grudging points for effort if not results.

Naggie Bauer, as she'd universally been known because she built her choir with sheer nagging, had eventually left for better opportunities in Sioux Falls. But she'd given him a gift that he could never repay: a feeling of accomplishment. He'd liked it. And closing cases gave him that same sense of accomplishment. But right now, he wished he'd stuck full-time with carpentry.

"Well, Marek Okerlund, I hoped to see you here at the musical festival, but not quite like this." The Bolvin matriarch's double, or even triple, chins wobbled as she cut into Marek's reminiscences. "But I will say, my boys gave Hal Birchard a good sendoff."

Marek wasn't at all surprised to learn the Bolvins had started the spontaneous tribute. In fact, he suspected Nick had been the tenor leading the way, and that suspicion was confirmed when Ned nudged his youngest brother, nearly dislodging him from the riser.

"Lightweight," Ned muttered, but it was subdued, especially since he was busy scowling at Marek. "If you're gonna start throwing around accusations again, I'll pop you one."

"Let them do their job," Patty boomed. "They didn't find anything last time and won't this time. Because there isn't anything to find. So don't get your undies in a twist."

But Marek noted that young Josh squirmed under her hands. Beside him, Karen must have, as well, because she asked the boy, "When did you last see Mr. Birchard, Josh?"

The boy ran a hand through his lion's mane of hair. "I don't know what time it was, exactly." Marek noted he had no watch, but probably few of his generation did. They had phones instead. "But right after his performance. I went to give him a high five and talk to him about a couple offers I got."

"Offers? What offers?" Nate stared down at the back of his son's head as if he'd never seen it before. "You never told me that. Why tell Hal?"

Josh hunched his skinny shoulders. "He's just... he knows stuff about the industry, okay? I just wanted his take, that's all. Got one offer to be repped by a big-time manager. And the record guy said he might sign me to his label depending on how I do at the concert... which won't happen now."

"Just the solo act tonight's been canceled. You've got the full concert with the band on Monday night," Nick told his nephew. "That's still on. I checked with the organizers."

Josh all but twisted into a pretzel to see his uncle's face. "No shit?"

His grandmother bopped him on the head. "Watch your mouth."

"Ouch." Josh rubbed his head, but the half-smile held no animosity, nor did his grandmother's. This was a close-knit family, one Marek had once felt part of.

With effort, Marek concentrated on the here and now. "What did Mr. Birchard say to you, Josh, about your offers?"

What could only be called a sulk took the affection out of the boy's face. "Not a single congrats or anything. All doom and gloom. Warned me off everybody and everything, said to keep doing what I was doing and I'd get where I needed to go on my own. As if. Like anyone's going to come offer me that kind of deal out here in..." He got the stink eye from Karen and behind his back, from his family. "In God's country."

Good catch. Boonies. Bumfuck. Nowhere. It was, however, somewhere for its residents. Reunion was hanging on to its population by its anxiety-bitten fingernails.

"They just did offer you that deal." His grandmother gave him another bop. "Right here."

Josh rubbed his head again. "Once in a blue moon."

Marek agreed with that. He wasn't sure how long the Big Jam had been going on, but so far as his memories went, the participants, judges, and crowd were all Dakotans. Maybe some Iowans and Minnesotans wandered over the border. But he admitted his info was outdated.

"You made your own luck," the proud papa said. "They came for you."

His son ducked his head.

Aw shucks? Or something else?

Karen asked, "Was that your setup back there? The guitar and drums and everything?"

Josh winced. "Yeah. It was all set up for the concert tonight. Guess I'll need to haul it all back to Hal's..." He stopped when Karen shook her head. "Or not."

Marek's mind went back to Hal and his fiddle. "Were you all here for Hal's performance?"

"Sure. He's family, or as close to it without blood." Nick pulled out his phone. "I even videoed it." He cradled the phone in one hand, swiping with the other, until he brought up the video and turned it so Marek and Karen could see and hear.

Marek knew nothing about fiddling, but he knew what he liked. Though the music definitely had a folk flavor, it had a modern flair to it, almost close to folk rock. And as Seoul had said, the man had thrown a musical kitchen sink into it. Maybe it was the poor quality of the phone speakers, but somehow, he'd made the fiddle sound as resonant as a cello, then bright and cheerful as it morphed into a reel. Only when Karen stepped on his toe did Marek realize he was tapping his foot.

When Birchard finished with a flourish, bowing deeply, the unseen crowd gave a huge cheer—and he rose again, flushed, with a look of... almost epiphany. Like he'd found his calling.

"Does he play a mean guitar, too?" Marek asked. "Birchard."

Josh looked nonplussed. "Guitar? Acoustic, yeah, but not electric. But he could pick up just about anything and play it, so I guess he just didn't want to." He frowned. "Weird. He knew how to score a..." His mouth clamped shut.

"Score a what?" Karen pressed when Marek didn't.

When Josh kept silent, his grandmother shook his shoulders. "You tell 'em the truth."

"Score a hit. You heard him."

But Josh kept his eyes down.

CHAPTER 6

A S MUTED MUSIC LEAKED OUT from various points in the darkness, Karen decided to step things up a notch. She didn't really blame Marek for treading carefully with the Bolvins, but in a rural county like Eda, they often knew the players.

But the biggest player in this scenario was Hal Birchard himself. She didn't know anything about him or his people. The name Birchard wasn't in her mental rolodex. Was it French? Was he part Indian? She knew some of the early French trappers had intermarried with the native tribes. And some Indians looked as white as she was. "Where was Mr. Birchard from?"

That simple question drew only baffled silence. The Bolvin brothers looked at each other, and one by one, they shrugged. Nick spoke for all. "He never talked about being from any one place. I know he lived mostly in cities. Chicago, Kansas City, Twin Cities, and also overseas. Places like Taiwan and Puerto Rico. He was a rolling stone and went wherever the road took him. Said he liked it that way. I never expected him to stay here as long as he did."

Karen pursed her lips. "Why here?"

"Change of pace," Nate contributed.

Closemouthed Ned finally spoke. "Told me that he was looking for musical traditions off the beaten path."

"Was music his business or just a hobby?"

Ned snorted. "Was basketball just a hobby to you?"

Stupid question. No, it wasn't. Even now, although she was no longer a player, Karen followed the game and helped a bit here and there with young local players. And she still spent time in the high school gym when she had the time. She missed her one-on-ones with Larson. And any pickup game she could participate in, she did. "Point taken. But I meant, how did he make his living?"

They all shrugged, a wall of disinterest. Nick finally said, "Computers of some sort. He was self-employed. So far as I can tell, it was computers and music. That was his life."

Karen wasn't sure that was a life, but maybe it was. After all, many would say she didn't have a life. Work and... what? A little of this, a little of that. A little life. If Larson ever managed to get untangled from his obligations to his kids... oh, what was she thinking? She admired that he'd taken them on and wouldn't have it any other way. But would *their* time ever come?

"He had a big heart, Hal did." Patty dabbed at her bloodshot eyes. "He took our Josh under his wing, let him use his place as a base for practice—"

"For which my wife is forever grateful," Nate said dryly.

"—and did whatever magic he does on those computers to make that video. The one that went... infectious?"

"Viral, Grandma. Sheesh."

That earned him the third bop, and it was harder than the others. "Mind your elders. Seems strange to me, to call something after a sickness, but maybe that's what it is. In all my years—and don't you be adding them up—coming to the Big Jam from the time when my crew were just a twinkle in my eye, this is the first time we've had any violence. Hot words, sometimes. But that's it. A good family outing. Now that's changed forever. Not just a man got murdered tonight. Music did, too."

"'American Pie' all over again," Nick muttered.

Karen knew that song but couldn't recall all the details of

its origin. Something about a day in history when a bunch of famous musicians had died. But she couldn't remember their names. So much for a lasting legacy.

"At the risk of getting hit up the side of the head," Ned said to the back of his mother's head, "music will never die. Not here, not anywhere." He gestured toward the muted sounds of campground music, little pockets of melody in the dark meadow where the moon silvered everything below it. A serene serenade with a nasty undertone. "It's how we deal."

His mother made a musical hmm. "You may be right. But what happened to Hal wasn't right." She looked straight at Karen then Marek. "You'll find who did this."

"We will," Karen said, hoping it was true. "However long it takes."

"Aren't you effing done over there?" came a too-familiar female voice from out of the dark.

"Hold your horses!" Karen shouted back. She made one last pitch to the Bolvins. "Is there anything, anything at all, that was odd about today, that Hal confided to you? That he was worried or upset or anything that might have led to this?"

Nick pulled on one satellite-shaped ear. "Well, he scratched on the Jam Off initially. I asked him why, and he said he was at a fork in the road. I thought he'd decided to cut out on us, as well, and I was more than a bit upset, as we needed him. But he was... somewhere else. In his head. Just walked off before I could say another word. Then he showed up as the last contestant, and I was like, 'Great, we're good.' Then..."

And then. Hal Birchard would never walk that road again.

Ignoring the pacing of Ms. Heavy Metal Rip-off, whose name Karen still didn't know, she went for the judges' tent, another ship in the night, but shrouded. Marek was a silent shadow, dark on dark, behind her, as she ducked into the tent.

Unlike the Bolvin brothers, the three judges looked like

they'd made a deliberate attempt to be as far apart from each other as physically possible. Inside, the tent smelled of sweat and alcohol. A large fan was the only sound. She recognized only one of the men—Axel Knutsen, a fixture at any public event that required a musical flourish, from taps at funerals to the national anthem at basketball games, always wearing red suspenders and his trademark straw hat with a band bearing musical notes. The seventy-something-year-old looked relieved when he saw Karen.

"What can you tell us, Sheriff?" he asked.

"Nothing," a dry voice answered. "Good grief, man, don't you ever watch TV?"

Karen looked over at the dim corner where a sleek, silver-haired man stood, swirling a glass of red wine. But by the curve of his mouth, he seemed more amused than disdainful. She gave him a slight nod. "You're right, Mister..."

"Kuhl. Anton Kuhl." He also seemed amused that he had to tell her. He must be the big-time label guy that Josh Bolvin was so excited about. "You?"

"Sheriff Mehaffey." She tilted her head in Marek's direction. "Detective Okerlund."

"Detective?" That lifted Kuhl's eyebrows. "I may not know much about rural policing, but isn't that unusual?"

"Very." Eda County was, to her knowledge, the only rural county in South Dakota to have a detective on staff. "But it works for us."

Marek cleared his throat. "I'm only part-time."

"Not exactly encouraging." The slightly slurred voice came from the final judge, a pudgy, compact man with artificially dark hair. He looked about the same age as Kuhl, though in a lot worse shape.

Karen narrowed her eyes at the man. "And you are?"

He squinted up at her from where he sat at the lone table. Like Kuhl, he also clutched a drink, but it looked like a much harder one. "Sal... Marmo." He swatted at a mosquito and missed. "I'm getting eaten alive. Can we go now? Shoulda never come to this hellhole."

"A man died tonight," Axel chastised him. "Have some respect."

For a moment, Karen thought she'd have to step in between the two men, as Marmo sent Axel a glare hot enough to reduce the tent—or Axel—to ashes.

Kuhl took a step forward. "Drink your whiskey and calm down, Sal. Before our Mayberry duo arrests you for being a royal asshole."

Marmo lifted a finger. "Fuck off."

Axel went almost apoplectic. "Watch your language in front of a lady."

"Lady? I don't see no lady."

Before Karen could respond, Kuhl took two long steps and grabbed hold of Marmo's shirt lapels "Snap out of it, Sal, or you're going to be staying in this town for a much longer stretch than you signed on for. Capiche?"

Something in the man's hard, lean face made Marmo shrink back. He batted ineffectually at the hands that held him. "Get away from me, you bloodsucker."

More animosity. Interesting. "Do you two know each other?"

Carefully, Kuhl released his hold on the sweaty man then ran his hands down his pant legs, as if he'd touched slime. He looked up at Karen without a hint of his earlier amusement. "A long time ago, we crossed paths and locked horns. Let's just say we're not BFFs."

It would have been better for their investigation, Karen thought, if they were mad at the victim rather than each other. "Did any of you know Hal Birchard?"

"I did." Axel tweaked his suspenders. "Not well. But he was with the Bolvins, and where they went, he went, and where the Bolvins went, I often went. We competed at SPEBSQSA events."

"Speb-squaw?" Karen tried out the strange word.

"An acronym for the Society for the Preservation and Encouragement of Barber Shop Quartet Singing in America. Over forty thousand members. They hold various contests across the country. Old music and new. The Bolvins and their Quartertones quartet have, I admit, done far better than my humble crew, the Mellowtones."

Who knew barbershop was still a thing? "What do you know of Hal specifically?"

The elderly man took a moment. "Got a voice like a bull horn. He anchored that quartet of theirs. Heard he also did his share of arrangement. Some say he took their music up a notch, but I don't agree." He seemed both abashed and defensive as he continued. "He took liberties."

"He added creativity," Kuhl murmured in correction. Then as Axel looked ready to argue, he teed his hands. Time out. "Water under the bridge." Kuhl looked at Karen. "Unless you think one of us murdered Mr. Birchard for his creative fiddling?"

"Was that the bone of contention?" Marek asked.

Kuhl's mouth twisted. "We couldn't come to an agreement. I was pulling for Birchard, Mr. Knutsen for the jazz singer—your deputy, I believe?—and Sal for that heavy metal gal."

Surprised to hear that Seoul was in the running, Karen turned to Axel. "Seoul? I don't imagine she did anything traditional."

His chin lifted. "Within the tradition, that's what's important. Jazz is always ad-lib." When Karen blinked, he clarified. "Supposed to go off on tangents and play with soul."

"Ha-ha," Sal mumbled over his drink. He seemed to have dowsed his fire in it. "I was looking for an edge, for something new, something young."

"For you to fleece," Kuhl bit out.

Sal lifted his drink to toast the man he'd clearly like to roast. "'Zactly. Don't tell me you don't do the same. You just pretty it up in shtick."

Axel pursed his lips. "Music is its own reward."

The other two just stared at him as if he was nuts. Obviously, neither wanted to waste their breath trying to convince him otherwise. Axel was a bit like her senior deputy—everything in its place, its box, or its drawer. She'd even bet his pencil case had all the nubs sharpened. She just hoped that Kurt would be back to work soon, as his attention to detail had saved her butt more than once.

His day shift partner, Walrus, was many things, but a stickler wasn't one of them. She was still figuring out where her youngest deputy fit on the attention-to-detail scale. So far, Seoul got high marks on procedure. She'd controlled the scene, controlled the uncontrollable, and given a coherent report.

Marek asked, "So after you took a break, did you three stay here or leave?"

Kuhl broke the silence first. Again, he looked amused. "I took a long walk to clear my head." He indicated a flap she hadn't noticed before at the back. "Not much for an alibi. I went around the park trails. I'm afraid I can't recall any particularly notable landmarks. But I can tell you that you have a nice little trail down to a stream across from a trailer park." He lifted one loafer to show the mud on the edges. "Is that the Big Jam?"

"No, that's Connor Creek. The Big Jammer, its official title, is a proper river." When she got no further comment, she turned to the elderly man. "Mr. Knutsen?"

For the first time, Axel looked uncomfortable. "I needed to talk to somebody about... something." A hint of desperation in his eyes made *her* feel uncomfortable, but she pressed on. "As you said, Mr. Knutsen, someone died. We aren't gossips, we're the law."

Flags of color flickered into his sunken cheeks. "Well, I..." He threw a glance at Marek. "Can I tell your detective? It's... personal."

She wasn't as quick as her detective, but even she could deduce it was something that wasn't supposed to be mentioned in front of the ladies. "Forget I've got an X chromosome." When he blinked at her, she sighed. "I'm the sheriff. I don't count as female."

He looked doubtful but plucked up his suspenders—and his courage. "I went to find Doc Hudson for a... a personal matter... a prescription ran out... related to a certain..." He floundered, and Karen, understanding, held up a hand. Male-type problem.

"You can stop there. We only need your alibi. I can check with Doc."

Regretfully, Knutsen shook his head. "Well, that's the thing. I couldn't find him. Nowhere. I even started toward the instrument tent, thinking maybe he'd gone to talk to Birchard. I'd checked everywhere else, so I headed back there." His hand shook as he readjusted his straw hat. "Almost ran into that... that young woman with the painted face. Made a rude gesture at me, and I turned right around." He fingered his middle finger on his left hand. "She's the one that made such a godawful racket in the Jam Off."

"That, you old fart, was mighty fine music. I could make money off that girl. She calls herself Rad Wilson. Radical." Sal Marmo had finally provided them with Ms. Heavy Metal Rip-off's name. "She's got more balls than anyone else in this room... tent... whatever."

Karen now wanted to talk to the rocker, but first, she needed one last alibi. Well, that and some fingerprints. She'd already collected them from the Bolvins, for elimination purposes. "And you, Mr. Marmo? Where did you go?"

"Where d'ya think?" He lifted his drink. "Concession stand. Long line. Then came back here to drown my sorrows. Tastes like piss but does the job." He lowered it. "Go do yours, so I can get outta here."

She'd like to give him her finger but restrained herself. She didn't think Axel Knutsen would approve. Though given the way he was glaring at Marmo, maybe she was wrong.

Karen just hoped that Rad Wilson had killed Birchard or knew who did.

CHAPTER 7

AS HE EMERGED OUT OF the judges' tent, Marek almost bowled over Rad Wilson. Had she been listening?

"You want an obstruction charge, Ms. Wilson?" Karen demanded as she exited the tent behind him.

"Obstruction? You're the one who put *me* on ice. I've been waiting to 'cooperate'"—she slashed the quotation marks with black and scarlet fingernails—"since, like, forever."

Marek was tired from dealing with a sick daughter the previous night, it was getting late, and he'd had to cancel his date with Nikki. They'd had tickets—very *expensive* tickets—to a much-anticipated concert at the Washington Pavilion in Sioux Falls. She'd gone with a teacher friend instead. "Let's find somewhere to sit."

"Fine." Rad whirled and launched herself into the nearest tent.

"I swear," Karen said as she followed reluctantly. "I *will* arrest her for being a royal pain in the ass. The wonder is that she wasn't the one that got killed."

Marek ducked under the flap. Pencils, papers, and a cash box were strewn over a long table. Seated in one of the folding chairs behind the table was a familiar face.

"Connor."

A harmonica held near his mouth, where his shiny new wedding ring glinted, the Grove Park manager blinked eyes the color of fall acorns under graying red hair. "Detective. Should I leave?"

"Yes," Rad snapped just as Karen said the opposite.

"You choose the venue, you take it as-is," Karen told her. "And that means Mr. Connor stays. So long as he keeps his mouth shut."

Sulkily, the girl dropped into a folding chair and stuck her black leather boots up on the table. Must be hotter than hell. And all the metal buckles and body-piercing rings that dangled off any available exposed skin gave a new meaning to the term "heavy metal."

"Shoot," Rad said.

"Happily," Karen muttered and actually got a snort. In the background, Connor softly began playing "Camptown Races" on his harmonica. Marek had to hold back a snort of his own. *Camptown ladies sing this song.* If Marek were betting on the races, he'd choose Karen hands down. She was still a rookie when it came to homicides—most rural sheriffs were, no matter how long their tenure—but she had the talent for it. She just needed the patience.

Karen crossed her arms over the back of a folding chair as she straddled the chair backwards. "All right, what is it you're so desperate to tell us that couldn't wait?"

For all her hurry, the heavy metal rocker now seemed content to draw it out. In fact, Marek thought she was acting like the cat that got the canary. Her edge was gone. But what replaced it wasn't any prettier. She smirked. "I know who killed the freaking fiddler."

Karen just shook her head. "If you tell me it's my deputy, I'll cuff you on the spot."

That got a return snort. "S&M's not my scene."

"Funny. I thought S&M Records was exactly your scene." Karen lifted her eyebrows at Rad's sound of disgust. "Oh, you meant sadomasochism? My bad." Karen tapped fingers on the metal chair back. "But murder isn't funny. Just who do you think killed Hal Birchard?"

"Boy Wonder."

Marek didn't like that answer. At all. "Josh Bolvin?"

Rad rolled her eyes. "Everybody's tripping over their shitkickers to asskiss the kid, but it won't last. Just a one-off, that's all." She pulled on her sterling silver nose ring. "Talk about a shitkicker name. Bolvin. Chewin' his cud—that's what he was doing. Tame, just like his tunes. Not an ounce of rad. Kinda like the guy who got offed. Trad's bad, not rad. Dead tunes."

Dead tunes? Hardly. Hal Birchard had given an inspired performance. And if he'd been involved in the arrangement of some of the oldies that the barbershop quartet had sung to the delight of the July Fourth crowd, Hal Birchard was not only good but something more. It took real talent to spin a classic so that it sounded new.

Connor tuned Marek back in with Simon and Garfunkel's "Sound of Silence," which this time, Rad took note of. "If you want the real thing, not the piss-poor original, listen to Disturbed's take."

Connor lowered his harmonica and studied the girl. "I'll grant you, Disturbed nailed that one. And I like it, a lot, depending on the mood. But Pentatonix is their equal, just in a different way."

"Oh, please. They're just barbershop rebranded as 'a cappella.'" More slashes of those killer fingernails. "Dead, dead, dead. But at least you've got some clue." She looked pointedly back at Karen. "Unlike some others."

The girl's default was sulky, snarky, and self-absorbed. She was looking out for herself; that was clear. Whether the truth aligned with her goals, that was the question.

"Music isn't my business. Murder is," Karen said evenly. "Why do you think Josh Bolvin killed Birchard?"

After a slight pause in the musical play-by-play, Connor switched to "Killing Me Softly." Apparently, he was no more excited about Josh as the killer than Marek was.

Rad grinned so hard that the lightning bolts painted on her face turned into sideways smiles. "Because I saw him come out of the instrument tent, really steamed."

That was not news. Danielle had said the same.

"When?" Karen sounded almost bored.

"Do I look like a clock watcher?" The rocker raised her left hand, dangling a bracelet with little daggers buried in broken hearts. Not a watch in sight. "That's..."

"Lame. Got it." Karen leaned forward. "Hal Birchard was a competitor of yours."

That got a reaction. "Hardly. Not for a California record label."

"You listened in on the judges' deliberations. Don't deny it. You knew that it was a three-way race and that the judges were leaning toward Birchard to break the deadlock."

That was news to Marek. Was it true?

"That's a freaking lie. They were leaning toward your dep—" Rad's mouth snapped shut. Then she crossed her arms, metal clanging. "Doesn't matter. I'm a sure thing. I don't need any freaking trophy from some pissant festival in bumfuck."

Talk about bravado. But there was still something of the cat with the canary in there.

"You're full of it." Karen leaned back, as if ready to call it a day, then paused. "Tell me, Ms. Wilson, do you do a lot of presentations?"

Marek blinked at that. Usually, he was the one who asked off-the-wall questions. Connor segued into "The Land of Confusion."

"What do you take me for, some nerdy prof or something? I perform, I don't 'present.'" This time, the slashes ended in a claw. Rad shot a look at Connor. "And Disturbed did that better than Genesis. Kickass graphics on the vid."

Before Connor could reply, Karen pulled the conversation back to herself. "I just wondered why you were playing with a laser pointer."

That, Marek knew, was a stab in the dark. He bit the inside of his lip as Connor played the theme song to *Jaws*. Unfortunately, the musical play-by-play broke the suspense—and the moment.

Karen's jaw tightened as she glared over at the park manager. "Cut it out."

Connor gave her a sheepish look and pocketed his harmonica. Too late.

Rad didn't break. "I don't know what you're talking about."

"No, I'm sure that would be too juvenile for you, right? And being all-knowing, I'm sure you know that using a laser to mess with people is a federal crime with significant penalties. It's considered an assault." Karen rose to her feet. "Lots of people take photos, even videos, at events like this, you know? I haven't had time to sift through them yet, but who knows what I'll find."

"So freaking what? Nothing to see."

But Marek saw more than a hint of fear in her heavily mascaraed eyes. He pushed with his own question, not off-the wall, but hoping to catch her off-kilter. "Why did you give Axel Knutsen the finger?"

The rocker jolted toward him, metal jangling. "Who?"

"The judge with the straw hat."

"That dried-up old man couldn't play himself out of a cardboard box. Everything has to be *in* the box. Out of the box, that gives him the willies. In music, in life. I'm outta here." And she suited word to deed and jangled out.

"That girl's hiding something," Connor said.

"No kidding," Karen returned.

Connor sighed. "I meant that she's hiding pain. A lot of it. I've been there."

A PTSD vet who'd finally gotten his dishonorable discharge reversed and his opioid addiction from painkillers under control, the park manager was now married with a stepson. He was one of the most live-in-the-moment people Marek had ever met. Perhaps he had to be, to survive.

"I'm sorry I messed it up for you," Connor told Karen.

She blew out a breath. "My fault. I told you to stay. And I'm not sure I'd have gotten anything but more lies, more evasion. If we're lucky, we'll find a photo or video to use as leverage against her."

Video. That triggered a thought. He turned to Connor. "Do you still have motion cameras set up in the park?"

"You mean the trail cams? Ah..." Connor looked sheepish again. "I took them all down after I got the job." Before Marek could bemoan the loss, he finished, "Except the one at the footbridge I built over the creek to the trailer park. I want my wife safe when she comes and goes from working there. It's not a fancy system by any means, but when I get back home, I can check if it was triggered."

"Home" was a house in Grove Park, part of the low-compensation package.

Karen nodded. "That's something, at least. One of our judges took a walk down that way, or so he claims. If we could start eliminating at least some of the thousand people there, that would be good."

Two Fingers ducked his head in to the tent. "Sheriff, we've finished taking statements and obtaining photos and videos."

Karen let out a big breath. "All right, let's call it a night. Tomorrow, Marek and I will go to the autopsy first thing. The rest of you can start slogging through the photos and vids."

Two Fingers gave her a salute and did an about-face out of the tent.

"That's also someone who's hiding some hurt," Connor murmured. When they turned to look at him, he shrugged. "Takes one to know one. Vet, right?"

"Right. Air Force. Ordered to drop a bomb on innocents. He's... mostly better."

That got an understanding nod. The military was a bond Marek didn't share. He didn't think he would have lasted a day under a drill sergeant. Fortunately, Karen wasn't hardcore spic-and-span and only required that he wear his detective hat. Marek was more than willing to follow her orders. Maybe Nikki had at least bought him a CD from the concert he'd missed. Or a T-shirt.

CHAPTER 8

KAREN HATED THE SPOTLESS AUTOPSY room in the basement of the Sioux Falls hospital. The antiseptic didn't fully mask the odors, and rather than give hope of life, the shiny medical instruments dissected death. No matter how much she believed in justice, exposing the naked body was a desecration of that life. So she stood a bit straighter, breathed through her gritted teeth instead of her nose, and looked at the pathologist instead of the body.

Dr. White was not, for once, wearing a dress shirt and slacks with his trademark bow tie. Instead, he wore a brand-new Chicago the Tour T-shirt with worn jeans. But it was a Saturday, so Karen gave him a pass. Besides, Hal Birchard would likely have approved.

Beside her, Marek twitched. "I had tickets to that concert," he told the pathologist, obviously having finally registered the T-shirt. She'd noticed his processing abilities were often delayed in the mornings, particularly if he hadn't slept much. Not that her brain powers were much better, as she hadn't even had time to make coffee.

"Had? Oh." Dr. White's smile flashed like cream in his coffee-colored face—and with as much gloat as gleam. "I suppose I should be thankful that my work can be delayed a bit, unlike yours, Detective."

"How was the concert?" Marek asked, as if hoping it'd been terrible.

"Some people gave up on the band after lead singer Peter Cetera left, but I must tell you, the experience was absolutely superb. Even though I had a man-crush on drummer Danny Seraphine, I'll admit his replacement—or is it his replacement's replacement?—did well enough. I didn't want it to end. The drum riffs? To die for."

Taking up a couple scalpels, the pathologist beat a tat-tat on an empty gurney. The sharp sound was precise and ear-cringing, but the beat was strong. Karen had to stop her foot from tapping. Then she sucked in a horrified breath as he finished it off by flinging the scalpels in the air... and catching them again by the handles. It was a *very* close call.

He winked at her. "I played a pretty mean drum myself, back in the day."

Her heart was still pounding to the beat of his stupidity. "If you'd missed, we'd be transporting you up a level to the ER, and you wouldn't be playing with drums... or dead bodies."

Though she hadn't meant to sound disapproving, he put the scalpels aside. "My apologies for the levity."

"None needed," Marek said before Karen could. "Our victim was a musician."

Dr. White's shoulders relaxed. "So I heard on the radio coming in." Picking up one of his discarded scalpels, he went to work on the neck, delicately and with as much precision as his playing, but without the beat. "Offed at the Jam Off, that was their lead. I've heard of a Folk Off before, but I like your take better. Now... let's get started."

The rhythm of scalpel and saw was far more grating than the impromptu drumming, but she survived it. When the maestro laid down his instruments, Karen let out a breath. "So... cause of death?"

Dr. White lifted a hand toward his own neck, as if to tweak his missing bow tie, then let it fall to the table. "As you've already noted, he was garroted."

Karen kept her mind on the case, not the body. "That was

an even cut, not down or up. Straight on. So it had to be somebody strong. *Really* strong. Birchard was built and just under six feet. That narrows the field considerably. In fact, I don't think anybody fits that profile so far."

Marek made a soft sound of dissent. "Could still be anybody. Mud underneath the blood."

"Under?" Karen frowned as she tried to fit that into her scene. And drew a blank. "So..."

The pathologist helped her out. "Your victim was garroted after he fell to the ground."

Karen blinked then nodded. Regretfully. Finding a Marek-sized perp would have been fairly quick work. "He had no defensive wounds?"

"Correct. Your conclusion?"

"Unconscious when he was killed?"

"Almost certainly. Your notes said he was playing an electric guitar." Dr. White picked up one of Birchard's hands and considered it then went down to the feet. "Hmm."

That sounded like he'd just confirmed something. "What?"

"Burn marks. Very faint. I wouldn't have noticed them if I wasn't looking for them. Often, you don't find them. He was electrocuted."

Karen exchanged a look with Marek. "Larson said the amp was dead—and unplugged from the guitar. I thought it happened from the fall. Maybe not."

"Or maybe that's what happened," Marek mused. "And limited the shock."

"That's not my call." Dr. White looked down at the body sadly. "But to continue with what *is*, I'd say Hal Birchard lost consciousness from the shock and fell forward. That's where he got the bruises you see on his face, especially his nose. I don't think the shock itself was fatal. But he may have been out for some minutes. If he lived, he may have had some residual paresis, even brain damage." He looked at the bare feet. "Was there water in the area?"

"Grass was damp," Marek told him. "Maybe a puddle."

"And he was barefoot. Not a good combination. It may not have taken a huge jolt. We could be talking fairly low voltage. Keep that in mind."

Karen was itching to get Larson's input. "Will do. Anything else?"

The pathologist stripped off his latex gloves. "I will get the tox screen to you ASAP, but I don't see any signs he was a user. A few old scars here and there, but it's hard to say at this point where they came from, so I can't rule for or against a rough childhood. Some extensive dental work done later in life might suggest he was from a poor family—or neglectful. Do we have a next of kin to release the body to?"

Karen shook her head, happy that she didn't have to do a notification but sad for Hal Birchard. Everyone deserved someone who cared. "He doesn't seem to have any kin, at least in the area. Doc Hudson told me last night that Birchard used the Bolvins—his musical buddies—as his emergency contacts. If no one else comes forward, I expect the Bolvin family will take care of arrangements."

"Good to know he had friends, if not family. Oh, one last thing." Dr. White opened a cabinet and took out a plastic bag that held a pair of silver behind-the-ear hearing aids. "These are a pretty powerful model, so I'd say a significant hearing loss, at least in the high frequencies. He wouldn't be the first to lose what I can only imagine was his most valuable asset." Dr. White touched the backs of his own ears, turning his head slightly. For the first time, Karen noted he had discreet black-colored hearing aids. "I've been there, done that, though my loss is only moderate. Even without them, I do okay in quiet settings. Still, it's a loss. I keep telling my kids they'll blow their ears out, too, with the head-banging stuff they listen to, but they don't listen to me."

"Already can't hear," Marek suggested.

Dr. White smiled ruefully. "It's a very selective hearing loss."

"Been there, and still doing that," Marek returned.

Karen felt a twinge at her loss—not of hearing, but of having a child to yell at. That she had reunited with her adult daughter had to be enough, and truthfully, it was more than she could have hoped for. And she couldn't imagine Eyre blasting music of any sort. Eyre used headphones or played only when she thought she was alone. Classical, mostly, with some Celtic fiddling and new-agey mishmash thrown in.

Jessica Baake, however, was blasting something Karen couldn't identify but was definitely under the hard rock category when Karen and Marek arrived at the Sioux Falls DCI office a quarter hour later. Karen herself was a classic rock fan.

Whatever Jessica's music was, it had Marek wincing. Did the older generations always wince at the music of the younger? Probably.

"Sorry," Jessica said when she caught sight of them. She clicked the music off. "Larson never lets me rock my tunes when he's here. Yells at me to watch my hearing. Which kind of defeats the purpose. And... what's so funny?"

"Nothing." Karen slid onto one of the stools. She admitted to feeling disappointed that the young woman was alone. "Where's your fearless leader?"

Jessica grinned, pulling on the scar. "Facing the move. Today's the fill-up-the-truck day. Tomorrow's zero day. He put it off three times already by saying he had to work. I told him to stop crapping out and get it done. I could handle the case until Monday."

And Larson hadn't even told Karen that this was the big weekend. Well, she'd take care of that. He'd learn what it meant to move into a town like Reunion. "So what've you got for us?"

"Well, we've got some prints lifted from various items in the tent. The triangles had none except the Bolvins but highly smudged, especially around the grip area. The fiddle string had nothing that I could lift, but that's about what I expected. Another stab at the fiddle came up clean, so you can take that with you. Lots of lifts on the amp and guitar and mic. Birchard's on the guitar and amp, naturally, and at least half a dozen others. Some are too smudged to lift. We'll check the good ones against our databases, but I'm guessing they'll be from Josh Bolvin and his uncles. You'll want to get those for elimination."

"Already done."

"Larson also said we should hold on to the amp and mic, as he wants to check the wiring."

Smart man. He'd seen something there that Karen hadn't. But she gave herself a pass. He'd been doing this stuff for a lot longer than she had. "Dr. White said Birchard was electrocuted before being garroted."

"Oh. Ouch. But I suppose that's good, that he wasn't... aware. No wonder he didn't fight back. Don't you hate it when Larson's right? A few minutes at the scene, and he's already figured out stuff that hasn't even occurred to me yet." Jessica moved over to a metal table and picked up a bagged Samsung Galaxy phone and a handwritten list with notes. "I only just started on the list of calls. We'll have to wait for the phone company to cough up the details, but I can tell you that he made a couple really interesting ones yesterday afternoon."

"You look like the cat that ate the canary, Baake." When Karen just got a smug smile, she ground her teeth. "Spit out the hair ball."

Jessica brightened. "Have you seen Hairball?"

Baffled now, Karen said, "No, I don't have a cat."

Marek chuckled while Jessica doubled over on her stool. When she caught her breath, she got out, "No... Hairball... the band. Explosions, lights, over the top. Arena rock. Great stuff. My uncle and cousins took me to a concert in Cedar Rapids. Even the local band that opened didn't suck. Vicebox."

Karen held back her horses and played the game. "Sounds... criminal. What vices?"

"I didn't dare ask. But they might be able to use the services of a good lawyer." Her grin widened. "That's what Hal Birchard did. Actually, he called two of them. Thanks to the magic of Mr. Google, I identified them as Andrew Van Doren, an estate lawyer in Sioux Falls, and Daryl Link, an intellectual property attorney in Los Angeles."

CHAPTER 9

MAREK DECIDED THAT HAL BIRCHARD wasn't much into home maintenance.

The 1960s ranch-style home backed up to the new recycling center, and in his opinion, it should just be shoved right into the facility. Though he wasn't sure any of the raw materials were salvageable. The roof sagged, the paint-stripped shutters that still remained were cockeyed, and the concrete drive looked like a moon shot, cratered and cracked.

Karen stalked up behind him on the walk. She still looked pissed. She'd been unable to reach either lawyer, even after going through a gauntlet of answering machines and admins. On the way back from Sioux Falls, she'd cranked up the radio in the Sub and simmered to classic rock on B102.7.

"Not looking to me like Hal Birchard had anything to leave anyone." Karen waited impatiently on the cracked step for him to open the door. "Maybe that call to the estate lawyer had to do with him getting property, not leaving it."

Marek took out the key that Nick Bolvin had given to him. All of the Bolvins, including Josh, had one. Apparently, the sorry-looking house was their man cave.

After pulling out his XXXL-sized latex gloves, Marek slid the key in and pushed open the wedged door with a shove. He whistled as he got a good look inside.

Karen gave him a push in the back. "What? Does he have girlie pics on the walls?"

"No, he's got a seriously expensive sound system in here." Marek took a step inside so Karen could get around him. "I've got Paradigm speakers at home that cost me a couple thousand, but these? I'd say he's got at least a couple hundred thousand just in this room alone. Acapella Audio Arts. Pivetta. Wavac."

"Boys and their toys," Karen muttered, obviously not familiar with the high-end audio brands. "But it does explain why he bothered to lock the door. Think the Bolvins killed him for these?"

Marek took that as a rhetorical question. While Karen went for the small open kitchen, he moved into the side hall beyond the living room. The first door led to a basic bathroom that didn't look like it had been updated since the 1960s. It reminded him strongly of the boys' locker room at Valeska High, with dented tiles and grimed-in body odor not even heavy-duty bleach could get out. The bedroom attached to the bathroom had at least made it into the 1970s, with zigzagging orange-and-lime walls. The basic white-and-gray bedding was twisted up and hung drunkenly over the side of the king-sized mattress. Had Birchard had a lover?

An unwelcome thought stopped Marek in his size-fourteen Blunnies. What if Josh and Hal were involved? That would certainly explain the boy's evasive replies when his father—and, good grief, his grandmother—could hear every word. And if they'd fallen out, it might also explain why Birchard wanted to change his will.

So far, though, Marek pictured Hal Birchard as a loner who only connected with those who shared his passion for music. Had that passion bled over to the bed? Well, they could test the sheets for semen stains. DNA tests would be a much longer process since the case wasn't high-profile.

"Kitchen is a step up from that bathroom, but that's not saying much," Karen said behind him. She surveyed the bed and the rumpled sheets. "Sloppy or..." He could see her mind run down the various possibilities, and when she pinkened, he was pretty sure she'd seen the same ones he had.

"I'll bag the sheets." Karen looked around the bare walls. The dresser top held only a Mason jar of pocket change and a discarded pair of socks. "No family photos. No art. Nothing personal."

Marek went to the nightstand. "If he moved around, he probably traveled light." Marek jerked his thumb back toward the living room. "And that high-end equipment is all from the last several years, so he must have bought them after he got here."

Karen pursed her lips. "Putting down roots?"

Marek shrugged as he noted a box of condoms. Unopened. "Or that's just the way he operates. Decides one day he's had enough of one place and up and sells everything, takes the cash, moves on, and buys the latest and greatest wherever he lands next."

Karen placed the sheets into a large plastic bag. "Are you going to upgrade your Paradises?"

"Paradigms." Marek hid his smile. "And no, probably not until Becca is out of school, if then. I'll be lucky to still have a house if she goes to college then grad school."

"At least you'd do something with this place." Karen cocked an eye to a water stain on the ceiling. "It's falling down around his ears. Or was. I bet they raze the place after it's sold."

Marek closed the nightstand drawer. "I won't take that bet. If he'd hired me to do a remodel, I'd've turned him down flat. Better to start over."

Karen closed the last drawer in the dresser. "Clothes. All wash-and-wear. Cotton and fleece." She opened the closet. It held nothing but a pair of Nikes and well-worn hiking boots. "Wow. Not a single hanger. The man must not own a dress shirt, much less a tux."

"I don't own a tux." Marek let his hand snake back to the

gun at the small of his back when someone knocked on the front door. "I'll get that."

"Let's." Karen followed him into the living room then peeked through the dusty blinds. "It's Seoul. What's she doing here? Her shift isn't until midnight. She should be sleeping."

Marek opened the door. "What are you selling?"

The young deputy stuck out her tongue. "Girl Scout cookies."

"Thin Mint for me," Karen replied. "What are you doing up? I don't want you crashing your not-so-snazzy ride on your shift. Unless, of course, you drive the Sub. In that case, be my guest."

"Couldn't sleep. And the guys ran me out of the station when I tried to help them with the photos and vids, so I decided to come over and..." Seoul trailed off as she got a good look at the contents of the room. "Oh, wow. That's some serious—" She snapped back her hand before she touched a speaker then whistled. "Is that a baby Steinway?"

Marek blinked as she went directly to a dark corner, where a baby grand piano, black and gleaming, stood. Karen hissed when Seoul reached out again. Putting her hands under her armpits, the deputy shrugged in apology. "It's hard not to touch. That's a Steinway. Serious moola."

Karen pulled out extra gloves from her back pocket and threw them over. "You play?"

"Since I was a tyke. We had a vintage Yamaha upright." Gloved, Seoul tinkled the keys, making a face. Marek guessed that the tactile feel of the keys was lost, because the pitch sounded fine to him. Nevertheless, she launched into Scott Joplin's "Maple Leaf Rag."

"Just what we need," Karen drawled. "Music for a scene search."

To Marek's regret, Seoul stopped mid-rag and held up her hands. "Have gloves, will search. Where do you want me?" She grinned. "And don't say in bed."

Karen just shook her head. "We've got one room left on this level. Then the basement."

Marek followed her into the last room off the hallway. Even before Karen flipped on the light, a low-level hum and small blinking green-and-red lights told him the room contained at least one computer.

"Well, we just jumped into the twenty-first century." Karen put a hand on the back of an ergonomic office chair and surveyed the Spartan but loaded room. "This must be where he worked. The question is, what was that work?"

Marek jiggled the mouse to disengage the screen saver on the large monitor. The screen that appeared showed various stock indices, and he could see icons for financial apps. "Stock broker?"

Karen looked up from a stack of prospectuses pushed into a cubbyhole on the desk by the window. "Usually, you deal with clients if that's your gig, and there's zero indication of that."

"He could do it remotely. Or..." Marek thought about the gold mine in the living room. "He was a stock picker. Market timer, perhaps?"

"You need money for that," Seoul said.

Karen picked up a paperweight in the shape of a musical note. "Or be very good or very lucky."

Whichever the case, that kind of "job" would allow him to come and go. Marek tried to bring up the financial programs, one at a time, but they were all passcoded.

Karen pursed her lips. "If he had a lot of money, or inherited it, then changing his will would be a big deal and a motive for murder."

They spent another half hour in the office, gathering various papers from the desk, but nothing else flicked a switch. So they tromped down the rickety stairs to the basement. When the three of them stood at the bottom of the stairs, blinking under the fluorescent lights that had snapped on, Marek shouldn't have been surprised by what greeted him.

But he was. And he wasn't the only one.

Seoul practically hummed. "Look at all these instruments. And that has to be a recording studio back there." She reached out to touch a Martin acoustic guitar and got her hand slapped. "Sorry. This is just so... badass. No wonder the Bolvins came over here whenever they could. I thought it was just a cappella that they did, but it's so much more. And look at all those tapes and CDs." She walked over to the wall, where hundreds of them were stacked in specially made shelves. The deputy tugged the latest addition out and read the Sharpie-written handwriting through the clear case. "Dated last month. Listed as accordion. Polka. Frank Mazurek. Valeska, SD."

Marek nodded. "Danielle said he was interested in local, traditional music."

Seoul looked at the wall in awe. "If this is all traditional folk music, it's a gold mine. Some of those are ancient cassettes and even..."

"Tapes," Karen supplied dryly. "What's it worth?"

"Worth? Priceless. Not many ethnomusicologists venture out this way. Usually, they go to exotic places like the Amazon or deepest Africa. The Dakotas are hiding in plain sight."

Karen seemed to lose interest. "So, priceless only to academics."

"Not just. Musicians mine that stuff, too. What's old is new. What goes around, comes around. Just think of the Celtic craze or jazz or world fusion, all that came from traditional folk music. Hal Birchard mined that in his performance, and it was a hit with the crowd."

Marek pointed out the obvious. "But the music is all here. Not a motive for murder."

Karen eyed the polka CD dubiously. "Not unless we're

looking at an academic interested in ancient history. As far as I'm concerned, polka can remain dead and buried."

"Spoilsport. My music history prof would go batshit crazy over this stuff. If it isn't recorded and the next generations don't carry it on, that music is lost forever. Like the ancients. We don't have a clue what their music sounded like before scores were invented." Seoul moved on to a series of deep black cabinets with drawers. She pulled one open, her tawny eyes as intent as a cat's on a leaf of catnip. "Sheet music." She sifted through a handful. "Mostly printed. Rare, I think, as I don't recognize any of them. Bygone era. Ragtime. Big band. Barbershop. Gospel."

Marek wasn't surprised when Karen let out a frustrated breath.

"So... nothing particularly valuable except to academics and old-timey collectors."

Seoul moved on to a cabinet shoved behind a music stand in a corner. When she pulled on a drawer, it didn't budge. She tried another. Same result.

"Locked." Marek moved forward. "Let me try."

Karen breathed down his neck as he jiggled and pried. "There you go."

Seoul slid the first drawer open slowly, as if starting a striptease act.

"We don't have all day," Karen told her, glancing at her watch. "It's almost lunchtime."

"Where's your sense of drama?" Sighing in mock disappointment, Seoul pulled it all the way open. More scores. Only these were originals handwritten on preprinted musical notation paper. Seoul hummed the first bar under her breath, a catchy tune that sounded faintly folkish but with a more modern slant and rockish rhythm that had even Karen twitching.

Seoul perused the sheet. "No songwriter, no date, just the music. Kind of hurriedly penned with some changes and annotations. Not bad. Not bad at all. For its type, that is."

Karen began to pace. "But again, nothing to pin a murder on."

"Sadly, I agree, but..." Seoul's jaw dropped as she opened the last drawer. "Oh. My. God." The Catholic deputy actually crossed herself, either in penitence or in reverence. With shaking fingers, she picked up the first sheet in a thick sheaf of faintly yellowed music. The notes were handwritten, as before, but much neater. "I can't believe it. Look at the date. And the name."

Marek focused, but he hadn't gotten much beyond the T-R-I before Karen beat him to the punch. "Trick Legrande. Sounds faintly familiar. But..."

Marek took a stab. "Wild Abandon?"

"Of course." Karen snapped her fingers. "Classic rock. Boy band that hit it big in the eighties and nineties. But they're long gone. All of the band members are dead, right?"

Seoul didn't look up from the music. "Right. Trick Legrande held that group together. But the thing is, he went solo after the band broke up when the lead singer overdosed. Danny Cooper."

"Oh, yeah." Karen made a whisking-away-the-heat motion. "Heartthrob with the flowing golden locks and dreamboat eyes. Killer voice. 'Rock On' was a major hit. We played it for all our high school ball games."

Which only went to show that what went around, came around. Josh Bolvin had tapped into a long history of Boy Wonders. Hopefully with a better outcome.

"OD, car wreck, and suicide," Karen murmured. "So... I assume that the music you're holding is worth something, Deputy Durr? Are we looking at a collectible?"

"Collectible?" Seoul looked back up, dazed, awed, and clearly beyond excited. "Some would sell their soul for this. If it went out on auction, I'm guessing millions, easy. My dad is a big fan of Wild Abandon. He has the entire collection. Well, along with Genesis, Kansas, and Chicago. Thing is, I've heard all of it. Many, many times. But these? They've never been recorded. Ever. And the dates? They're all after the band broke up."

Marek dredged a stray memory out of the swamp he called a mind. "Legrande committed suicide, didn't he?"

"Yes, he..." As Seoul trailed off, her face went from awed to dismayed with the swiftness of a mime. "Oh, crap. Crap, crap, crap."

Karen's face sharpened. "What? Not so collectible after all? Forgery?"

"No. This one?" Seoul lifted the sheet she'd been perusing. She hummed a couple bars. "That's Josh Bolvin's viral hit. The one he took credit for. It's Legrande's music."

CHAPTER 10

LOOKING MORE LIKE THE GAUNT and pale Boy George than the golden all-American Boy Wonder, Josh Bolvin sat in the crowded interview room with his head bowed, his guitar-callused fingers tightly clasped. His father and uncles held up the walls between bulging file cabinets. Nothing would convince them to leave the room, and Marek hadn't even tried, even though Josh wasn't a minor.

Go after one Bolvin, deal with all.

Marek wondered if they'd topple the filing cabinets over on him if they didn't like what they heard. Though his stomach roiled with the hot dog he'd nuked for lunch, his head knew it was the right decision for him to lead the interview. He knew Josh at least fleetingly. Using a relationship to twist a confession out of a suspect was basic investigative technique. Right now, though, he wished he were back in Albuquerque, where he rarely knew the victims or the suspects unless he'd already had the misfortune to run into them in the criminal justice system.

Marek supposed he was lucky the Bolvins hadn't already crushed him when he read Josh his rights. At least they hadn't pulled the lawyer card. The deep distrust most Dakotans had for lawyers had no doubt warred with the Bolvins' desire to protect their kin. So far, distrust had won. And the Bolvins' distrust in Marek would certainly follow, no matter the outcome.

Sometimes the job sucked. On the table, Marek placed an enlarged photo of Josh storming out of the instrument tent. "Josh, all we want is the truth. Whatever that is." When the boy raised his head, his dreamboat eyes skeptical, Marek met them head-on. "If you play straight with me, I'll play straight with you. Is this you?"

Josh poked one finger on the printout, turned it, and nodded.

"You'll need to speak for the record," Karen murmured from her place by the door.

The reminder of being recorded sometimes sent suspects running, but it didn't faze Josh Bolvin, perhaps because he was used to being recorded. "Yeah. That's me." He brooded over the clear expression of fury, the balled fists. "I was pissed."

The time stamp on the photo from a Sioux Falls fan of Josh's viral video was 6:27 p.m. Marek could just make out Rad Wilson near the platform on the side of the judges' tent, her mouth twisted into what looked like satisfaction—or maybe it was just the face paint. But whatever it was, she'd told the truth. And why not? Josh Bolvin had what she desperately wanted: the notice of the music industry and the chance for a bigger stage.

"Pissed about what?" Marek asked.

Josh hugged his skinny torso. "I told you. He dissed my offers."

Marek leaned back, letting off some of the pressure. "You like to write your own songs?"

The dreamboat eyes lidded. "Sure. Who doesn't? I mean, someone like me, who grew up with music all around, it's just natural."

"Your family does mostly traditional music, right? But you chose rock."

A low rumble from Ned had Marek's shoulder blades itching. He wasn't sure what the eldest Bolvin was objecting to—that the boy had chosen another path or that Marek had called their music traditional. He supposed it might be considered an insult, though it wasn't meant as such.

Josh actually smiled over Marek's head. It lightened his entire face to the carefree young man Marek had seen running after his younger cousins on a July Fourth cookout at the Bolvin farm. Still in his teens but a recent high school graduate, he'd been on the cusp of adulthood.

"Uncle Ned thinks I've sold my soul to the devil. I was supposed to get old enough to be the perfect fourth."

"Diminished fourth," Ned returned.

Josh burnished his knuckles against his chest. "Augmented."

Karen looked totally baffled by that return, but while Marek didn't remember all the specifics, he knew it had to do with chords. Sharps, flats, whole and half notes. Once upon a time, he had been able to talk that language, but even with his dyslexia-survival-mechanism, a good memory, he couldn't recall the exact differences.

But if this panned out, he knew the Bolvins would be permanently diminished. "The video that went viral, who did that? You?"

Josh frowned at Marek, as if his mind were going back to overheard whispers about the Dumb Polack. "You saw it. It's me."

"Yes, singing, playing the guitar. But the keyboards, the harmony, all the backing tracks?" Marek saw the hit register. "Who mixed it? Produced it? That was a very high-level video."

Marek had taken the time to watch it again on YouTube on his phone. The kid had panache, he had charisma, he had the voice, and he played a decent guitar. But so did many others. There'd been far more to that video than the boy's contribution. Even Marek's relatively untrained ear could tell that.

The boy curled in on himself. Nate leaned over and put a hand on his son's rounded shoulder. "Go on, tell the man.

It's no secret. Then we can get back to the festival before we miss the Barn Off."

Marek wasn't sure he wanted to know what that was, but he waited. Would the boy come clean, or would he implicate himself?

The boy uncurled in bits and pieces until he was upright again. "Hal did. Mr. Birchard. Have you seen his place?" When Marek nodded, Josh went on, his awe clearly visible. "He's got a freaking studio. Harmonizers, mixers, synthesizers—you name it, he's got it. He even lent me his Boomerang loop station for my solo act. I thought he did that stuff for work, like a remote producer or something, but he said that would take the fun out of it. We worked together on the video, and he added a lot of the tracks and special effects and all that jazz. But he didn't want any part of the public face of it. That's the honest-to-God truth!"

Marek didn't doubt that. Hal Birchard seemed to crave a low profile—at least until his last performance. Time to do a bit of mixing of his own. "How long have you and Hal been lovers?"

"Whaaat?!" Josh backed away from the table so fast that his chair fell back and hit one of the filing cabinets. "Me and... No way. You're way, way off, Mr. Okerlund." His father pushed him vertical again. "I've got a girl. Evie Hahn. She's in Minneapolis with her family this week for her sister's wedding, but she'll be back on Monday, and you can ask her. We're tight. I'd never... especially with a guy... and an *old* guy. Older than my dad!"

The hand tightened on Josh's shoulder and shook. Hard. "Have some respect."

Marek wasn't sure who that was directed at, Josh or himself, but he forged ahead. "But it was all a lie, wasn't it. The offers, the accolades--they shouldn't have come to you. All you were was the pretty face, the showman, the frontrunner."

Ned slapped the table in front of Marek. "Josh *earned*

those offers. Anyone who says different won't walk out of this room without a busted face."

Marek didn't look up. Face or no, he had a job to do. He kept his eyes on the boy. If he got sucker punched, so be it. "You didn't write that music, Josh, and we can prove it."

The boy froze.

"What the hell are you talking about? He worked night and day to..." When he got a guilty silence from his son, Nate jerked him around. "Josh?"

Faced with the implacable wall of Bolvins, the truth burst out of Josh Bolvin. "I *promised*."

"Promised what? And to who?" Nick's "aw shucks" face now said "aw hell." "You told us you wrote that song. You *lied* to us."

Josh upturned his calloused hands in supplication. "Hal made me promise. We had a deal. You all taught me not to break my word."

His father said, "Hal's dead. You aren't. Come clean, Josh. Whatever it is, we'll deal." But Nate's face was tight with tension and dread.

"Don't look like that, Dad. I only did what he wanted, I swear." Josh swung back to Marek. "Hal didn't want to be involved in any performances, Mr. Okerlund. He just wanted to write, mix, produce. The ultimate behind-the-scenes guy."

Ned crossed his arms. "So you didn't write any of those songs?"

"I wrote the ones for the cancelled solo act but not for Monday's concert. Look, Hal's like... on another level. I heard him playing that song, the one that went viral, when he didn't know I'd come downstairs. I asked him if I could get a copy of it, as it would make a great cover. At first, he said no. But a couple weeks later, he changed his mind. Said he wanted it out there, you know? That music only lives when it's shared and heard by others. But he didn't want to be on the road or deal with all the crazy stuff. I figure that's why he was so down on my offers. Told me taking a deal with a label or signing on with a manager was like selling out the farm for the pleasure of becoming a tenant on my own land."

"Makes sense," his accountant father said.

"What else?" Marek asked. "You weren't mad just because he was against you signing a label. It was more. It had to be more. You're not a firebrand."

Josh looked down at the table, and his shoulders slumped. "He said he wasn't going to let me use that video or any of the music we'd already recorded and were going to perform at the concert on Monday. So yeah, I was royally pissed because I worked my tail off to get things just right on vocals, on the guitar, so I wouldn't embarrass him or the guys he found for backup for the concert, or hell, you guys." He looked at his father and uncles. "It was my big chance to make it. He knew that. And he tried to kill it, just like that." He snapped his fingers.

Marek watched him carefully. "So you killed him."

Josh just shook his head. "No. Just no."

"Will you take a lie detector test?"

"Yes. Hell, yes." No hesitation.

Marek backed up. "How much money did Hal Birchard want as his cut? Was it a set amount or a percentage of any income?"

"Hal didn't want money. Said he had enough already. And I believed him. I mean, the house is the pits, but the equipment? The basement studio? You probably don't realize just how expensive that stuff is. I could only dream."

Finally, Karen spoke, as they'd prearranged. "But it wasn't Hal Birchard's music, was it, Josh? That's just another lie. It was Trick Legrande's."

Josh blinked up at her. "Who? Is this a trick?"

As a performer, Josh was an actor of some degree, but that was a very convincing baffled expression. Behind him, though, the faces ranged from disbelief to shock to blankness.

"From Wild Abandon."

That got at least a glimmer. "Some old rocker?"

"Some dead rocker," Ned told his nephew then glared at Marek, which Marek didn't think was fair, since Karen had made the accusation. "You're off your rocker."

Marek had one last question. "When you left Hal, what was he doing?"

"Cleaning that old fiddle. The last thing... the very last thing I said to him... was that I hated him. I didn't kill him. I wouldn't. But I said that to him." Josh lowered his head into his folded arms on the table, and his shoulders shook with silent tears. "And now I can't take it back."

Can't take it back. The words of many a regretful killer. While Marek reserved judgment, he had no way of either proving or disproving the boy's innocence, as much as he'd like to.

"Are we done here?" Nate asked, his hand on his son's back, his eyes hot—and worried.

Marek glanced at Karen and got her nod. He'd like to put his head down on the table and cry as well. "We're done. For now."

And likely forever when it came to Marek's friendship with the family. The Berlin Wall had nothing on the Bolvin Wall.

CHAPTER 11

ONCE AGAIN, KAREN PARKED THE Sub in the lower lot of Grove Park and began the trek up to the festival grounds by foot. She was surprised that the Big Jam was so still so well attended, given that there was a murderer on the loose.

Beside her, Marek easily matched her stride. Neither of them had said a word on the drive. She hadn't even turned on the radio. Normally, she liked to talk out her thoughts, but at the moment, she had none. Whether Marek did, she didn't know, as he thought in silence. More likely, he was brooding about being on the Bolvin blacklist again.

Josh Bolvin was still a suspect, but they had no real hard evidence and a lot of questions about just what had transpired. If he had killed Birchard, knowing the music was actually Trick Legrande's didn't seem to be the motive. Birchard may well have passed it off as his own. Her men were still working on a timeline from the huge number of statements, photos, and videos. Her senior deputy, Kurt Bechtold, was leading that effort. He had returned to work with a huge batch of kolaches his sister had baked and so was forgiven for his time away caring for her. Karen had been reviewing the work already done when her phone had rung, sending them back to the festival.

Edging around the hooting and clapping crowd, Karen took several steps toward their target before she realized she'd lost Marek. He'd stopped and was staring at the stage. Only then did she really register the racket... music?

Incredulous, she watched as half a dozen beefy men in overalls and Saint Patrick's Day bright-green shirts beat a rat-a-tat-tat on milk cans while a woman in traditional Irish dress tapped an old hammer against a series of water-filled milk bottles arranged down a long milking bench. Each jar produced a different note.

"What the hell...?" Karen breathed as she stopped next to her detective.

"It's the Barn Off." With a silly grin on his face, Marek bobbed his head to the beat. "All the instruments have to come from inside a barn."

Unlike the previous night, when the crowd was far more restrained and the musicians more intense, this crowd was good-naturedly rowdy, and the musicians were hamming it up on the stage. One of the overalled men lifted a cowbell and beat it while the woman went after the jars like a whirling dervish. It was actually pretty good. And under other circumstances, she'd enjoy it. She'd had no idea it was a thing. Now they'd switched from some Irish reel to "Old MacDonald Had a Farm" and were really going to town—or country—working the crowd.

"I wonder what she does if it rains," Marek mused.

Karen tugged Marek's arm. "Come on."

Reluctantly, he turned away.

When they ducked into the registration tent, they found Connor hooking up an old VHS tape player to an even older tube TV. "Where did you unearth that setup?" Karen asked then tucked tongue in cheek. "In a barn?"

"Very funny." Connor switched on the power strip and rose to his feet. "If it still works, it still works. Old tech is harder to hack. And cheaper."

"The clarity isn't anywhere as good," Karen fretted as she watched the grainy picture that came on.

"That doesn't matter to me. It's good enough."

Was it? She just hoped she didn't have to watch endless footage of Bambi and the birds before they found out. But he'd obviously cued it up close to what he wanted to show them. She appreciated the effort. It was just too bad that he wasn't as tech savvy as his predecessor. Crouching down, Connor hit the pause button on the player as the time stamp of 6:56 p.m. jumped onto the screen as the camera was triggered.

"When was the body found?" Karen asked Marek.

"Seoul's call came in at 7:17 p.m.," her human recorder replied. He didn't have photographic memory, but it was pretty darn close.

"So Danielle found Birchard maybe five minutes before, ten at most. It's only a couple minutes from the creek back to the judges' tent, and Kuhl was back at seven." Karen took out her phone, set it to record, and pointed it at the old TV. She didn't think she had a working VHS player lying around. "Go ahead, Connor. Roll it."

Connor hit one of the clunky buttons, and the tape player groaned to life again. The camera was set maybe a yard from the trail and footbridge. The figure who passed by was blurred, but the silver hair, the easy grace, and the pin-striped shirt identified the man easily.

Anton Kuhl stopped at the footbridge and looked around, then he stooped down out of the camera's sight, perhaps retying his shoe or dragging a finger in the water. Then he stood, put his hands in his pockets, and held that pose for a moment, taking in a deep breath. Nature time, perhaps. A California thing? After checking his watch, he turned around and passed the camera on the way back up the trail. The camera snippet ended and jumped to someone Karen recognized.

Seeing the ball cap, she smiled. "Bobby made the team?"

Connor's stepson had once been told he wasn't good enough to play baseball, period.

"Not only made it, he's the team captain. Hitting .320

and plays first base. Wears that cap everywhere. He's in hog heaven."

A big step up from being homeless. "It's been a hard slog for all of you. At the risk of jinxing things, I'm glad to see things turning your way. It's not something I see very often in my business."

"I appreciate it each and every day."

Unlike many who blithely parroted such greeting card fodder, Chee Connor actually meant it. Homeless once in this very park, he now lived in the park in an actual home. Karen would take his hard-won Zen of living in the moment over Kuhl's nature-immersion minute any day.

"Did that video help you?" Connor asked as he ejected the tape and handed it to her.

Karen pocketed her phone and took the tape. "We're still working up the timeline. But it does confirm Kuhl's story."

"The record label mogul? Was he a suspect?"

"Everyone's a suspect," she said in dark tones, but a clang of cowbells from the Barn Off ruined the effect, and Connor just laughed.

"Well, I was in here." His laughter died. "We set record attendance for the Jam Off this year because of Josh Bolvin's viral hit. That's what drew the sharks. That manager? Marmot?"

"Marmo," Marek corrected. "Sal."

"Yeah, him. He was stinking drunk by the time the judging started. Crashed into a tent pole and almost brought down the concession stand. Axel Knutsen had to sober him up." Connor hesitated then shrugged. "For what it's worth, I've heard through the grapevine that Marmo and Birchard had some kind of run-in before the Jam Off started."

That got her mind humming. "Was it over Josh Bolvin?"

"No one I talked to had any idea. Apparently, Birchard and Marmo walked into the woods before anyone could get wind of it. Came back one at a time, alone. Neither looked happy." Marek asked, "What time was that?"

Connor shrugged. "All I know is that it was after noon and before the Jam Off, which started at three."

As they turned to go out, he said nonchalantly, "All I know personally is that Tommy Fogler came in before we got the Jam Off started and changed places with Birchard."

Karen did a full three-sixty. "You didn't think to mention that?"

"I already did." His eyebrows lifted. "To your Deputy Two Fingers."

She really needed to set up an incident meeting so they were all on the same page. But with so many statements to cull through, it wouldn't be soon.

Connor shifted on his feet. "Any more questions?"

"Yes," Marek said. "Where is Kuhl right now?"

Connor blinked. "Kuhl? Umm..." He picked up a printed schedule from the table. "He's doing a talk on songwriting down on the lower campground. He should be wrapping up soon. We were lucky to get him to agree to do that besides the judging. Not many would. Once word got out, we had to limit attendance. Not all were happy."

Nor was she. Once again, Karen and Marek trekked across the meadow, this time listening to a group of burly men in Lederhosen play the Liechtensteiner Polka on wheel spokes and vats. Shaking her head as beer steins were raised and clunked, Karen led Marek down a short trail past the lower parking lot to another opening in the woods, where a canopy rippled in the wind.

About thirty attendees sat in a half circle on folding chairs as Kuhl wrapped up.

"Remember, sometimes the most powerful music, the most powerful note, is..." Kuhl paused, leaning forward, and when the attendees did the same, he finally whispered, "Silence." He waited another beat. "The pause, the rest... is it the end? Or just another motif, a buildup, to something new, exciting, different? Is it unfinished or will it resolve?

Anticipation, timing, is everything. The sound of silence is powerful. Use it."

And Kuhl got in return... a very loud round of applause. As he smiled, he looked up then caught sight of them, and his mouth twisted wryly.

Karen noted that neither Josh Bolvin nor Rad Wilson were in attendance. Had they signed up and been turned away? Or had they decided they were already good enough? It took a while before Kuhl was able to free himself, but eventually, the attendees, buzzing like a hive, moved off in search of the nectar of inspiration.

Uncertain why Marek had decided to talk to Kuhl, Karen let him take the lead.

Marek cleared his throat. "Mr. Kuhl, we have just a few questions."

Anton Kuhl took a swig of bottled water then gestured toward the vacated chairs. His light-colored shirt was damp, and he flicked a finger over his upper lip, where sweat had gathered. "I must say, when I think of the Dakotas, which admittedly is not often, I think of cold weather, not hot. But I am revising that opinion as we speak." He took another swig. "What can I do for you?"

"I'd like your take on the competition," Marek said.

"My competition?" Kuhl's silver eyebrows shot up. "I don't believe I have any, unless you count Sal, which I don't."

Marek looked abashed, but Karen didn't know if the expression was real or faked. "No, I meant the contestants at the Jam Off."

"Oh. I see." Kuhl slowly screwed the plastic top onto the nearly empty bottle. Karen was glad it wasn't being used as an improvised instrument. Idly, she wondered if the record mogul had signed up for the talk just to avoid the Barn Off. Probably not his cup of Dom Perignon. "Well, let's just say that it was a unique experience."

Karen felt her spine stiffen. "Yet you came here for the local talent."

"You misunderstand me, Sheriff." Kuhl turned his hands up in an I-come-in-peace gesture. "Actually, I've been pleasantly surprised at the high level of musical knowledge. Most can sight-read and score, an art that is getting harder and harder to find these days. And there were a few very good acts at the Jam Off that would not be amiss on many a concert floor, if only they had the branding. But it's still not the kind of talent I rep. You can be good, *very* good, and not make it to a label. It's always the X factor, isn't it?"

"And you think Josh Bolvin has that?" Marek asked.

"Ah. The 'Boy Wonder,' as one of your more colorful denizens calls him."

Karen was pretty sure that would be Rad Wilson. "Josh said you offered him a contract?"

"I offered to talk contracts, yes, but not until I heard him live. That's why I came all the way out here in the first place. A video can be deceiving." Kuhl looked at the vacated chairs. "I had hoped to see him here. He was signed up."

"He was a little busy," Karen said neutrally.

"Oh? Surely he's not a suspect." True alarm flickered. "He seemed a level-headed, if a bit naïve, young man. And he's got an openness—a genuineness—that would draw both men and women of varying ages. Please don't tell me it's all fake. Usually, I can spot that kind of thing."

Karen didn't think it was fake. But that didn't mean Josh wasn't a genuine killer. "We haven't arrested him, if that's what you're asking."

"I hope it stays that way." Kuhl unscrewed the bottle and took the last swig, wincing at what must be overly warmed water.

Marek asked, "What's your take on Josh Bolvin's video? Of his songwriting?"

Kuhl pitched the empty bottle into a garbage can, which made a very unmusical clunk. "It was remarkably... mature. In content, in presentation, in production. Not at all what you expect from a nineteen-year-old boy. That's why I'm here. Why Sal's here."

Unfortunately, both would soon find out that maturity was the product of a dead man's music.

Marek shifted on his Blunnies. "Do you know what Marmo and Birchard were arguing about before the Jam Off?"

Kuhl's face went blank. "Arguing?"

Karen nodded. "Heated enough to draw eyes—and have the two of them going into the woods to duke it out in private."

Kuhl pursed his lips. "I wasn't aware of that. Nor would Sal have confided in me. He's a man addicted to hard drink and a quick buck at the expense, literally, of the talent. Perhaps Birchard tried to get Sal to manage him and got turned down flat? Fiddling, no matter how well done, isn't the kind of music that draws Sal's ilk. He might take a flier on Rad Wilson, and he'd dearly love to leech off Josh Bolvin's success, but he'd never touch Birchard."

Someone had, though. Was it the music or the man?

CHAPTER 12

K AREN WALKED INTO THE OPEN bullpen on the first floor of the Eda County courthouse. With its huge glass windows, her transparency-in-government sheriff's office looked out across Main Street to a small park with a bandshell. She couldn't remember the last time an actual concert had been held there. Vaguely, she remembered getting all bundled up as a second grader to sing holiday songs with her class. The hot apple cider and cookies afterward were more memorable.

Karen paced the room, weaving her way through the desks, peering at her men's work. Only when Two Fingers gave her a steady dark stare did she stop. She'd never been good at waiting. The festival would break up after Monday night's concert, and while she'd heard that it was still on for that night, developments could sink that.

As Marek dropped into his chair and stared at his screen saver, Karen stopped playing micromanager and sat on her desk. Then she popped back up. She might as well see what Nails was saying about the investigation. She clicked on the radio that sat behind her desk.

—not much to report. Most people I talk to think the killer had to be one of the contestants of the Jam Off. Makes sense to me, since Hal Birchard was, in a manner of speaking, hoisted with his own petard—or fiddle strings. But I have also confirmed that young Josh Bolvin was questioned and

released. The Bolvins are keeping pretty closed-mouthed about the whole affair. Nate Bolvin—that's Josh's father, if you don't happen to remember which N the boy belongs to—said that there was nothing to talk about. And I couldn't reach Sheriff Mehaffey for comment. I was told she was out gathering statements.

As she switched the radio back off, Bork looked up at her with bloodshot eyes over his stack of statements. "Fake news. We were the ones who gathered statements."

"Sorry. Blame Josephine," Karen told him, sure that their semi-retired secretary had been the one to deflect Nails with the lie. Well, okay, not really a lie. She and Marek had talked to people, who'd made statements. But that reminded her. "Kurt, can you find me the statement of Tommy Fogler? He switched places with Birchard for the Jam Off."

Her hatchet-faced senior deputy turned from the chalkboard, where he'd been working on the timeline. He went to his desk and leafed through a stack of neatly sorted papers. Within a minute, he had it. That was why she loved him, even if he and Walrus were the bickering odd couple on her roster. She'd decided they must enjoy it and had stopped trying to smooth things out between them. At least Walrus was out on a call.

Karen skimmed the statement and, seeing Marek's quirked brow, summarized. "Fogler says Birchard approached him, not the other way around. Birchard told him that he wasn't feeling well but hoped to perform later. Going last meant he could scratch and not leave a hole in the lineup. Fogler jumped at the chance to go earlier because he gets antsy if he has to wait."

Marek tilted his head back. "Was Birchard really sick? Or just upset because of his run-in with Marmo?"

"What run-in?" Bork asked.

Karen explained briefly. "We need to talk to Marmo. Anyone have his contact info?"

After Kurt gave her the cell number, she called, but it

went straight to message. When she called Connor to find out where Marmo was, she was told that he was "indisposed" and wasn't planning to return to the festival that day. Connor didn't know where the man was staying, either, only that it wasn't locally. Frustrated, she hung up—and gave up.

"Mmm. Indisposed? Drunk, more like." Bork rubbed his eyes. "One of the statements called him 'Smarmo.' Like *smarmy*. He may have connections in the music biz, but he's bad news. Josh Bolvin would be a fool to dance to his tune."

Two Fingers cracked his knuckles before entering data in an open spreadsheet. "If Marmo's got the connections and can catapult Josh into the industry, that tune may change fast."

As her men began working on the timeline again, Karen paced, avoiding the desks, and eventually ended up in the break room. She'd already had too much coffee, but she was hungry, so she headed for the battered old fridge. She pulled it open... and saw the bird box.

Her stomach rebelled. What idiot had put that there? Marek? No, they'd all left directly for the park. She hadn't even thought about it until now. Maybe Tammy had stuffed it in there.

But at least it was something to do. Karen went back out to the office, started to dial the resident FBI office in Sioux Falls, then remembered it was Saturday.

Oh, what the hell. She tried it anyway—and was gratified to find The Seasons were both in the office, wrapping up a case from Pine Ridge Reservation.

Looking around the room at her bleary-eyed men, she decided to put the call on speakerphone.

"What can we do for you, Sheriff?" Agent Sommervold, summer to her partner's winter, asked. She sounded tired but satisfied. "Just don't tell me it's urgent."

Karen tucked her tongue in her cheek. "We've got a body."

Bork coughed, and Two Fingers looked up with a gleam

in his dark eyes. Kurt turned, obviously baffled, as he'd missed the punchline.

Agent Wintersgill came on the line, his clipped New England accent icier than snow cones in July. "If this has to do with your fiddler in Grove Park, call DCI. We don't do state parks, only national."

"I'm aware of that, Agent Wintersgill." She hoped her polite, even tone grated him. Not that she had anything against the man, but he was looking forward to the rest of his weekend—and she wasn't. "Grove Park isn't a state park, actually. It's a county park. This has nothing to do with that case. We have another body that, regretfully, has been delayed a bit because of said case."

A pause followed, along with mumbling too low to hear, other than a few choice curse words. Then Summer came back on. She, too, could do polite—and skewer you in the process. "Delaying reporting of a body earmarked for federal custody is not standard procedure, Sheriff. Nor, I might add, SOP for any jurisdiction. Just how long did you wait to call us?"

Karen waited a beat. "Coming up on twenty-four hours."

"In this heat?" The momentary heat in Summer's voice chilled. "Sheriff, I realize you're busy, but that's—"

"Criminal? Don't worry. We put it on ice for you."

Winter reentered the fray. "And the scene?"

As Kurt frowned at the swing shift duo of Two Fingers and Bork, who shook with soundless laughter, Karen steeled her voice to keep from doing the same. "Sorry, it was blown to bits. Dynamite."

Karen could practically hear the gnashing of teeth over the airwaves. Then Summer let out a windy breath. "You're pulling our leg."

Karen leaned back in her chair and splayed out her legs. "No, actually, I'm not. I do have a body to transfer to you, and it definitely falls under your purview. I'm afraid there's not much left of it, but the chain of custody hasn't been broken." Thankfully, the box had been properly sealed. Tammy ran the evidence room, so she was the most likely one to have done so, but Karen wouldn't rule out Josephine.

"All right, I'll play your game, Sheriff." Karen heard a click of a pen and paper being ripped from a notepad. "Who is the victim?"

"There's some question of that, as well." Karen looked over the heads of her men, not sure how much longer she could keep it together. "Either Kirtland or Wilson. Male. Indeterminate age. Short in stature and build. Yellow on blue."

"And why does Kirtland-or-Wilson fall under our jurisdiction?" Then Summer hesitated. "Yellow on what? Did you say *blue*?"

"That's right."

"A State fan?" The agent sounded concerned.

The South Dakota State University colors were blue and yellow. Karen had never inquired as to Sommervold's collegiate forays, but she was a South Dakota native. "Doubtful. I believe the victim is possibly an out-of-stater. From Michigan if he's Kirtland. If Wilson, anything's possible."

"Did he cross state lines in the commission of a crime?" Wintersgill sounded less clipped but still skeptical, more intrigued, and just faintly... very faintly... amused.

"Not that I'm aware of, but I know very little about either."

Karen heard fingernails tapping on the legal pad. "Sheriff Mehaffey, I get the distinct feeling you are enjoying this. And I am not. Why is this our business... and why do I hear nothing but a suspicious silence in what has to be a very busy bullpen?"

Bork lost it first, then Marek. Karen doubted the agents could hear his subsonic rumble, though. Two Fingers just put his head on his desk and shook. Kurt refused to make it a quartet, his trim figure almost rigid with disapproval.

"We really do have a case, Agents. And I can give you

chapter and verse." She paused. Silence. Kuhl was right about anticipation. "You'll find it under the Endangered Species Act."

Karen counted five seconds of silence on the other end, then Agent Sommervold finally blew air through what must be gritted teeth. "If I were there, Sheriff, I'd roast you—then toast you with the Pilsner I'm going to drink while you have to toil to the fiddler's tune."

"Ouch. We really do have a case. Or you do. But it depends if it's a Kirtland's warbler or a Wilson's warbler."

"Pull my leg once..." Summer began.

"No, I'm serious." Karen snorted. "Well, no, I'm laughing, but you know what I mean. The case is being pushed by a local birder, whose brand-new gravel road got blown to bits by his neighbor because it meandered over into the neighbor's property. The bird was collateral damage."

"Pull my leg twice..." Winter finished.

But Summer was already laughing. "It's got to be true. Only in the Dakotas. Or should I say, only in Eda. I know a few farmers who'd do just that. Did the farmer have a permit?"

"For the dynamite? Yes, he did. His nephew, who is also my night jailer and a volunteer firefighter, got it from the state fire marshal. So that's all legal. But I'd like to unload the body. It's been sitting in our breakroom fridge."

Sounding as tongue-in-cheek as Karen had earlier, Sommervold replied, "We'll send a courier."

Karen had the distinct feeling that this case was going to be part of FBI lore. Still grinning, Karen had barely hung up when the receiver rang under her hand.

She stopped laughing when the caller identified himself. The estate lawyer from Sioux Falls.

"Thank you for getting back to me, Mr. Van Doren."

Finally. Something in her voice must have alerted him to that unsaid word. "My wife was in the middle of labor when your call came through to my admin. She didn't pass it on until now."

Oops. Karen warmed her voice. "I hope all's well?"

"More than," he said, sounding elated—and exhausted. Karen guessed that the child was his first. "We've got a little girl. Hannah Michele. I wouldn't normally answer a call on the weekend, but Doreen said you were quite insistent. What was it that you needed to speak to me about? I'm assuming this is about Hal Birchard. Your role, perhaps?"

Karen blinked. "My role is as sheriff."

A blank silence greeted that statement. "Is Hal in trouble?"

Now Karen was truly confused. "Have you watched the news?"

"No, we had *Looney Tunes* on the TV in the birthing room. The real news is enough to scare a newborn from entering our world. Why? What's happened?"

"You had a call from Hal Birchard yesterday at 4:21 p.m."

"Did I? I'm afraid I haven't checked my work messages. I'm calling from the hospital. I don't give out my cell. Otherwise, I'd never be able to unplug from the office."

"I'm afraid I'll have to ask you to meet us at your office. It's important."

Now the lawyer sounded less than elated. "Sheriff, I don't see why this can't wait. Unless it's life or death, I would prefer—"

"It is. Death."

"Mr. Birchard has died? I'm very sorry to hear that. But the reading of the will can wait, surely."

"Mr. Van Doren, I have a feeling that we're talking at cross-purposes. Hal Birchard was murdered last evening at a music festival in my jurisdiction. Before he died, he called you. I need to know what that call was. It lasted almost a minute, so presumably, he left a message."

"Oh, my. I thought this was about his will... well, no matter."

"Who are the beneficiaries of the will?" Karen asked.

The lawyer hesitated. "Well, this is a bit awkward."

All eyes—and ears—were on her. "Why? Do you get something?"

"No." He hesitated. "You do."

CHAPTER 13

A NDREW VAN DOREN MET THEM in the lobby of his office in a new development off I-229. Not yet thirty, the young lawyer had raked his fair hair into spikes with worried fingers, though Karen wasn't sure if that was from his wife's labor or Karen's browbeating. Despite her pressure, Van Doren had refused—politely but firmly—to divulge anything further about the will. He'd said he needed to check with the firm's senior partner.

All the way up to Sioux Falls, she'd racked her brains, trying to figure out why a complete stranger would name her as a beneficiary. Marek had leaned toward some kind of charitable role. She'd said if it was to replace the Sub, she'd take it in a heartbeat, no matter the ethics. As the Sub had sputtered on that declaration, she'd patted the steering wheel and assured the old Suburban that she was just kidding—even as she crossed her fingers behind her back.

"Congratulations on your new fatherhood," Karen told Van Doren with a smile. "And sorry I've pulled you away from your daughter and wife on this special day."

"Thank you. It's... well, amazing. Though getting there was much less so." Van Doren rubbed at his temples. "I'm sorry for the delay on the will. But I didn't want to proceed without permission. We've never dealt with a situation like this before." He looked uncertainly at Marek. "We can go back to my office. But I'm not sure the chairs are big enough for your..."

"Detective. Also my uncle. Marek Okerlund."

"I'll stand if I can't sit," Marek told the lawyer.

After a curious look between the two—probably noting the lack of familial resemblance—Van Doren beckoned them down the hallway. "Follow me."

The deep burgundy carpet silenced any footfalls—almost eerily so. Karen felt more like she was in Tish's funeral parlor than in a lawyer's office. Perhaps they'd consulted the same architects? Her eye was drawn immediately to the blinking message light on the high-tech black-and-silver phone on the mahogany desk. She'd told Van Doren not to queue up his messages until they got here.

"I did just as you said." The lawyer gave her a weak smile. "Even though it was tempting not to." He sat down in the cushy leather chair and tapped the folder that lay open on his desk. "Instead, I went back over the will and codicils."

"Plural?" Marek asked, making the man start.

"Yes. Mr. Birchard was a frequent amender. Good for business but not something I suggest."

Karen got to the chase. "How did I come to be a beneficiary of the will of a man I never met before? Something for the sheriff's office, perhaps?"

Van Doren considered her for a moment, as if trying to gauge her. "You get only a nominal percentage of the estate. What you do have is a great deal of power. You're named as trustee." He must have registered her shock—and dismay. "From your earlier response, I gathered he didn't discuss this with you, as I strongly suggested he do. All along, I assumed you knew—and knew him. To find out otherwise means I failed as Hal Birchard's lawyer."

"Seems to me the failure's all on him," Karen muttered.

"The only explanation I can offer is that he must have decided you were a trustworthy person to conduct the role he gave you, especially given the main beneficiary. You can decline, of course, but it leaves the estate in limbo and, frankly, could throw the entire will into legal jeopardy."

Great. Just what she needed. Strong-armed from the dead into more legal responsibilities than she already carried with her badge. "All right, let's put that aside for now. Who am I trustee for? Josh Bolvin, perhaps?"

The lawyer blinked. "Who?"

"Guess not. Go on."

Van Doren clasped his hands together. "I must tell you first that Hal Birchard came into my office back at the end of May and completely redid the entire will. Before, much of the proceeds went to charitable organizations and museums and archives. Many to do with music. Some of that remains in the current will—and you, by the way, are getting far less than was specified in the original." Van Doren waited for her response. Perhaps he expected her to challenge the will?

She shrugged. "Can't miss what you never had."

He looked relieved. "For the most part, in the new will, there is only one main beneficiary. And frankly, if you tell me you don't know her, I will have a hard time believing that."

Karen searched her limited family members for a clue. Did Eyre know Birchard? Seemed unlikely, but stranger things had happened. Her biological daughter had gone to Vermillion to see her adoptive mother but was expected back tonight. Perhaps Eyre hadn't heard of Birchard's death. "What's her name?"

Van Doren watched her curiously. "Danielle Mehaffey."

In the background, Karen vaguely heard Marek grunt in surprise, but her vision seemed to waver in and out before she could focus again on Van Doren.

He tilted his head. "Your daughter, perhaps?"

Karen tried to get her brain back in gear. "My late husband's half-sister. She's a waitress in Fink and served Birchard at the diner there. But that's it as a relationship, so far as I know." Had Danielle lied? "She's a minor."

"Yes, I am aware of that. Sixteen, he said. That's why a trustee had to be named. And that doesn't end until she's forty or your death. He was concerned how a significant windfall might affect her if he died when she was still relatively young."

Karen hesitated before asking. She wasn't sure she wanted to know. But her job demanded it. "Did he say why he left his estate to her?"

"A way to pay a debt."

"A debt?" Karen was more confused than ever. "Danielle doesn't own much more than the clothes on her back. What could he owe her?"

"Not a monetary debt?" Marek shifted on carpet-silenced feet. "To a man alone, maybe just her attention at the diner was enough. And he knew she'd had it rough."

The lawyer looked as doubtful as Karen felt. Then the blinking light caught her eye. "Why don't you play your messages?"

After three messages, all from heirs lost in the probate maze and looking for a helping hand out, a deep voice with a faint rasp came on.

"Hal Birchard here. Look, I know you said to cool it with the changes, but I need to set up another appointment with you as a new spin's come up. It's kind of complicated, so I want an in-person meet. Just let me know when's good for you. Oh, and get me the name of another IP attorney if the one you referred me to doesn't pan out."

Birchard hung up with a click that sounded like a gunshot in the silence.

"IP?" Marek asked.

"Intellectual property. Not my area. Something about rights and music?"

Karen exchanged a look with Marek. Legrande's music. That was a tangled web. "We've got a call in to Mr. Link. He hasn't returned it. Perhaps you...?"

Van Doren looked abashed. "Sorry. I don't know the man. I found him the way most people do: Google."

"Can we have a copy of the will and codicils?" she asked.

The lawyer took out a sheaf from below the originals. "Here you go. I made them while I waited." He hesitated. "But..."

She hated buts. "What?"

"Mr. Birchard also wrote a sealed codicil that I wasn't privy to, although he assured me that it was properly notarized, to be opened only in the event that the will was challenged. It's kept in our safe. You would need a court order to open that. I'm sorry. The senior partner was adamant."

"Can't I just challenge the will?"

He smiled faintly. "You could. You'd be waiting months, if not years, to get on the docket to trigger that provision. Better go to a judge for a warrant." His phone beeped, and he took it out of his pocket and smiled. The new father turned it to show them a red-faced baby with a bow on her bald head. "First picture."

"Go be a daddy," she told him. "And thanks."

On the way back, Karen had Marek drive, so she could read the fine print—all ten pages of it. Mostly legalese. "It's really pretty vague as to what his estate actually holds, but it looks like whatever is in his trust, whatever property real and personal, whatever rights held or to be held by him, are to be held in trust for Danielle. At my discretion. Minus five percent for myself. Minus ten percent to various charities and special bequests."

"Bolvins?"

"Not mentioned. I wonder if that was going to change. To exclude or include Josh, I wonder?"

"As a motive to murder..." Marek trailed off and concentrated on the road, looking grim.

"It's not how I'd see Josh Bolvin, but you never know."

He didn't look away from the road. "Not just Josh."

"Then who... Danielle?" That had completely gone over her

head—or under her heart. "You're seriously suggesting that Danielle found out about the will, perhaps told by Birchard himself, then discovered he was going to change his will and killed him? What about the electrocution? Did she do that, too? Look, I get that you don't want it to be Josh—"

Marek drove around a dump truck. "And you don't want it to be Danielle."

"—but Josh knows his way around amps and guitars."

"Still could be an accident. Garroting him? That could be a crime of opportunity."

"And juveniles are often impulsive." Karen palmed her phone and called Jessica. "Do you have any results yet on the amp?"

A pause then a polite, "Hello, Sheriff Mehaffey, how are you? I'm tired, it's Saturday, and I might actually finish what I'm doing if people stop calling me. First Larson, now you."

Karen took a deep breath. "Sorry. It's been a long day."

"And the day is yet young," Jessica said in a muffled voice, sounding like she'd cupped the office phone between shoulder and ear while she worked away at a computer. "All I can tell you is that the amp was tampered with, but the amount of voltage—45 watts—doesn't match the effect. Larson thinks the mic stand may play a part. If they come in contact, that can do some damage. Add bare feet and water, and it's a recipe for a good shock. Basically, the amp tampering's not accidental, but he could have shocked himself with the mic. Or fallen into it and... ha ha... amplified the effect."

Karen rubbed her forehead. Would they ever get a break? "Any prints on the amp?"

"Plenty on the amp. I also found one inside where the amp was tampered with. Lifted it. It's clear and clean. A real beaut."

Karen straightened in the Sub's passenger seat. "Any matches?"

"I don't have the power of Larson. I can't intimidate the

fingerprint guy into coming back in to work when he's out dangling innocent worms into the river with his buddies on a fishing trip. Of course, your tamperer may not be in the system. Our guy will need to look at the prints you submitted for your main players. But if there is a match, you should have it on Monday."

"All right. Thanks. Really. I mean that."

"Got that. But I'm running near to empty. Need fuel. See you tomorrow."

Karen looked blankly out the windshield. "Tomorrow?"

That got a faint laugh as the typing paused. "You should have Sunday circled in hearts, Karen. Red-letter day."

"Oh, yeah. Right. Larson. Moving day."

When Karen hung up, she relayed the information on the amp being tampered with to Marek, who didn't seem overly surprised. Sometimes it grated on her that he kept his thoughts to himself so much.

When the Sub's fuel light lit up, her stomach rumbled. "Let's stop for some gas in Aleford. I'll order pizza to go, and we can take it back to the office and do some research on Hal Birchard."

That got a double thumbs-up—fortunately Marek's hands were huge, and the Sub didn't end up in the ditch.

CHAPTER 14

WHEN MAREK BROUGHT IN THE stack of pizza boxes that had been killing him not-so-softly all the way back from Aleford, heads lifted, noses flared, and the bullpen rushed him en masse. After the pillage was complete, he was left with just one box of pepperoni, which he held on to only by putting it over his head. Even the normally restrained Kurt bent enough to "remove" two pieces from Walrus's pie, saying he was saving Walrus a heart attack. Walrus had too much pie in his mouth to argue, but if looks could kill, the piper would have been playing at Kurt's funeral.

Karen was the first to speak after the gorging was complete. She dabbed tomato sauce off her cheek onto a cheap white napkin that smeared more than absorbed, but she kept at it until the sauce was gone. "Anything break on the timeline while we were gone?"

"Geez, I'll tell you one thing." Walrus kicked back in his chair, letting out a satisfied belch. "That Rad Wilson is one nosy parker."

Marek had a pretty good idea what that meant. Rad had her nose in everything. Except a book, he'd guess.

"Nosy parker?" Karen shook her head. "Have you been watching Brit mysteries again, Deputy Russell?"

Walrus worked a bit of cheese out of his mustache and popped it in his mouth. "Laura gets the remote on Sunday nights. Gotta do what you gotta do. And they aren't half bad, even if you need a translator sometimes. I thought they spoke English over there. Anyway, that girl was everywhere. Sneaky."

"Mmm." Bork swallowed hard on his last bite of Canadian bacon. "I've got a photo that caught her eavesdropping on the judges' tent."

"And I've got one of her giving the finger to Axel Knutsen," Two Fingers added. "The look on Axel's face is priceless."

"Girl's got balls," Walrus admitted.

"And chains." Karen pitched her box into the trash. "I can't imagine wearing leather in July."

Marek looked at the last slice of pepperoni and let it lie in a pool of congealing fat. He didn't want to think about what it was doing to his stomach, to his arteries, or to his brain. He booted up his computer. "We need to find out more about Hal Birchard."

At that, Kurt started to sort through papers on his desk.

"You gonna spill on the will, boss?" Walrus asked Karen. "You got us all curious."

As Marek started his online search, Karen filled them in. "Bottom line is Danielle's now a suspect, given she is the main beneficiary of Hal Birchard's will. That's motive. And she supposedly found the body, meaning she had opportunity."

"Geez, I'm sorry."

And Walrus really was. The rest of the roster looked equally dismayed. They'd worked long and hard to save her only a few months back.

After clearing his throat, Kurt picked up a piece of paper. "Hal Birchard has a sheet. Juvenile is sealed. As an adult, he first shows up at age nineteen for distributing marijuana. Pleaded down to possession and escaped jail time by enlisting in the Navy, where he did time in the brig for insubordination and marijuana possession."

Looking up from his computer, Marek frowned. "I wouldn't have pegged him for a vet. More a creative type."

"Obviously a bad fit," Two Fingers said. "Though there are plenty of military who are musicians. Whiles away the time. Was he kicked out?"

"Birchard finished out his tour and was honorably discharged." Kurt sniffed in clear disapproval that the man wasn't dishonorably discharged for his behavior. But Marek didn't think the black marks against Birchard were that bad or that unusual. "After discharge, he had a dozen other encounters with the law—all misdemeanors or pled down to same—in almost as many places."

"Born a ramblin' man," the good old country boy, aka Walrus, quoted.

Marek pursed his lips. "Where was the last?"

Kurt scanned down. "Drunk and disorderly in San Juan. Did some time for that one. Sentenced to six months but only served two."

Walrus pulled on his mustache. "Guess he finally grew up."

What Marek wasn't hearing was any suggestion that Hal Birchard went after young girls like Danielle. No dings for soliciting, domestic violence, or anything that would raise flags. Of course, Birchard could be flying under the radar.

Marek consulted Mr. Google. Fortunately, there were very few Hal Birchards and only one currently living in Reunion, South Dakota. One of the background-check sites gave Marek a long list of residences. Ramblin' was right. Previous to South Dakota, he'd been in Taiwan. Prior to that, Atlanta, Memphis, and St. Louis. All had strong musical traditions, Marek supposed. And that was all in the last ten years. Before that, Birchard had been in the Bahamas, Puerto Rico, Chicago, and Dublin.

Karen asked her senior deputy, "Where did Birchard get his first charge, Kurt?"

"Bellevue, Nebraska."

Marek's mind jumped tracks. "How far from Omaha?"

Karen looked over at him, her fjord eyes hooded. "Just south, near Offutt Air Force Base." She got up and started to pace. "May just be coincidence."

Walrus pursed his lips. "What may be?"

"That Danielle is from Omaha. As was my husband."

"Ah." Walrus creaked back in his chair. "Not touching that one."

"Maybe there's a connection to Birchard, maybe not. We need his birth certificate." Karen pulled on her ponytail as if it was parachute rope. "Did Seoul log the contents of his desk into evidence?" Before anyone could reply, she'd stalked over to the basement door, jerked it open, and disappeared down the stairs. The door snapped shut behind her with a discordant screech.

"Whew. This ain't good." Walrus blew out his windsock of a mustache.

They fell into a silence that wasn't broken until the door slammed open again. Karen held an evidence bag filled with papers. She dumped it on her desk and pulled on gloves. With a set expression, she began going through the papers. "Tax returns for the last three years. Receipts and warranties for some of that equipment in the basement. Passports going back several decades. Old VA card. He must not have visited the doctor often. Discharge papers. Black-and-white photo of an enlisted man. Air Force." Karen turned it over. "Airman Lucien Birchard. Offutt AFB. Hal's father? Doesn't favor him, though. The elder's got a full head of hair, for one."

Marek glanced at the photo of Lucien Birchard, which Karen laid down to grab more papers. Young, he thought, and still slim. Middle-aged, he might look more like Hal. The eyes were both dark, the faces roughly the same shape, and the ears close to the head.

"Here we go. Birth certificate." Karen held it up to the light as it looked creased, and the typed print faded. "Harold

Lucien Birchard. Born at the base hospital to Lucien Arnold Birchard and Janet..."

Marek waited, but nothing more came out. "Mehaffey?"

"No. Not Mehaffey. Not originally." Karen cleared her throat. "Janet Brigid Rose Plunkett." She lifted her eyes to Marek's, and he could see the bleakness. "She was Patrick's grandmother."

Only the hum of the air conditioner broke the silence for a long moment.

"Whoa. Back up." Walrus waved tomato-stained fingers. "Danielle is Patrick's much younger half-sister, right? That makes Hal Birchard her..."

"Half-uncle," Marek murmured. "Patrick's mother...?"

"Was Lianne Mehaffey." Karen's face was tight with restrained emotion. "Lianne's father, John Mehaffey, didn't stick around. Lianne had Patrick when she was sixteen. Patrick never knew who his father was. I'm not sure even Lianne knew. She dumped Patrick on her mother, Janet, almost from day one. Patrick said his grandmother wasn't perfect, but she did try, and she did love him. But she died when he was only six. Lianne hauled him around with her for a couple years until Social Services got called in after she abandoned him at a gas station. She was higher than a kite—and tried to fly like one. Ended up in the hospital, where she got hooked on painkillers then went on to worse. Patrick got shuffled between her and foster parents for years. He finally ran away to Boys Town and stayed there until he got into the Army at eighteen."

Marek had known Patrick had it rough. Just not how much so.

Almost blankly, Karen stared down at the birth certificate on her desk. "Birchard was only two years older than Lianne. No way Danielle doesn't know him—or *of* him. Like Patrick, Danielle did hard time with Lianne."

"Mmm. Maybe Danielle did know of him. But I'm not so sure Birchard knew about her." Bork rubbed his temples.

"He only started going to the diner and changed his will after Nails broke her name—and her relationship to you—on his radio show."

"All right, I'll grant you that Birchard may not have known about Danielle." Karen crossed her arms. "I sure didn't. Nor did Patrick. But that doesn't fly the other way around. Danielle knew about Patrick, and she would've known Hal Birchard's name the same way."

Deciding that Karen had gotten through the worst of the shock, Marek leaned back in his chair. "How did Birchard know about you?"

"We've had a couple cases hit the national news," Two Fingers said when no one else spoke up. "One of them was when Patrick was murdered. Birchard may have recognized the name or face, or was curious enough to follow up on it, and discovered the connection. That may explain why he came here in the first place. You were the last of his family."

"And then he didn't bother to contact me?" Hurt edged her voice. "I mean, I understand why Danielle didn't let me know who she was. She was a runaway and under sixteen until a couple months ago. I'm the law. What's Birchard's excuse? I know I'm only an in-law, not blood, but surely that's better than nothing."

Marek felt for her. She and Patrick, she'd once told him, had wanted a big family. But a land mine had ended that dream. And while her biological daughter Eyre reappearing in her life had given Karen a taste of family, that she'd been snubbed first by Danielle and now Hal Birchard, had to sting.

"He trusted you to look after Danielle," Marek pointed out.

She blinked then tilted her head. "Okay. That's something. But I'll never know for sure, now. So much I'll never know. Patrick was very open about where he'd come from, what he'd been through, and I admired that strength. I thought

Danielle... well, I guess we'll find out, if her strength was character—or in pulling a wire through her uncle's neck."

Taking a deep breath, Karen pulled out her cell phone, braced her shoulders as if readying to take a block on the basketball court that would drop her to the hardwood, and made the call.

CHAPTER 15

BECAUSE DANIELLE WASN'T YET EMANCIPATED and still a minor, Karen had to do a song and dance with the case worker in Omaha. Technically, because it was currently a noncustodial interview, they were covered just with notification. But if they ended up arresting Danielle, then it would get dicey.

Understandably, the case worker that she'd tagged was cautious. They'd worked together over the emancipation—which may never come. Finally, they came to an agreement that if Danielle voluntarily waived her rights and understood she could leave at any time, the interview could take place. If she requested a de facto guardian to be present, that would be honored. And if they took her into custody, all questioning would cease and a lawyer called in.

As they'd signed off, the caseworker, an old pro who'd gone through the system herself, said, "We've both put in a lot of time on this case, so I will be really pissed if you end up locking Danielle up."

"You won't be the only one. But if she did the crime..."

"Yeah, yeah. She'll do the time. But she's got rights. Make sure you respect them."

And Karen would. If Danielle had killed Hal Birchard, Karen wanted to get the girl the best defense she could. Which really ticked her off, because defense lawyers were the scum of the earth. Unless, of course, it was one of your own under the gun of justice.

When Danielle finally appeared with a sleepy Harlan just after eight o'clock that evening, Karen was strung as tight as a... well, as a bow. Boy, did Karen not want to play first violin in the interview, but she agreed with Marek that she was the right choice, just as he had been with Josh. Karen had developed a relationship of sorts with Danielle over leisurely lunches at the diner in Fink after her young boarder and cousin, Mary Hannah Mock, had left for the summer, taking her culinary skills along with her.

At least Danielle hadn't requested that Harlan sit in on the interview, though he asked her if she wanted him to do so. She'd shaken her head. "No, I've got this." She looked at Karen. "You had more questions about my statement?"

Karen could answer that quite truthfully. "That's right."

"No problem." She followed Karen and Marek into the cramped interview room, which seemed a lot bigger without a wall of Bolvins. It made Karen feel bad, that the person Danielle should be most able to count on in the room, Karen herself, was instead going to try her best to play the devil's advocate. Briefly, she thought of the fiddle and its little devil. An omen?

After getting the Miranda rights and voluntary waiver completed, Karen took Danielle through her previous statement, lulling her into an easy rhythm. Nothing, so far as Karen could recall, differed more than wording from the more informal questioning at the park. That was good, she told herself, but she felt her stomach roil with the last vestige of her black olive pizza as she eased into the rhythm with a discordant note. Or tone. Tune? Marek probably could tell her the right term.

Karen kept her tone friendly. "So... tell us more about your uncle."

"My..." Danielle wrinkled her nose. "I don't have an uncle.

Oh, do you mean Patrick? I know your husband was, like, old enough to be my uncle, but he was my half-brother."

"When did you find out about the will?" Karen pressed.

Danielle blinked. "Will? Who is Will?"

"Not who. What. Come on, Danny. We know about the will, know he was going to change it, and you saw easy street slipping away." Karen hated herself, hated her words, and hated the look on Danielle's face. Utter shock. Utter betrayal. While she'd expected a reaction, Karen hadn't expected anything that extreme. But she reminded herself that the girl had faced many, many rejections in her short life. Trust came harder.

"What are you talking about?" Danielle backed away from the table as if it had just become too hot to touch. "Are you saying Patrick left me something?"

"Get a grip. Look where you are. Hal Birchard."

Danielle was starting to look at Karen as if she'd lost her mind. Maybe the girl thought that was better than being betrayed by her. "Hal left me something? I barely knew him. I mean, I knew him from when he'd come into the diner, but I told you... there was nothing there between us."

"Just blood."

"Blood?" As her nose stud flashed red, so did the Mehaffey fire. "I didn't kill him!"

An interesting and sad reaction. When talking blood, the girl thought death, not kin. "You failed to tell us Hal was your uncle."

"No, he wasn't." Danielle sought out Marek as if he were the only sane adult in the room. When Marek nodded, she leaned back in the chair. "Uncle? How... I don't understand."

Her gut roiling in protest, Karen kept up the pressure. "You had to know. Hal Birchard isn't a common name. Come clean."

"I *am* clean. You think with a junkie mother like I had, I'd go there?"

"You knew about the will. Hal told you, and then

something happened, and he changed his mind. When did he tell you? At the diner, or before he participated in the Jam Off? That must've been a shock. Harlan was ready to go, so you took your chance. You went to see him, bringing him a drink to sweeten him up, and when he told you to forget it, that he'd already talked to his lawyer, you lost it." She gentled her voice. "I get that. You just lost it."

Danielle's lips trembled. "No, I didn't. You've lost it. I didn't know I had any uncle. Or any other family other than my mother, except Patrick. And that wasn't until he died and my last foster parents got the notification."

Was that even possible? "Lianne was only two years younger than Hal. She had to talk about him, if only in passing, even if you never met him."

"My mother never said anything about family." Danielle hesitated then took that back. "Except once about her mother. 'A twitchy mouse of a woman who drank too much because her heart got broken. Boohoo.' That was her saying that, not me. I got more respect." Her chin jutted as she rose to her feet. "Why didn't *you* recognize Hal Birchard's name? Patrick was your husband. *You* should've known." As that struck home, she nodded. "Exactly. You didn't even know I existed. I wish you'd never known. I wish I'd never come here. No, I take that back. I found something here, not with you, but something good—something you're trying to take away from me."

Karen controlled her inner shaking, afraid it would show on the outside. With every ounce of her remaining control, she asked, "Oh, what's that? Your freedom?"

Now Danielle got into her space. "You think if I was such a money-grubbing gold digger that I'd be working for peanuts in Fink? With the media coverage back in May, I could've milked that into some serious money. But I came to Eda County looking for family—and I found it. But not with you. Harlan, Cookie, the regulars at the diner—they believe in me. You don't. They're my family now. Even my foster parents, all unlucky thirteen of them, weren't as bad as you. I'm done. With you, with this." Danielle jabbed her finger on the table in a rhythm of hard knocks. "I. Did. Not. Kill. Hal. Birchard." A pause then she got in one final jab. "Period."

With more control than anyone of her age should possess, Danielle Mehaffey walked over to the closed door, opened it, then closed it so gently that only a whisper of sound escaped into the silence she left behind. When Karen thudded her head onto the table, she felt Marek's big hand slip over her shoulder, reminiscent of Nate's for Josh.

She felt bone-deep hatred for herself—and her job. And she felt so relieved that she could cry. "Danielle's not our killer," she mumbled into the scarred wood. "That wasn't anything but heart, no acting."

"I agree. But we had to do it. And you played it just right."

Karen raised her head to look at her half-uncle. "Then why does it feel so wrong?"

"Give her time. And a killer on a silver platter. She'll come around."

Karen wondered if Marek realized how doubtful he sounded. Maybe because he'd had to deal with the Bolvins and like her, wasn't sure that their relationship would survive. Was any job, even justice, worth the cost?

With effort, Karen pushed to her feet, feeling like she'd just gained a weight she would never lose—that of loss. When she went out, no trace of either Danielle or Harlan remained. They'd hotfooted it out of the office quicker than Karen thought possible.

She'd been outflanked, outrun, and outdone. But Danielle was free. And Karen would do everything she could to make sure her young sister-in-law stayed that way, come Monday's hearing.

CHAPTER 16

A FTER LETTING HER MEN OFF for the night with orders to show up for an incident meeting at eight sharp on Sunday morning, Karen finished up some lingering paperwork and drank coffee until her head started to pound. Then she drove the short way home, the Sub sputtering all the way.

"Come on, you can do it," she urged it. "Just get me home. Please." Another hiccup. "Pretty please, with an oil change on top."

The Sub complied then died just as she pulled in front of the Arts-and-Crafts-era bungalow on 22 Okerlund Road. Cursing the clutch-fisted county commissioners, she called for a tow truck to haul the sorry piece of... that is, loyal but aging and solidly built piece of metal... away to Gotsch's garage. Until she had the keys to a new ride, she wasn't going to jinx things by dissing the venerable Chevy, her family's preferred brand.

She just hoped she didn't have an emergency. She'd tried that argument with Harold Dahl, the longest-reigning county commissioner in Eda County, but he'd just said that she could appropriate a cruiser from one of her men. Right. Like she'd pull them off the road.

To say Karen was in a bad mood when she stalked into the house was... well, absolutely correct. When she heard violin strings crashing into her pity party, she didn't immediately realize that the sound was real. And for a dumbfounded moment, she wondered if she'd just gone bonkers. Then she got it. Must be the radio or a CD.

Eyre was back. Good. She had a favor to ask her daughter.

Karen wandered back toward the bedroom her parents had shared. She'd felt too weirded out to take it over as her own when her father, Arne Okerlund, had deeded the house to her after he married Clara and moved down the road. She preferred the attic room she'd grown up in, where she could see across the street to her grandfather's, now Marek's, bungalow. At least the Okerlunds had—mostly—mended fences. Her father still muttered darkly about the Marek family always being trouble, but Clara wouldn't let him get away with anything more than that.

As it had turned out, Marek—the last to carry that troublesome name in Eda County—was no trouble, and his daughter had brought life back into Arne's world after his stroke. Eyre had been one more piece to glue the Okerlunds back together. Karen's daughter looked the image of Karen's mother, one of the stolid Mocks from the little Brethren enclave of Eder near Fink, with their plump bodies, softly rounded faces, and rich brunette hair.

But the startled eyes that rose as Karen trod on a creaky floorboard were all pale-winter-sky-blue Okerlund. The music, something classical but faintly familiar, ended in a squeak of strings. Not a recording but the real deal. "Oh, Karen. You scared me. Sorry. I'll just put this away." Karen's twenty-something daughter tugged over the case on the bed. "I brought my violin back with me from Mom's place as she's downsizing. Or so she says. I'll believe it when she starts culling the books in the twenty-or-so bookcases."

Karen was glad that Eyre no longer stumbled when saying "Mom" in her presence, when referring to Dr. Anne Leggett, professor of English and all-around decent human being. Anne had engineered her adopted daughter's residence with Karen after Eyre's rented rooms behind the county archives where Eyre worked had burned down. And Eyre was far more like her adoptive mother, studious and academic—in a word, a nerd—than Karen.

But over the last year that they'd been living together, they'd slowly been learning to appreciate those differences as complementary instead of opposite. Obviously, Karen had more to learn of this daughter she'd held only for a short time then not seen again until she was fully grown.

"Why didn't you bring it earlier?"

"Well, I didn't want to bother you."

And... they still hadn't found the right balance. "Eyre, this is your home so long as you choose to live here. You can play your violin when I'm here." Karen smiled to reassure her. "Assuming you don't sound like a cat of nine tails."

"That's for you to judge."

"Sounded good to me. What is it?"

Eyre paused as she opened the case. "Vivaldi's 'Four Seasons.' Didn't you recognize it?"

Another gulf. Her own mother hadn't grown up with music other than the human voice, and her father hadn't really cared one way or the other, though he'd regularly shouted up the vents for her to tone down that godawful noise on her boom box. Meaning rock. "Vaguely. I mean, it sounded familiar." Like music used as background for commercials, maybe. But she was wise enough not to say that.

Eyre smiled wryly. "I also play some folk. Reels. Celtic. Whatever." Proving it, she lifted the bow and did a little jig.

Now Karen was impressed. "Cool. You can do that as much as you like." And then tried to balance that out. "I mean, the other is fine, too. But I really like the folk."

Eyre laughed. "Not what my parents said when I started. But unlike Jane, I stuck with it. Even won a few contests. I may not have competed *on* the hardwood like my sister did, but I competed *with* the hardwood." Eyre tapped the body of the violin as she nestled it back into its case, reminding Karen of Hal Birchard's fiddle. Only the violin looked different somehow. Maybe it was just that it wasn't decorated like Hal's but very simple, very plain, with a deep cherry color that looked pretty good against the black cheek thingy.

Eyre opened a little alcove in the case, filled with tools of the trade, from extra strings, polishing cloth, balled-up white gloves, and a small block of what looked like wax.

And that took Karen right back to the case as Eyre closed hers.

Oblivious, her daughter went on, "I thought some about trying to find a group to play with but..." Now Eyre looked up. "What is it?"

"Nothing." Karen had to focus back on Eyre. "Just a case... I mean, not *this* case." Karen gestured at the violin case. "I take it you haven't heard about Hal Birchard's murder at the Big Jam?"

"The big what? And who is Hal?"

Good question. "A local musician. You up for doing some research?"

Pleasure put roses in Eyre's cheeks. "In the archives? Always."

"No, online. Hal Birchard was from Omaha but was a rolling stone. And it turns out that he's the half-uncle of Danielle."

"Your Danielle?"

Not hers any longer, sad to say. "I had to question her tonight. It didn't go well. Birchard left her the bulk of his estate, and it looks like that's another big tangle, as I'm the trustee. Birchard was passing off some music—or actually Josh Bolvin's—as his own, but it was actually written by the legendary Trick Legrande."

Eyre blinked owlishly. "Who? I mean, I know who Josh Bolvin is, but not Legrande. Have you seen the video Josh Bolvin did that went viral? It's great. I mean, really great."

That distracted Karen. "You listen to rock?"

"Sure. Not heavy metal or anything, but there's some good stuff out there."

"Well, for your ears only, that viral hit was actually written a couple decades ago by Trick Legrande. Maybe you've heard of his band, Wild Abandon?"

"Not off hand, no. Sorry."

"If you're going to do research on Hal Birchard, then I'd appreciate you do some on Trick Legrande, as well. From what Seoul told me, that music shouldn't even exist. Legrande supposedly took his music with him to the grave— the deep blue sea."

"Really? Sounds fascinating." Eyre pushed aside the violin case and reached for another instrument she excelled at—her laptop. "Give me the details, and I'll get started. When do you need it?"

"Um, tomorrow at eight sharp. We've got an incident meeting."

"Got it. Tomorrow's Sunday, so no work. I can stay up late."

Leaving Eyre happily cracking her knuckles and attacking her keyboard like a concert pianist, Karen made her way up the stairs to her attic room, with its sloping roof and mullioned windows. Across the street, she could see Nikki Forsgren Solberg trying to wrestle a tennis ball away from Gun Shy, Marek's—or really Becca's—field-bred springer spaniel, while Marek and Becca watched from the porch. Gunny had failed life as a bird dog and was now living like a king at the foot of his mistress's bed or in a palace of a doghouse.

They looked like the perfect family, but Nikki wasn't Marek's wife, and Becca wasn't Nikki's daughter. They'd made an informal and loosely knit family nonetheless. Nikki lived and worked in the converted schoolhouse by the bluff. Karen doubted a marriage was in the cards between Marek and Nikki, given Nikki's independent ways. But the arrangement worked for them.

Why couldn't she have the same? She had made so many plans with Patrick, and they'd gone up in smoke. Then she let the envy go. She'd had her ups and downs, so had Marek, and if he was up now, and she was down, that was the rhythm of life.

Restless, Karen snapped on her radio, cleaned her attic room, attacked her closet, and wished she could play a pickup game with Larson, but he was no doubt too busy. With his new family. Which she wasn't part of. Dammit, she was getting maudlin.

Finally, she went to bed, but couldn't sleep.

CHAPTER 17

JUST AFTER MIDNIGHT, KAREN GOT a call from Seoul, who was on solo patrol while her nightshift partner Adam Van Eck was on vacation, visiting his old Broadway buddies in New York. After listening to the problem, Karen jumped out of bed and reached for her clothes. "Pick me up."

"I can handle it," Seoul told her. "I just wanted to let you know in case that—"

"Pick me up," Karen repeated. "I know the owner of the Prairie Rose." Formerly, the out-of-city-limits bar had been called The Shaft, and its irascible owner would have burned the place down rather than contact the police. "That Krissy Martin called us in is a first. I want to make sure it's not the last."

Seoul picked her up in her cruiser, and they drove out of town and into the starry night. By the time Seoul stopped on the slight hill that led down to the former Sioux quartzite quarry, Karen could see the brawl was in full swing—literally. In the light of a full moon and a lone streetlamp from the parking lot, she counted about half a dozen men on each side, surging into a swarm of arms and bowed heads like a scrum on a rugby field. Telling the sides apart was easy enough as Team Overalls took on Team Lederhosen.

"My God. It's the Barn Off gone berserk."

That had Seoul turning in the driver's seat. She looked like a kid playing cop in her new deputy's uniform that, like the hazmat suit, had to be special ordered. "Really? I was going to go to the Barn Off, but... you know, the case."

Karen had dealt with a drunk or two going at it, but a dozen beefy men intent on beating the crap out of each other? She tallied up her men and came up short. Marek would come, no questions asked, and he had a gentle way about him—plus the size to back it up. But even as she thought it, another wave surged out of the bar and dove in, moving the brawl over into the road. The new players were dressed in T-shirts, shorts, and flip flops—and one was hopping mad, literally.

This could get ugly in a real hurry. "Couldn't they wait until Marek got here?" she bemoaned.

"Marek... Good idea."

Karen put down her phone just as Seoul took up hers. "No time, Deputy. We *are* the cavalry." She hoped Seoul carried extra riot gear in her trunk, because they were going to need it.

Seoul just kept looking at her phone, swiping and tapping, then with a sound of satisfaction, she placed the phone in a holder on the dash. Then she hooked it up to a cord that snaked from the console and put the cruiser in drive. Before Karen could draw breath to ask what the hell her deputy was doing, Seoul hit the lights but not the sirens and floored the cruiser. Karen was flung back into the seat.

The ear-splitting tune of "The Lone Ranger"—Marek's longtime ringtone—blared out of the outside speakers. *Ta-da-da ta-da-da ta-da-dah-dah-DAH.* They galloped down the road.

"Have you gone stark raving mad, Deputy Durr?" Karen demanded once she got her jaw in the upright and locked position. They were almost upon the scrum.

Seoul shot her a gleeful, more-than-half-mad glance. "Just watch."

If they managed to survive, the only thing they'd be seeing was the inside of prison bars after being convicted of mass murder by cop cruiser. The scrum didn't move—but stilled as if flash frozen in varying states of confusion. As Seoul neared at full gallop, they surged again, parting like the Red Sea. Seoul stepped on the brakes in the middle of the road, neatly separating the two factions.

Karen just knew she'd have a welt across her chest. When she could draw breath, she said, "You're fired."

"No, I'm not." Seoul flung off her seatbelt. "This'll be fun."

Biting off an oath, and without any riot gear, Karen got out just as Overalls and Lederhosen started to surge back over the road.

Seoul marched right up to the beefiest of the Overalls-in-Green, who looked to be their ringleader. "Hey, what's your name?"

For a moment, Karen thought the bull-built man wasn't going to respond. She wasn't entirely sure that he even saw Seoul, given how much shorter she was—and how swollen the man's eyes were.

But he finally fastened on her. "Michael Galloway of Aleford. What's it to you?"

As Karen inched out her nightstick, Seoul pirouetted to the ringleader of the Lederhosen, a man not as big as Galloway but more than wide—with muscle, not fat. "You?"

"Dieter Hahn from Fink." He glared down at her. "Playing 'The William Tell Overture' ain't gonna win you any points." He spat on the ground. "Friggin' English."

On that, apparently, both sides could agree, as a dozen more splats were added, gleaming darkly in the moonlight. Probably a good thing that Karen hadn't called in Walrus, who was English. Like most Scandinavians, Karen was happy to stay neutral. Out of the fight, she might actually survive. She'd just keep mum about her German blood.

"So, what brings you gentlemen out on this fine night?" Seoul asked as if she'd encountered them on some sultry night on the boardwalk.

"Asshole Irish," Hahn said, glaring over her head at

Galloway. "Just a friendly ribbing over their loss in the Barn Off to the better team, and they fly off the handle."

The Overalls surged forward with fists raised, proving his point, but Seoul simply held up a hand. "I'm Irish."

That stopped the Overalls in confusion, awaiting a verdict from their leader. Galloway peered down at the Irish setter–colored hair. "That ain't a real red."

"Durr's German," a booming voice from the Lederhosen sang out. "She's one of ours. Level-headed. Controlled. Like our win. We did it with style—and real music. Not some half-assed ditty of 'Old MacDonald Had a Farm.'"

One of the Overalls jeered and started singing "John Jacob Jingleheimer Schmidt."

When the waves looked ready to crash back down over dueling ditties, Karen pulled out her nightstick with one hand and put Marek on speed dial on the other. At least when he found the bodies, he'd know who was responsible.

Seoul pulled out her shirttails and flashed her midriff. "I've got the tattoo."

The deputy bared tight abs and a shamrock.

"Nice. But no go."

Undaunted, Seoul dropped her shirt and belted out an Irish drinking song, or at least one about knocking heads and dying gallant deaths.

"Better, but no cigar. You're still a stinking Gerry."

A German. And that got snarls from the Lederhosen.

Karen gripped her stick tighter, but Seoul started doing an Irish step dance that had the Overalls-in-Green hooting and stomping their feet to give her a beat. When Galloway didn't join in, merely crossing his arms, Seoul did a nifty two-step skip then flicked up one booted foot—and hit his jewels.

He sang. And dropped.

A deadly silence fell. The calm before the storm. Karen wondered what it would be like to be the rugby ball in the middle of a scrum. Then, in a piping voice like a piccolo coming out of a tuba, the fallen ringleader said, "Aye, there's an Irish lass!"

"And a regular Brunhilde!" the Lederhosen ringleader boomed. "Drinks on me!"

A raucous cheer went up from both sides, and Seoul was carried off the field, grinning back at Karen like a mad leprechaun. Music had carried the day... or at least the musician. Crazy girl.

"Are you going to shut us down for serving a minor if I hand her a pint?"

Karen turned as the owner sauntered over with an unconsciously sexy swing of hip that had a Lederhosen straggler ogling then patting his heart. Or perhaps not so unconsciously, as Krissy Martin gave him a wink.

Karen told her, "My deputy's legal. Twenty-two. But Seoul's on duty, so if she takes even a sip of that Guinness or Pilsner, I'll have to fire her."

"You'd have to go through the crowd." Krissy glanced back at the bar. "I wouldn't want to restart that rumble if I were you."

"Good point." Karen realized she was still holding up the nightstick and lowered it with relief. "How's it going, Krissy?"

"At the bar? The name change—and my name on the title—have kept the gropers away. Now I can kick them out for good. I can't say we've gotten a more upscale crowd, but we've got a few more females dropping in. I should be grateful for that much, given what happened."

A lot of ugly revelations had been mined out of that old quarry-built building. "And you?"

Krissy shrugged nonchalantly, but even in the moonlight, Karen could see the scars—not physical but present nonetheless in an always-alert defense mechanism. "I still keep looking over my shoulder, waiting for the old man to boot me. I don't know if I'll ever feel truly comfortable out here alone, but the bar's mine now, so I'll stick. The old man taught me that much." Krissy waited a beat. "Are we going to chat out here until the sun comes up, Sheriff?"

"Is that a way of asking when I'm leaving? Don't worry, we'll go as soon as you boot out my deputy. Seoul's my ride. Mine's at Gotsch's."

"My sympathies." Krissy strode back into the bar.

When Seoul finally came back out, she looked smug.

Looking up from checking "The William Tell Overture" on her phone, finding it had been written by an Italian named Rossini, Karen glared at her deputy in mock disapproval. "If you say 'I told you so,' I *will* fire you."

Seoul paused, as if reprocessing, then grinned. "Oh, that? No biggie. My granny always said, 'It's better to whistle for your dinner than get it stuffed down your throat.' I got talking to Michael, and guess what?"

So she'd already gotten the Overalls ringleader's number. "He's your granny's cousin's nephew's second-cousin-removed's BFF?"

"Who knows? Could be. Granny's got a regular tribe back on the Emerald Isle. But Michael and his merry crew left for supper on Friday night before they took statements. He ducked into the instrument tent during the judges' break. Forgot his cowbell there as they were about to leave."

That sobered Karen. "And? Don't make me kill you."

"Don't want to ruin the punch line."

"Spill it." Karen made a fist. "Or I *will* punch you..."

"You wouldn't land it." She held up her hands when Karen lifted her fist. "Peace." And she spilled it.

Checking the hour, Karen texted Marek instead of calling him, as she guessed he was fast asleep—or otherwise engaged. He wouldn't be able to break the news until morning anyway.

CHAPTER 18

MAREK WOKE TO THE SOUND of music.
The hills may be alive, he thought, but he didn't want to be. Groaning, he rolled over and put the pillow over his head. And got a hard shove.

"Up and at 'em, cowboy."

"Very funny," he mumbled as "Git Along Little Dogies" floated down from the attic for the umpteenth time since Becca had started a music rotation in summer school.

"At least it'll be done by this afternoon," Nikki said, snatching the pillow back.

"Whoopee ti-yi-yo." But Marek rolled off the bed. He wished Nikki would stay over more often, but he respected her boundaries. Still, Becca listened better to Nikki than to him. "Sure you don't want to deal with that?"

Her muffled voice, with a Western twang, came through the pillow. "'It's your misfortune, ain't none of my own.'"

He was tempted to tell her that she was going to have a new home in Wyoming to complete the refrain of the old cowboy song. But he wanted her right where she was.

Shaking his head to clear the cobwebs, he made his way, yawning, up the creaking stairs to his old room. When he pushed open the door, he found his daughter sitting cross-legged on the rumpled bed. On the wall behind her, the faces of her mother and brother, Madonna and child, painted on the *retablos* hung above her head. Always, he would feel a pang for what might have been, if a drunk driver hadn't plowed into his wife's car, with Becca strapped into her car seat as Val slowly bled to death, along with their unborn son.

"Sweetpea, what did I say about playing that?"

His eight-year-old daughter looked up, taking her lips off the red plastic recorder that looked scratched and dinged enough to be the same one he'd used back in the day. Her black hair was tangled, something he'd have to take care of before long, and her dusky skin sun-kissed, popping her pale-blue Okerlund eyes.

"I have to practice my part. Teacher said so. We're playing today." When Marek just kept staring at her, she sighed with the long-suffering look of the put-upon. "'Don't play when people are sleeping.' But you aren't."

"Nikki is." But the sound of plates being pulled down from cupboards in the kitchen below told him that was no longer true. "Was sleeping." But the distraction did the trick. Becca abandoned the recorder and tore down the stairs. Marek followed more slowly, rubbing his eyes. Oh, to have that kind of energy again. Why did it all go to kids?

When Marek got to the kitchen after a pit stop, Becca was helping Nikki make French toast—and humming her class song instead of playing it. Progress, he guessed, but he got an eye roll of green eyes from Nikki.

Nikki leaned toward Becca. "Why don't you do some drawing this morning, Becca? Something with colors. Paints, I think. We haven't worked with those for a while."

Nikki was a multi-media artist by passion—the perfect tutor for his artistically precocious daughter— and an English and art teacher by occupation.

Always willing to indulge her passion, Becca ran off to get her paints before Marek could stop her. "She does need to eat."

"She can do both." Nikki handed him a plate of French toast. "I always hated it when my parents would take away my book and tell me, 'No reading at the table.' Yet the rest could talk all day long about the weather, the sports team, or corn prices. Didn't seem fair to me."

So while he ate, Marek watched his daughter ignore her cooling breakfast, her tongue between her teeth as she made a colorful montage that didn't look like anything he'd ever seen her do before. Sort of dreamscape with some weird shapes.

"What's that supposed to be?" he asked.

She didn't look up. "It's 'Git Along Little Dogies.'"

"You do know that dogies are just little calves? Like at the Bolvins?"

"No, it's what the song *looks* like."

Marek stared at her. Behind him, Nikki sucked in a breath. "Synesthete."

"What?" That took his head—and his entire body— around. He'd gradually relaxed his fear for his daughter's future educational attainments after she'd been officially declared dyslexia-free. Now that fear shot up to red-alert territory. "What's that? Is it curable?"

Nikki patted his head as she bent over his shoulder to get a better look. "Don't worry, Dad. It's not a bad thing. I've only met one other. Your daughter can *see* music. Colors. Shapes. It must be awesome."

Becca finally looked up, shocked. "You can't?"

"Afraid not. It's a gift given to few." Nikki squeezed Marek's shoulder. "Don't you have an incident meeting this morning?"

Marek surged to his feet in alarm then let out a breath as he registered the kitchen clock. "It's only just after seven. I've got plenty of time."

But he took a shower, got dressed, and picked up his phone. Only then did he see a text from Karen. Walking back into the kitchen, he stopped abruptly. "Damn."

"Daaaad," his daughter admonished.

"Sorry. My bad." He pocketed his phone. "I have to go,

sweetpea. Eat your French toast. And mind Nikki." He looked at Nikki. "Thanks for taking her while Arne's gone." His half-brother, Karen's father, was gone with his wife, Clara, and her toddler grandson to visit Clara's elderly aunt, who wasn't expected to last the week.

"My pleasure. Good luck."

He wouldn't need luck. He'd already gotten that.

When Marek rattled over the cattle guard at the Bolvin farm, the cows underneath the old oak trees by the pond sent him disgruntled, even glowering, looks. He didn't imagine that the Bolvins would object if their cattle decided to rush his Silverado, stampede him, and hide his body in the pond. By the time he slid out of the pickup, in between the homestead and the barn, he was surrounded—by Bolvins, not bovines. Three men and wives of two of them, one bulwark of a woman, and one shaking boy. A pug-nosed girl marched up to Marek and kicked him in the shin.

"I hate you. You hurt Josh. Get off our land." Then she bit her lip. "Mr. Okerlund."

Typical Bolvin. Straight up—and raised right. "I will, Em. But not until I deliver some news."

Josh Bolvin stepped up, chin up, and put a hand on his young cousin's shoulder. "Go ahead."

"I would've come sooner, but I didn't get the message until just now." Looking around at the set faces, the dread, and a few closed eyes, no doubt in prayer, Marek let out a breath. He looked straight into those dreamboat, or dread-boat, eyes. "I'm afraid you're out of the running, Josh."

"Running for what?" Nick asked when Josh just stared at Marek in confusion.

Marek smiled faintly. "For the Killer of the Year Award."

Obviously braced for something far different, Josh sputtered. "What?"

But his mother and his father practically knocked their son off his feet in a sandwich, while Em stood her ground and looked up at Marek suspiciously. "What's that mean?"

Nick picked up his daughter and Eskimo-kissed her. "It means Josh isn't hurt anymore."

And they joined the Josh sandwich, along with the rest of them... except for the matriarch. Hands on hips, she marched over. "Well, Leif Marek Okerlund..."

He hadn't been called by his full name like that since he was thirteen and his mother had found him coughing up his lungs after trying out a cigarette. But he felt his spine stiffen, his cheeks redden. "Yes, Mrs. Bolvin?"

She nearly knocked him out of his Blunnies as she rocked him back with a bear hug. After the shock, he hugged her back. The embrace turned into a rocking motion, as if she'd decided he needed to be babied. All that was missing was the lullaby. "You came right off to tell us. Knowing we'd be suffering. I knew my boy. I knew it'd turn out okay. And I knew it'd be hard for you, almost as hard as it was for my boys, both this time and the last, having to watch and wait. Now we can all load up for church with a good heart and lots to be thankful for."

Her lanky eldest son broke up the lovefest. "Let go of that man, Mom."

When Marek stepped back out of the bulwark's grasp, he dangled his arms at his sides, ready to take a hit. He might not like the black eye that resulted, but if it gave him any chance to get back into the Bolvin fold, he'd take it.

In a flash, Ned's fist contacted his chin—but with only a tap. "Next time, Okerlund, go after someone your own size."

"Yeah, take on one of us next time." Nate swung one arm away from his son so he could see Marek. "You've danced around the Bolvin family soft spots with our mother, my son."

Nick tapped Marek on the side of the head. "You're gonna take some licks if you go against us. Just the Bolvin way. You went hard at Josh." Now that the pressure was off, Nick turned and gave his nephew a soft clip to the chin. "But he wasn't straight with you right off."

Looking dazed, Josh asked, "What cleared me, Mr. Okerlund?"

"We've been working on a timeline from statements and photos. There's a lot of it, and we're still working it. But you were covered for the time after you left Hal Birchard until his body was found. And last night, one of the Barn Off contestants said he went into the instrument tent after you left—he passed you." And on the way over to the Bolvin farm, Marek had gotten confirmation of that from Karen. They'd found a photo to verify. "Birchard was alive and well."

The ecstatic relief leached out of Josh's face. "Somebody still killed him. And I'll never be able to take back what I said to him."

Marek shook his head. "If we all knew when we'd lose someone, our last words would be different. Mine to my wife was, 'Stop nagging. I'll get the damn milk.'" And she'd died going out to get that milk because he was still working a case. "From what I can tell, Hal Birchard wasn't angry with you, just about your offers. Can you remember anything else he said to you?"

"Didn't sleep a wink last night for replaying it all in my head."

"You told me you slept like a babe," his mother yelped.

He shrugged. "I didn't want you to feel worse than you already did, Mom. I know you and Dad weren't sleeping, either. It's been hell. The last couple days seemed like all the rest of my life was on the line."

And it might have been. "So, nothing."

"Probably not. But just before I stormed out, Hal said something kinda weird. That something was going to break and I'd understand why he was being such a hard-ass. That he'd make it up to me, one way or another, but I wasn't buying it." Josh scuffed a booted toe on the gravel. "As far as I was concerned, he'd just cost me the moon and the stars and all the friggin' planets. What was left to live for?"

When his parents tightened their grip on him, he grinned.

"But it ain't bad here, on Planet Earth, with the ground under you. Family." Unconsciously, he began to hum, and Marek could practically see a song form in the kid's head.

Not all were so lucky as Josh Bolvin. He doubted Rad Wilson or, for that matter, Hal himself, had that grounding. As Marek was about to turn back to the Silverado, Em came up and hugged his abused leg. "I'm sorry I kicked you, Mr. Okerlund. Can Becca come over soon?"

"After the concert this afternoon?" her mother suggested when Marek quirked an eyebrow at her. "Assuming we live to the end of it."

Death by music. Somehow, he'd survive. And at least Becca could carry a tune. She just needed to change the dang record. Or recorder.

CHAPTER 19

L EANING BACK IN HER DESK chair, Karen listened to Nails's first radio spot of the day with growing disbelief and anger.

—that we've got a real doozy of a lead today. So big that when I got the call, I didn't care that I only got three hours of shuteye last night. Now, I know plenty of folks out there, especially the older ones, won't know the name Legrande from the Grand Ole Opry, or the band Wild Abandon from Mutual of Omaha's Wild Kingdom. But I worked my way back from the dead with Wild Abandon's 'Washed Up.' 'Washed up but ain't sunk yet.' Kept me plugging away. So let's say I've got a vested interest when I get a tip that Josh Bolvin's viral video hit 'Plain Sight' was actually Legrande's music, not his.

"Geez friggin' louise," Walrus burst out into Nails's dramatic pause. "How'd he *get* that?"

All eyes went to Seoul. She held up her hands. "I haven't told a soul." Then she winced at the unintentional pun on her name. "Pinky swear. I wouldn't. I didn't. Not even to my dad. Maybe the Bolvins tipped him? They knew."

Marek frowned. "I don't see that."

Nails cut over him. *I just checked with Josh Bolvin, who confirmed. He says he had no idea about Legrande. Didn't even know the name. He thought Birchard wrote the song, just didn't want to tour it. That was their agreement. In even better news, Josh also told me that he'd been officially cleared.*

So now we've got a real mystery on our hands. I tried to reach Sheriff Mehaffey for comment before I aired this morning, but she wasn't answering. I'll update you later if I get through. If you're listening out there, Sheriff, give me a call.

Karen frowned, pulled out her phone, and found it dead. Her scrum with Seoul had disrupted her usual routine, and she'd forgotten to put it back on the charger after her return home. Cursing under her breath, she jerked open her drawer, rummaged around until she found the extra charger she kept in the office, and plugged it in.

She'd love to browbeat Nails over leaking such a crucial clue, but she couldn't. This one was on her. She picked up the phone and called him. "Who was your tipster?"

Only a slight pause from Nails. "You know I can't tell you that. Even if I could, which I can't, because it came in on my tip line. Can't even tell you male or female, because the voice was muffled. That's straight up. So... any comment?"

Hampered by the cord of her landline, Karen paced in a tight circle until she wound the cord around herself. She reversed course to untangle herself as she tried to formulate a response on the fly. "During the course of our investigation, we have cleared a number of suspects, including most recently, Josh Bolvin. And we will continue eliminating suspects until we have found who is responsible for ending the life of a very talented musician. That Hal Birchard apparently passed off Trick Legrande's music as his own is only one of many angles we are pursuing."

"You may not be aware of it, Sheriff, but as a fan myself, I am familiar with Legrande's entire output. 'Plain Sight' isn't one of them. Just how did Hal Birchard get ahold of that music, and when was it written? When the band was still together or after?"

That information, at least, was still under wraps. As was the news that there were a lot more songs where that one came from. But she could honestly say, "At this point, we are unaware of how Mr. Birchard obtained the music.

If it is relevant to our investigation, we will find out." She did some selective hearing of her own on the question of *when* the music was written. Let him think she didn't know. "Otherwise, I'll leave it to the audiophiles out there."

When the click sounded, signaling the recording was done, Nails said, "You might want to start screening your calls, Sheriff. Or have Josephine do it for you."

Good luck with getting the part-time secretary here on a Sunday morning. "Why is that?"

"Because the news about Legrande is going to hit the national wires."

Karen closed her eyes. "Any idea when that happens?"

"Well, since I contacted a buddy at the *Argus Leader* just before you called, I'd say you'll be hearing from the press within the hour. I just wanted to break the news first."

"Thanks a lot." She couldn't quite bite her bitterness. "You may have damaged our case."

"Sorry to hear that." And he did actually sound sorry. "But I went with what I had. If you'd picked up your phone..."

Karen clicked off before he could. After unraveling herself again from the cord, she turned off the radio, which was playing Legrande's "Washed Up." She looked around the room and noted Eyre wasn't there yet. She checked her watch. Almost half past eight. So be it. "Okay, people. We've lost our leverage on the Legrande angle."

"I don't get all this brouhaha over a bit of music." Kurt added another entry in the timeline.

Seoul looked at him as if he'd arrived in a spaceship from the deepest voids. "Music is about as basic as it gets. Just think of life without music. No rock 'n' roll on the radio or app, no dancing with your main squeeze, no "Hallelujah Chorus" at Easter, no *Phantom of the Opera* on the stage, no rousing organ at Wrigley Field, no national anthem to pull at your patriotic heartstrings at the Olympics, no mournful taps at military funerals."

Kurt did accede to the last with a nod.

"Geez, forget opera," Walrus grumbled. "Movies are where it's at. Some epic scores. Like *Rocky.*"

Seoul shook her head sadly at him. "All that dramatic buildup, the suspense, where do you think it came from? You can thank opera for pairing music and drama. That's where it all started."

Walrus blinked. "Seriously?"

Fortunately, Eyre rushed in before Seoul could launch into a lecture on the history of music. While the topic might be interesting, they didn't have the time, especially if the newshounds started nipping at their heels.

"Sorry I'm late." Eyre clutched her laptop and a notepad and almost lost both before Bork grabbed them for her. "Thanks. I was waiting on some info from overseas." She caught her breath and settled on Marek's desk. "Who do you want first? Birchard or Legrande?"

Karen sighed. "I'd prefer Birchard, but give me Legrande, since that news is going to hit the airwaves soon." Her phone burbled on her desk. The caller ID read out as a Twin Cities media number—one she recognized and didn't want to answer. "Or now." She transferred the call to Tammy with instructions to say "no comment." If the press was insistent on something to quote, they should contact Nails. Then Karen pulled out the cord. "Go on, Eyre. What do we know about the man and his band?"

"Um, let me think." Eyre bit her lip as if trying to corral her thoughts. Unlike Karen, Eyre was not the shoot-from-the-lip sort. "Okay. Patrick 'Trick' Legrande was born in Kansas City to a single mom on welfare. She kicked him out at thirteen, saying he was too wild for her to handle, and he ended up in a group home. That's where he met the other two founding members of his band, Toby Bryant and Alan Mohler. Apparently, they regularly snuck off to a hidey-hole in an abandoned building nearby to practice their music. When the three of them were turned loose at eighteen, they officially formed their band as Wild Abandon. You know, wild and abandoned."

"Geez. I never knew that." Walrus's mustache drooped. "That's really sad."

"Well, things got better... at least until they got worse. They headed for California in a beater and a rickety trailer they nearly lost on the way. But they finally made it and had some success doing gigs. They'd do whatever, whenever, and had been together for years by then. They mostly played popular songs but started adding some of Legrande's. By chance, they played one of his for the birthday party of a girl whose dad knew somebody in the business. That contact led to their first single, just entitled 'Wild Abandon,' which charted out at ninety-nine in the top hundred, and they got some buzz. Signed with S&M Records. From there, it was all up."

"Until it came crashing down," Walrus finished. "I remember that. The first to go was Toby Bryant."

"What of him?" Karen asked her deputy. "And I thought you were a country boy."

"Hey, I've got unplumbed depths. Besides, some of their early stuff was pretty close to country rock. Toby Bryant was the lead singer, the pretty face, and pretty screwed up."

Eyre nodded and picked up the story again. "Their signature song, 'Washed Up,' came near the end of their run when Toby Bryant was in and out of drug rehab. That single went platinum, but it didn't help Bryant. He overdosed in his hotel room before their big comeback concert."

"Ouch," Bork said. "Bad timing."

Under her breath, Seoul hummed "Hotel California."

Her lips twitching, Eyre continued. "Legrande and Mohler tried to keep things going. The label gave them a new front man, but it didn't work out. Lots of infighting, then the label dropped them but refused to relinquish rights to the earlier stuff. Big standoff, lots of lawyers, lots of heat. A few months later, Mohler crashed his Ferrari into a guardrail on the Pacific Coast Highway and flipped into the sea."

"Suicide?" Karen asked.

Eyre shook her head. "The newspaper reported that he braked hard."

"And then there was only one," Seoul said mournfully. "Trick Legrande."

Walrus blew out his mustache. "I hate a sad ending."

Two Fingers finally spoke. "Why? What happened to him?"

Seoul answered before Eyre could. "After his fight with S&M Records, Legrande was down to his last mil. Blew it on a fancy boat and died dead broke in the Caribbean. Now that *was* suicide. He left a note, saying he'd been driven to it by S&M. By that time, they'd not only refused to relinquish the rights but weren't even going to allow Wild Abandon's music to be played over the air. Essentially, they killed the band. And Legrande said he was going to take all the stuff he'd written since the band broke up, stuff he never recorded, to the grave with him. S&M claimed he'd signed a contract way back when, from when they were little more than kids, that said S&M had a right to *anything* Legrande wrote, even if he was no longer under contract."

"Is that even legal?" Bork asked.

"Probably not," Seoul said. "But you have to fight it out in court. That takes money."

"So both sides were pissing in the common well," Walrus said.

"What about the boat?" Bork asked. "Wasn't that worth something for his heirs? And were there any, after all the band was dead?"

Eyre consulted her notes. "His mother was long dead, according to his obituary. No sibs, no children. As for the boat, it foundered on a reef and wasn't worth the salvage cost." She looked up again. "If the boat had sunk, we wouldn't even know what happened to Legrande."

Walrus shrugged. "Just another Bermuda Triangle mystery."

"It wasn't in Bermuda," Eyre pointed out.

Walrus waved a hand. "Details."

But Karen noticed Marek's Okerlund eyes had lidded.

"Are we sure he really died?" her detective asked.

"Ah, the conspiracy theories." Eyre smiled at Marek. "S&M led the charge, claiming Legrande was just staging a grand exit to get out of the contract." Eyre held up another newspaper article. "Then six weeks later, what was left of Legrande washed up on shore. Autopsy confirmed." She held up more papers. "It turns out Legrande was a dead man either way. Advanced liver cancer. So endeth the sad saga of Wild Abandon."

"And yet their music lives on," Karen pointed out.

Marek tilted his head back. "Did S&M back off their threat?"

Seoul answered that one. "S&M went under after all the bad publicity. The rights got sold off wholesale to another label."

"Geez, so everyone lost," Walrus concluded glumly.

"Pretty much," Eyre confirmed.

Karen pursed her lips. Had they? "Who was behind S&M?"

Eyre consulted her notes again then an article in her folder. "Originally, it belonged to partners Lyman Skinner and Saul Merlini, hence S&M—"

"Here I thought it was for kinky music," Bork cut in to boos.

"—but was bought out by Merlini after Skinner decided to call it quits to go into a less stressful business."

Walrus asked, "Which was?"

Eyre flashed him a smile. "Mortician."

Before the jokes could begin, Karen's cell phone warbled. The caller ID showed a Sioux Falls TV station. KDLT. How had they gotten her private number? She blocked it. But she didn't have much time before she'd have to face the music. "Okay, enough about Legrande. Let's move on to Hal Birchard."

CHAPTER 20

THE INVESTIGATION WAS MEANDERING ALL over the place, Marek thought. Like jazz. Noodling a bit here and there, riffing here, reeling there—playing peekaboo with that elusive essential thread, the melody. Where was it? The thread, the string...

"So... Hal Birchard." Eyre settled back. "I couldn't find much at all other than what you already gave me from his sheet and his origins in Bellevue, Nebraska. But I did find a snippet on a newspaper site. It's a police report from San Juan, the capital city of Puerto Rico."

Marek stilled. He started to catch a whisper of the melody.

"It mentions a bar fight broke out at a place called the Dive 'n Dirty. One man was knocked unconscious with the edge of a glass pitcher. Two men were taken into custody."

Karen blinked. "Birchard wasn't charged with assault. Right, Kurt?"

"No report in the database," the senior deputy said stiffly.

Eyre held up a hand. "That's because he was the victim. And it says he was the music that night. I'm guessing that's how Birchard was making a living, cobbled together with a partial disability pension from the military. The report says Hal Birchard was treated on scene. I couldn't find anything more on the incident. Maybe the charges were dropped, if any were filed, but that's the last thing I could find."

Marek started to smile. "What's the date?"

"July second of..." Eyre looked up abruptly, excitement in her Okerlund eyes. She may not carry a badge, but she was an excellent detective in her own way. "The very same year Legrande died."

"In the Caribbean, you said," Walrus protested.

Eyre didn't bother to hide a smile. "Puerto Rico *is* in the Caribbean."

"Oh. I thought it was..." Walrus waved to the west. "Out by Hawaii or something."

Marek started to get to his feet. "We need those old passports for Birchard."

"I've got that." Seoul flew to the basement door. Within a minute, she was back, clutching the bag of papers. She wavered between Marek and Karen.

Karen made a magnanimous gesture. "Marek's idea, his honors."

After pulling on latex gloves, Marek culled the passports for the one he needed. "Birchard arrived in San Juan on January sixteenth and didn't leave until November eighth." Marek looked at Eyre, who was already typing away furiously on her laptop. "Was Legrande ever seen in San Juan?"

"Just give me a minute." The minute was long. Way too long for his liking. Building anticipation and suspense, in the words of Kuhl.

Eyre lifted a hand from her laptop and gave a fist pump. "Yes! A celebrity newspaper gives sightings of Legrande around Puerto Rico the previous year, including San Juan. And in April of that year, he bought that fancy boat in San Juan from a wealthy financier. It even has pics with him christening it." She squinted then let out a strangled laugh. "*Washed Up*."

Walrus sadly shook his head. "Man, that's some nasty gallows humor."

Marek felt the hum in his head of hitting the right chord. "Anything more on Legrande after that?"

Eyre scanned her hits. "No, not until his suicide."

Somehow, someway, the two men had intersected in their respective descents. Though Birchard hadn't had much way to go but up. Had he taken Legrande down on the way?

As if washing up on the same island, Walrus lifted his hand. "Hey, I got a theory on that. It's out there, I'll admit, but... what if it wasn't really suicide?"

"The conspiracy theories were disproven—" Eyre began.

"No, I mean, I know Legrande's dead. But what if, after Legrande gets the boat, Birchard encounters him, maybe they hit it off at the Dive 'n Dirty—both into music after all—and then get into a fight over something or other on the boat. Birchard bops Legrande over the head, dumps the body overboard, writes the suicide note, but he can't bring himself to destroy the music. Manages to get to shore, maybe with a dingy? Lays low for all this time with that music burning a hole in his pocket, maybe his conscience, but Josh catches him playing that music one day, and Birchard decides it's safe now to let it out under the kid's name. Who's going to believe that boy would have anything to do with ripping off the music of some long-dead rocker?"

When Karen cocked an eyebrow at Marek, he tilted his head. "More likely that Birchard got the music without resorting to murder. He didn't have a history of violence. But it *is* possible."

Walrus gave himself a point, swiping a finger in the air— in the direction of the skeptical Kurt.

"It would explain why Birchard never made himself known to me," Karen mused.

Then Eyre held up the autopsy report again. "Sorry, Mr. Russell, but Legrande wasn't bopped on the head. The body wasn't in the best of shape after being in the water, so they couldn't determine the exact cause of death. But there was no sign of violence. The conclusion was presumed drowned. I've got the full report if you need it. It was online to quiet the conspiracy theorists."

"As if," Kurt grumped. "Nothing discourages those sort."

Eyre scanned down the report again. "A handwriting expert at the time also confirmed the suicide note was in Legrande's handwriting."

"Spoilsport," Walrus muttered.

Karen got up and started to pace. "All right, let's get back to the here and now. Hal Birchard."

As church bells rang from the Congregational Church to mark the hour, Walrus piped up again. "You know, Birchard and the Bolvins sang at our church for special music a couple weeks ago. 'Amazing Grace.' I don't usually go for that kind of barbershop stuff, but—"

"A cappella," Seoul corrected.

Karen held up a hand. "That's all very nice, but not quite—"

"Wait, wait. I got a point." Walrus actually dropped his boots from his desk and sat up in his chair. "After, the Bolvins take off—to mass, I think—but Birchard sticks around and talks to the pastor. They disappeared into her office. Sort of stood out to me, seeing as I'd heard he's no believer. Maybe he had a confession on his mind?"

Marek shook his head. "More likely, music."

Walrus deflated. "Double spoilsport."

"But worth checking out," Karen acceded.

"I'll take that." Marek and the former psychologist were friends of a sort, which, given he wasn't religious himself, was a curiosity in itself. "When does the service start?"

"At ten thirty," the congregant answered. "I can do it."

"No, I want you here to take any calls," Karen countered. When Walrus's eyes swung to Kurt, she said sweetly, "Unless you'd like to work the timeline?"

Walrus held up his hands in surrender. "You're putting my soul in jeopardy."

"Our Seoul is just fine," Karen said with a smile. Walrus's phone rang then: Tammy, calling in a fender bender out on Bluff Road. Walrus trundled off with one last bite of pannekuchen.

"Where are we at with evidence?" Bork rubbed his eyes.

Karen pursed her lips. "DCI is still processing the scene, the prints are on hold until Monday, and I still have to weasel a court order out of Judge Rudy to unseal the codicil to Birchard's will. Not to mention the attorney in Los Angeles is still deflecting my calls." She opened the floor with an open-handed gesture. "Any and all theories on the case are welcome."

Something pinged in Marek's head, but it disappeared when Seoul turned around in her chair, propping her arms on the back. "Rad Wilson's all over this case. Eavesdropping, making snide remarks, taking out the competition with juvenile tricks."

Kurt frowned at Seoul. "The laser pointer? Is that proven?"

"Well, no, not yet. But I'd put money on it. It's her style. And I think she knows a lot more than she's saying."

"So take a harder look at her," Karen told her. "Report back. If we can verify the laser pointer, that would at least give us a lever."

That at least made Seoul happy. Whatever the case... Marek stopped mid-thought. "No, *wherever* the case." Marek didn't realize he'd said that out loud until all eyes turned on him.

Karen raised her fair brow. "Come again?"

He cleared his throat, his brain still scrambling for the thread. "Where's the case?"

"That's the question." Karen tapped fingers on her belt. "Did you get any sleep last night?"

"No, I mean, the fiddle case."

"Oh." Karen stilled. "I wondered about that, too, but got distracted. Maybe it was somewhere in the tent? Or Birchard stashed it somewhere?"

Marek creaked in his chair, tilting back his head. "Birchard was killed with the fiddle string. Was that just what was handy? Or was it deliberate?"

"You mean *significant*?" Seoul asked. "That takes us

back to Rad Wilson. She had a hard-on for the competition. Killing him with his own instrument is right up her alley. Are you saying there's something about the fiddle itself that may be a clue?"

"Maybe. I don't know. Where is it?" Marek asked. "The fiddle."

"Downstairs..." Karen began but had to take a step back, as once again, Seoul flew past her to the basement door.

"Sheesh. I want whatever she's having." Walrus stared at the shutting door. "She should be crashing as it's well past the end of her shift now and into her sleep time, right?"

But Seoul was bright-eyed and bushy-tailed as she trotted back out, holding the fiddle in a large see-through evidence bag from DCI. "No prints, right?"

"That's right," Karen confirmed.

"That's a beautiful fiddle. I've never seen one like it." Eyre came over to take a closer look. When Seoul placed it on Karen's desk, Eyre looked confused. "But there's something wrong with it."

"It's missing one string," Bork told her. "That was the murder weapon."

"No, that's not what I meant."

Marek leaned forward. "What's the problem, then?"

"It has too many strings."

"No it doesn't." Seoul blinked up at Eyre. "It's supposed to have sympathetic strings."

Walrus squinted at the young deputy. "The strings are supposed to tear up and cry when things go bad?"

Seoul stuck her tongue out at him. "It's a Hardanger fiddle. *Hardingfele*." Hands on nonexistent hips, she looked at Karen, Marek, and finally Eyre. "You guys are the Scandinavians. Don't you recognize it?"

"Is it rare?" Marek asked.

"Pricey, you mean? I don't know. Maybe. I mean, they aren't like a Strad or anything, but it's not my area. You'd have to find someone who could appraise it for you. I'd suggest the National Music Museum—"

"The Shrine to Music," Karen cut across at the same time then looked at Seoul. "I don't know where your museum is, but the Shrine is in Vermillion."

Where Karen had gone to school on a basketball scholarship, Marek knew.

"It's in Vermillion." Seoul's upturned nose wrinkled in puzzlement. "On East Clark."

"Name change?" Marek suggested when Karen blinked. "Can you get us in, Seoul?"

"It's a tourist site, but if you want to talk to the experts, I'm not sure." Seoul pursed her lips. "It took my major prof's letter of recommendation and a mini-thesis on my project to get through that door." She pulled out her phone. "But I know one of the staff. He practically lives there. Maybe I can catch him."

Seoul went through her contacts then triumphantly stabbed the number. The phone picked up right away, and Seoul did a thumbs-up.

"Yes, Dr. Lanski. This is Seoul Durr. I'd like to make an appointment, or rather, for my boss. No, not exactly, but..." Alarm crossed the deputy's face. "Wait! Wait, just hear me out. You helped me with a paper I wrote. Annotations in jazz." The worried brow unfurrowed. "Yes, I did publish that. And I thanked you in the acknowledgments. No... I didn't continue my academic track." She winced at whatever the reply was. "But I am"—she held up two fingers in the air and crossed them—"still engaged in serious work with a musical angle. And I wondered if you could help us out. It's about a Hardanger fiddle. Yes, it's in prime condition. I know that folk instruments are an area you have a great deal of knowledge about, so I... Monday at eight?" Seoul looked up and got a nod from Karen. "Perfect. Thanks so much. By the way, Dr. Lanski, my boss is Sheriff Karen Mehaffey of Eda County. She'll be accompanied by Detective Marek Okerlund. Bye!"

Walrus looked at her in admiration as she pocketed her phone as if it were a revolver into a holster. "You just hung up on him?"

"Before he could back out. Because he would have."

"So we've got things in process." Marek rubbed his temples. "But not much progress."

"I disagree." Karen nodded out the windows. "You may have just saved my bacon."

He turned and saw a satellite truck parked across the street and a reporter and camera crew unloading.

Karen straightened her badge and pulled her ponytail through her sheriff's cap. "Your San Juan connection will let me spin things out a while longer with the press."

"Have fun with that." Marek rose to his feet and checked his watch. He still had half an hour before the service started. "I'm off to church."

"Never thought I'd see the day." Walrus clasped prayerful hands. "You could get used to it."

Marek just shook his head and slipped out the back.

CHAPTER 21

W HEN MAREK EXITED STAGE COWARD, meaning out the back of the courthouse, he found the sky dark gray to the west, with the smudged look that meant rain. Hopefully, he'd get to the church and back before the storm reached Reunion. Already, he could hear the rumble of thunder, and he hoped that the festivalgoers were prepared for a deluge.

Next year, maybe he could make it to the Jam Off with Nikki. He'd have to ask her if she'd ever been. He hadn't. How many gems like that hidden musical festival existed in the backways and byways of America?

Seoul was right about one thing: a life without music would be a poor one indeed. Even the ancients had carried at least one instrument with them everywhere—their voices. Marek missed singing, he realized, as he stutter-stepped to miss a crack in the concrete sidewalk.

Step on a crack, break your mother's back.

Where had that come from? And why wasn't it "break *your* back"? Because that would be far more likely. Like folk music, he supposed, the origins of children's rhymes were a mystery. They were just passed down, generation to generation. Like music. Like religion. As he entered the church, he heard the rumble, looked back out at the far-off sky, thinking he'd misjudged the storm. But the storm was still a ways off yet and now looked to veer north.

Moving into the foyer, he realized the rumble was coming from inside the sanctuary. Drawn by the sound and the vibration under his Blunnies, he could only revel in the power coming out of the huge pipe organ that scaled up the far wall behind the choir loft.

Wow. Who knew? The case forgotten, he entered the mostly empty sanctuary and dropped down on a pew behind the magician playing furiously at the organ. He looked like the Wizard of Oz, a small man with grand aspirations. Only this time, they were real, his hands running over the four-level keyboard and his feet over pedals. Occasionally, a hand would flick out to pull knobs or push them back in.

Only vaguely did he realize Pastor Cantor had dropped down next to him. The organ crescendoed into a wall of sound that equaled anything he'd heard at a rock concert. Building and building up to the finale, which made the hair in Marek's ears scramble for cover and his bones vibrate like he was straddling a Harley. What a ride.

But like all good things, it came to an end.

"Never heard an organ before?" Tricia Cantor asked him into the resounding silence.

"Not like that." What, he wondered, would that music look like to his synesthete daughter? Maybe he'd bring her and find out. "Ah... just the elevator music kind. That was simply... amazing."

The man at the organ turned, red-faced, as if he'd just completed a high-intensity training bout. "Always good to make another convert."

Tricia laughed as Marek squirmed. "Not your religious beliefs, Detective. Organs. What was that, Charles? It sounded very familiar, but I can't quite place it. Bach, perhaps?"

"Yes. His 'Toccata and Fugue in D-Minor.' Took me years to conquer that." Charles's bright-blue eyes assessed Marek, as if trying to decide if the appreciation was sincere or just polite fiction. "Many people think of the organ as outdated.

And I suppose it is, for many purposes, at least in our mobile society. But it's been around a long time—the first mechanical pipe organ was invented in 3 BC in Greece—and I expect it will outlast us all. That's my hope, anyway." He got to his feet as someone beckoned him. "Pardon me. That's the choir director. Perhaps you'll come again? I give a concert here at least twice a year."

Marek nodded as the man scurried away. The Jam Off, Barn Off, and organs? What was next? However much he enjoyed listening to his own music collection at home on his Paradigms, nothing really substituted for the live experience. Like the missed Chicago concert.

"I'm guessing you're not here for my scintillating sermons, Detective."

Marek blinked and reddened. "Sorry. Thinking. You know the case we're working?"

Tricia rose as people started to file into the sanctuary. "Let's go into my office." She led him back and closed the door. "Will this take long?"

"Shouldn't," he told her, not bothering to settle in the comfy chair, the pastoral version of the psychologist's couch. All he could think of was *Monty Python*: Not the comfy chair!

The pastor sat behind her desk, hands clasped, her multicolor stole a bright spot in the dim room behind the sanctuary. "As for your case, yes, I do know about Hal Birchard and was very saddened to hear of his death. He actually came a few times to Charles's concerts. Like you, I think he got a kick out of the sheer physicality of it."

That was a good description. Physicality. "I've been told that after Birchard sang with the Bolvins here last month, he engaged you in conversation and that you brought him back here."

Her eyes danced. "Are you suggesting I've fallen into sin, Detective?"

He reddened again, remembering that he'd once accused

her of that. "No. I am trying to find out more about the man. If you tell me that you just talked music, I'll believe you."

"Well, we did talk music. Mostly."

When the pastor said nothing more, Marek sighed and looked over her intimidating wall of books written about arcane topics in theology and psychology. "And you're going to pull the confidentiality card."

"No, I'm thinking. I can't recall that he said anything that would help you. Nothing about any conflicts with others. It was an odd conversation, to be honest."

Marek turned back from the wall of books. "How so?"

"At first, we talked church music, which I've always loved, going back to when I took a summer semester of classes in Oxford. I spent many a pleasant time going to evensong in cavernous cathedrals where the choir outnumbered the congregants. The entrancing mix of organ and the pure tones of boy sopranos was a revelation." She looked at a photo on her desk, one he hadn't seen before. "After I lost my family, music was one of the only things that could speak to my grief."

Marek exchanged an understanding look with the pastor, whose husband, son, and future daughter-in-law had lost their lives one snowy night in Chicago. After Val died, Marek had sometimes hooked up Val's phone to the stereo system, brought up her playlist, then rocked his daughter in his arms through the night. Anything to fill the silence.

After tapping the photo of her family away from her view, Tricia looked back up. "There's also something unique, though, about participating in music. Whether a choir or a rock band or an orchestra—it brings you together in a way that can't be done otherwise. Our choir director often says that she wouldn't walk across the street to hear the 'Hallelujah Chorus' but she'd walk a mile to sing it."

Out in the sanctuary, the organ fired up again, but this time, with a far more meditative sound. When the pastor checked her watch, he asked, "What was odd about your conversation?"

"Oh. Right before he left, Hal Birchard turned and asked me, 'Do last rites done by a layman count?' I told him that we didn't do last rites in our tradition. That he should ask a priest."

Marek couldn't see a connection to the case, but it was certainly odd. Unless Walrus was right and Birchard had mortally wounded Legrande? "And that was it?"

"He said the day he went to see a priest, he'd probably kill him. Seeing the shock on my face, he said he'd had some unpleasant experiences with the breed. My take was that he'd been abused, but that wasn't necessarily so."

A knock on the door had the pastor jumping to her feet. "That's the sexton. Time's up. If you'd like to stay..."

"Sorry. Work." Marek smiled at her. "Not unpleasantness."

"There's that. Go in peace, Detective."

And with the organ rumbling at his back, he did, though none the wiser.

CHAPTER 22

BY THE TIME KAREN STOOD on the front steps of the courthouse to give her statement, the street was crowded with media. Most were from Sioux Falls and Sioux City. One from the Twin Cities, she recognized as being affiliated with Bates McClain, a decent reporter when it came to sniffing out stories. His was the call she'd ignored earlier.

Karen had majored in communications and had worked as a dispatcher for years, but her stomach still fluttered as she walked up to the mic. She wished Marek had stuck around, because though her close-mouthed detective rarely spoke, he was a solid support—and intimidated reporters with his size. And he just looked the part, when she often didn't. Sad, but true. But she made do with Kurt and Walrus flanking her. At least they wouldn't bicker with her between them.

Taking a deep breath, Karen began outlining the basic facts of the case and evading direct revelations of just how lost they were in finding the killer. Doublespeak, in other words—a hated but necessary tool in the hyper culture of media, where every word, every inflection, was picked apart for something to criticize, spin, or offend.

"As you have no doubt recently learned, Hal Birchard obtained a previously unknown song written by the rock legend Trick Legrande titled 'Plain Sight.' That song, which

Birchard claimed as his own, was recorded and videoed in Birchard's home studio with a young local musician, Josh Bolvin, who initially took credit for the song at the behest of Birchard."

The Twin Cities reporter muscled through the crowd. "How did he obtain that song? And when was it written?"

Karen silently thanked Marek that she wouldn't have to find a way to say, "Sorry, I'm just a sheriff in bumfuck, female to boot, and I haven't a clue." She looked directly into the camera. "We can't be certain." When she saw what almost looked like satisfaction—or at least a gloat—in the Twin Cities reporter, she went on. "However, we can tell you, due to the excellent research of my staff, that both Hal Birchard and Trick Legrande were in San Juan in Puerto Rico the same year that Legrande committed suicide. The obvious conclusion is that, either legally or illegally, Birchard obtained a copy of 'Plain Sight' at that time."

That turned the gloat to a shocked surprise, allowing a veteran Sioux Falls reporter to sidestep neatly into the gaping silence. "Sheriff Mehaffey, I've been informed that Josh Bolvin, despite being seen looking very upset after leaving Hal Birchard in the instrument tent, was cleared of the murder. Can you confirm?"

On safer ground, Karen relaxed enough to smile at the grizzled reporter. "Josh Bolvin and our victim had words— that's quite true—but Josh Bolvin's movements after leaving the instrument tent where Birchard's body was found can be accounted for by photographic and video evidence. And a witness, also confirmed on video, saw Birchard alive in the instrument tent after that encounter. Unless a nineteen-year-old has unplumbed depths—in his pocketbook—to hire a hit, I'd say he's cleared."

The Twin Cities reporter elbowed back, receiving disapproving glances from the more well-behaved Dakotans. "The motive is clearly the music. Do you have any idea how much a new song from Legrande would be worth?"

His tone said she didn't. And to be honest, she didn't. "Priceless, to his fans. I'll let the music industry put an actual number on that. And at this time, we cannot judge motive."

"Is it true that you are named as beneficiary of Hal Birchard's will?" called out a young reporter, who she was dismayed to realize was her cousin. Well, sort of. Blake Halvorsen was the son of her beloved Uncle Sig Halvorsen, her father's cousin.

Blake must have gotten another internship over the summer with the same Sioux Falls TV station he'd worked with previously. And damn him, he'd have local knowledge that might jeopardize her case if he pushed it. But she wasn't sure how he'd gotten that tidbit, since his father—always in the thick of gossip at his butcher shop—was out of town for the weekend at a sustainable agriculture conference.

The Twin Cities reporter actually turned to glare at the young man, who kept an admirably straight face—or at least a neutral one.

Karen pulled the Twin Cities reporter back with her answer. "Yes, that's true. I was named as trustee of the will with a nominal benefit, without my knowledge or consent, as I had never even spoken to the victim before." She saw mouths open like carp in a feeding frenzy but held up a hand. "We've recently uncovered the reason for that choice." She waited a beat, just because she could, and was rewarded by an anticipatory silence. "Hal Birchard was my late husband's half-uncle."

"How could you not have known that?" Twin Cities snapped out. Attack mode. And it hit, but not for the reason the reporter thought. It echoed Karen's question to Danielle. Karen just hoped she could handle it with as much control.

As Kurt stiffened to attention beside her, Karen said in a very, *very* even voice, "Because Patrick Mehaffey drove over a land mine while driving to the aid of a Muslim teenager injured in the Bosnian War." Take that, she thought, as silence fell. "I had little time to get to know Patrick's relatives, and he had few to start with, none of whom he acknowledged."

"Not even his half-sister, Danielle Mehaffey, who inherits the bulk of Birchard's estate?"

Damn him. Blake was good. He must've gotten hold of Andrew Van Doren. "He was, as I was, unaware that his mother, Lianne Mehaffey, who was a teenager when she had him, had a second child much later. Danielle came to Eda County over a year ago in search of Patrick's family. She was a runaway and didn't want to contact me until she was of legal age. If you can throw back your memories as far as last May"—a millennia to the press—"you may recall that Danielle was, among others, abducted in a sex trafficking scheme. Fortunately, she was rescued before that scheme was put into action. And that was when I learned of her existence and relationship to Patrick."

"Shouldn't you recuse yourself from the case, given your connection?"

Hearing Walrus's uncontrolled snort behind her, she stared down Twin Cities. "If I recused myself from all the cases where I knew the players, I wouldn't have anything to do, nor would my men. You might want to brush up on Rural Policing 101."

The Sioux Falls crowd smiled openly, though Karen winced inwardly. Her habit of speaking off the cuff did get her in trouble sometimes. "Anything else?"

Her young cousin wasn't done with her. "Has Danielle Mehaffey been cleared of the murder? She was, after all, the one who found the body."

Oh, she'd like to strangle him. In Karen's mind, Danielle was clear. Marek agreed. But that wasn't evidence. Not a done deal. "To date, we have found no evidence that Danielle Mehaffey was aware of the connection to Hal Birchard or the contents of his will. She has been interviewed and released. Our investigation is ongoing."

"Where is your detective?" the grizzled reporter asked. "I'd like to get his take."

Karen didn't tell them that Marek was at church. Not what they wanted to hear. "Detective Okerlund is out in the field, working the case, while I take valuable time off to answer your questions. It's time I got back to my job. Thank you."

Ignoring other called questions, Karen did an about-face and pushed through the double doors, letting Walrus and Kurt keep the reporters at bay. Her phone pinged with a text as she walked into the office, and she grabbed it with the intention of turning it off. But it was Jessica.

Where are you? Trucks are here. Have tidbit for you.

Slipping out of the back, she found Marek rounding the courthouse, as well, somehow having evaded the eagle eye of the grizzled reporter. "We're on."

"A lead?" he asked, gesturing to his Silverado. Her ride was still impounded for repairs.

"We'll see. We're meeting Jessica."

Driving down an alley to avoid the press, he asked, "Where are we headed? Sioux Falls?"

"Larson's new home." She texted her roster. "Moving Day."

Marek just nodded in easy acceptance. From murder to moving in a blink of an eye. Rural Policing 101. But Larson hadn't gotten the memo. As they piled out at his grandmother's newly painted gingerbread home in Reunion, Karen's men straggling in behind and neighbors coming out of the woodwork, the DCI agent's face was priceless.

Seeing Blake getting out of his press car, Karen stalked over.

He held up his hands. "I'm here to help."

Reaching in, Karen put her hands around his neck. "Consider yourself strangled."

"Hey, just doing my job." Though he didn't have the same easy gregariousness as his father or his twin, Blake had his own brand of a winning smile. He showed it more often now that he'd settled into his dream job instead of working in the family butcher shop. The only butchering he did now was of competing reporters. "*And* I took and passed Rural Policing 101. You're off the record as of now."

"You can live." Karen paused, tightened her grip a notch, then let go. "Barely. Don't you have to go back to your overlord and masters, the nefarious media?"

"Nah, they let me off the chain for good behavior. I'm Boy Wonder at the station." Apparently deeming it safe, he got out of the car. "Besides, Dad's due back tonight, and we're having a cookout. Prime cut. He grills the best."

"You're lucky I don't strangle you for that alone." Karen gave him a light push toward the truck. "Be useful."

He gave her a lazy salute. She started to look for Jessica when she was waylaid by Larson.

"Break in the case?" he asked warily as her men headed for the truck.

"In a manner of speaking. We're taking a break from the case." She snagged a lamp from Bork. "Where do you want this?"

Larson still looked completely baffled, not just by the question, but also by the help.

Hauling a clothes bag over one shoulder, Walrus stopped and slapped him on the back. "Get used to it, Larson. That's how it works here. People come out to help, whether it's harvesting or moving." He glanced back at the U-Haul truck. Short. Stubby. Barely enough to hold a room's worth of belongings, Karen thought. "Shouldn't take us long."

"That's mine. The kids' stuff..." Larson pointed at a huge unopened pod to one side of the driveway. He looked at it as if it were an alien lifeform ready to spring open and suck out all life on the planet. "Ex sent it last month, and it finally got here... along with the bill. Think she padded it with a lot of stuff she didn't want—just another FU."

Hopefully the last FU. And good riddance. Karen

would never understand the woman who'd given birth to two children, turned them against their father with vile accusations, then dumped them on that same father with a blithe and careless ease when she found herself a better sugar daddy. The wonder was that the kids were sane.

Obviously hearing the exchange, Marek stopped, as well, putting down a heavy metal floor lamp. "Might want to get a dumpster, then."

"Mmm. Let people pick it over first," Bork suggested as he joined the group, a garbage bag full of clothes slung over his shoulder.

Walrus concurred. "Free stuff attracts people like flies on hamburger. Gives 'em a high. They regret it later, so they leave it on the curb, and somebody else'll repeat the cycle. Win-win."

The door to the old gingerbread house opened, and rap beat its way out into the street in a blast that had Larson wincing. "Shut that noise off!" he yelled.

Nothing happened. At least, not until a surprisingly strong voice coming from a diminutive elderly woman yelled, "Please!"

That did it. Sweet, sweet silence.

Walrus backslapped Larson. "Don't sweat it, Agent Larson. I've got boys and it's the same in my house. They don't listen to me, but boy howdy, they listen to their grandmother. Comes from spoiling them, I say. You get to take the rap." Walrus gave Larson a comforting—or possibly commiserating—pat on the arm and headed for the pod. "Let's see what we've got here."

A lot of crap, as it turned out, judging by the pile of dated and broken furniture and bags of bedding and clothes left by the side of the street when they were finished. But Walrus claimed a few things. Somehow, Karen kept her mouth shut. Privately, Karen thought they'd likely be vetoed by Laura and end up on their curb.

When it was all done, Karen took a good look at the

parlor where she'd interviewed a frail old woman in a frilly dress. The delicate wire furniture was gone, as was the fragility of its owner, who told Karen that she'd started working out with her basketball-mad granddaughter. Not that she'd been a slouch before, they'd discovered, as she had a hidden workout gym in the basement. Apparently, a lady of a certain age wasn't allowed to sweat. The frowning wall of ancestors on the parlor wall hadn't been taken down but instead were now looking almost benevolent as they contemplated a bunch of newly found descendants, from the snap of an endearingly scowling and baffled Larson to basketball-playing Maddie and computer-gaming Brandon.

Now those staid ancestors had a chance for immortality.

In a track suit and sneakers but somehow looking as classy as if she'd worn an evening dress, Eleanor Larson beamed. "The house feels... alive. *I* feel alive again." She looked over at her great-grandchildren, who were bickering over the placement of a TV. "The house will go to them when I'm gone, and I want them to be at home here." Her lips twitched as Larson came in with a bag of his daughter's tampons, looking like he was holding an unpinned grenade. "Though there have been a few... adjustments... over music."

"Rap. Not music," Larson muttered darkly.

His son scowled. "It's got a beat."

"So does a cop. Doesn't mean squat."

"So sad, I got a dad, a bad dad, who's never rad." Brandon riffed a nonexistent cymbal.

His sister gave him the raspberry. "That's so lame. You want real music, try the Jonas Brothers. 'Only Human' rocks."

"Sucks rocks," her brother countered.

And the bickering resumed as Maddie and Brandon jockeyed for position up the stairs to distribute their belongings in their respective rooms on the second floor. She'd noted that Larson's room was on the opposite side of his grandmother's on the first floor and looked out onto an ancient oak with a swing in the backyard. The room in between the bedrooms was being converted into an office for him.

"Parenting is always a work in progress." Eleanor patted her grandson's arm much as Walrus had. "Give it time."

Eleanor had had her rebellious daughter young, who'd had Larson even younger. Unaware that his grandmother was still living, Larson had grown up in the Chicago projects with a drug-addicted prostitute for a mother. How different his life might have been if Eleanor had known about him and vice versa. Karen had no doubt that she'd have taken her grandson in and given him the love she'd been aching to give her daughter, who was long since dead and now buried in the family cemetery near the less-than-stellar father she'd adored.

Eleanor lifted her voice. "Who wants lunch?" Into the sudden silence, she announced, "I ordered enough Mex-Mix for an army. I see the delivery van's pulling in."

That stopped all other conversation for a good half hour as they snarfed down the spicy offerings. Only when Jessica headed out the door to get back to Sioux Falls did Karen remember the tidbit. Karen hurried out after her. "Give."

"Give what? Oh, yeah. I forgot." Jessica wiped a stray streak of green chile sauce from her scarred cheek. "*Excellent* huevos rancheros. I've got a fingerprint match for you."

Karen blinked. "I thought your print guy was out fishing."

"Our fearless fisherman fled at the first hint of rain. His misfortune, your gain."

Anticipation hummed. "The print inside the amp?"

"No, the mic. Plenty of prints from Josh Bolvin, but I heard you eliminated him as a suspect. The handprint on the mic matched Sal Marmo."

Karen whistled. "We'll have to see what Mr. Marmo says to that." Assuming they could find the man. That, in itself, was suspicious. But maybe he'd show back up at the festival. Becca's recorder concert was coming up, so maybe they'd catch him then. Two birds, one stone—or one stoned manager.

After Jessica sped off, Larson came out of the house before she could return inside, tugged her down to the porch swing, and laid a juicy one on her. All frustration and heat. His forehead to hers, he got out, "Doctor, doctor."

Karen pulled back in alarm, putting a hand on his forehead. "Did you overdo it?" She felt heat but not fever. "Aching bones? You're not twenty any longer, Larson."

"Got a bad case."

Karen wondered how he'd caught a case and still managed to get the truck here, before she got it. Robert Palmer. A bad case of loving her. She sighed and swung. "Ditto me for you. What are we going to do about it, Larson? When is it going to be our time?"

He reached out and kissed her hard again. "Don't know."

"Enough of that," Walrus boomed as he came out with a big bag of leftovers that Karen suspected wouldn't make it to the office. "We've got children present."

Channeling Seoul, Karen stuck out her tongue at him.

With a huge parental sigh, Walrus shook his gleaming bald head. "Kids these days."

Behind him, Brandon yelled out, "Elders these days!"

That's a wrap, Karen thought. And grinned.

CHAPTER 23

AKING HIS WAY THROUGH THE crowd at the festival, Marek felt far more nervous than his daughter, who swung between Nikki and Karen in his wake. While some of the festivalgoers called the kids' concert the Tot Off, it wasn't really a contest. Or rather, it was the participation-trophy kind: all in good fun, with no pressure. At least not for Becca's summer school class. For others, he suspected, that wasn't the case, especially for one shaking little girl whose father drilled her on her fingerings while her mother adjusted her costume. Why did parents do that? The joy of being a kid, the joy of music, should be enough in itself without adding adult expectations.

But Marek kept his mouth shut. Because Becca had plenty of pressure on her art—mostly self-imposed. Some of it, though, came from her maternal grandmother, who Skyped every month or so to check on her progress. Marek knew that if Adrienne Fiat had her way, Becca would be in New York City under the tutelage of the top art instructors in the country instead of in Reunion, South Dakota, where the art program, along with music, struggled mightily to remain on the curriculum at all.

That said, Marek knew his daughter was driven to do art, and perhaps that shaking little girl had the same passion for music, and her parents were only doing what they could to make sure she got her chance at her dream. Nerves didn't mean lack of desire. But at least that wasn't plaguing his daughter. Spotting the small group of recorder-holding kids, with a harried teacher at their center, Becca took off to join them. She hugged Em Bolvin as if they'd been parted for years instead of... two days. Sheesh. Friday seemed to have been eons ago.

By the time the Tot Off started, though, Marek had more nerves than a rookie on his first domestic violence call. He sat cross-legged on the grass between Nikki and Karen with the Bolvins just to Karen's right. Noting that Nick Bolvin looked faintly ill, Marek felt a bit better.

"Relax, Daddy," Nikki told him. "It's not like it's opening night at the Grand Ole Opry."

Marek rolled his shoulders, but that didn't help much. As he listened to a slightly older crew of kids play a wildly out of tune "America the Beautiful," he decided that he'd be glad if Becca never pursued music over art. At least his ears wouldn't have to suffer through art exhibits.

By the time Becca's group—the last—trotted onto the stage, his body was rigid, his ears screaming, and his heart thumping. Becca caught his eye, waving at him as Em waved to her parents. He gave his daughter what he hoped was a smile, not a death's-head grimace, and managed to give her a thumbs-up. Then the teacher raised her hands and released the little dogies. Somewhere in the wandering notes unleashed—yelps and squeals—he heard a melody, but it was as elusive as the case.

When the song was mercifully over, the crowd gave them a rousing round of applause, many getting to their feet in what appeared to be a standing ovation. Just like they'd done for Hal Birchard. But Marek was fairly sure that this time it was mere relief—and the need to stretch their cramped legs.

After relinquishing her recorder to her teacher, thankfully for the final time, Becca ran straight from the stage into his arms. "Did you like it?" she asked.

"That was..."

"Okerlunds never lie," Nikki reminded him under her breath.

"Unforgettable." Marek looked over her head at Nick, who'd hefted a bubbling Em. "I've truthfully never heard anything to equal it."

"We were the best!" Em yelled, raising her arms in victory.

"Ah, so humble, so self-effacing, that's my Em." Tweaking her daughter's nose, Penny Bolvin laughed. "You ready to come home with us, Becca?"

His daughter practically jumped out of Marek's arms. The two girls raced through the crowd toward the Bolvins' Ford F150.

"Thanks for taking her. I appreciate it."

Nick Bolvin poked him in the pecs. "Just molding the next knockout Okerlund voice."

Baffled, Nikki and Karen turned on Marek. "You sing?" they asked in unison.

Marek hunched his shoulders. "Not since high school."

"Which is a royal shame. It's a crime to hide that voice," Patty Bolvin boomed out, making heads turn. One of those heads belonged to Anton Kuhl, who was walking up from the lower level, probably from another workshop. Good plan to miss the Tot Off. Marek had seen suspiciously few actual musicians in the crowd, other than those whose offspring were participating.

Meeting Marek's gaze over the milling crowd, Kuhl beckoned to him and not, Marek was sure, for an impromptu audition.

"No rest for the weary." Karen sighed. "Back to work."

Going on tiptoe, Nikki pecked Marek on the cheek. "You can give me a private concert later."

He'd rather give her a private concert of another kind, but wisely said nothing. He followed Karen toward the waiting Kuhl, hoping that the record mogul could point them toward Marmo's current whereabouts.

"I only just heard about Legrande's music from one of

my workshop students," Kuhl told them, gesturing toward a vacated picnic table. As they sat, he gave them an ironic look. "I felt I had better come clean before you came for me."

Marek, his mind still on Marmo, hitched mid-thought. And he reached into his pocket to get the mini-recorder he always carried to dictate his reports for Josephine to type up. Sometimes, it also came in handy to interview witnesses.

"No need to read me my rights, Detective." The twist grew on Kuhl's long face. "I'm not confessing to murder."

Exchanging a glance with Karen, Marek dropped down to the nearby picnic table, the worn wood almost bare of paint. "If you're okay with it, Mr. Kuhl, we'd like to do so anyway."

When Kuhl hesitated, Karen said, "We'll need your official statement if this is going in the direction we're thinking. It's routine. And less paperwork for you."

With a resigned shrug, he acceded, and Marek engaged his recorder. The rights process was quickly completed, and Kuhl resumed. "When I said I'd better come clean, I simply meant that I have a vested interest in Legrande's music."

Now Marek got it. Label guy. "You bought the rights?"

"My company did, yes."

Karen blinked then picked up the melody. "At a bargain price."

"Also true. Saul was desperate at that point, up to his neck in debt, so I—"

Had Marek's recorder-abused ears deceived him? "Did you say Saul?"

Chagrin crossed the man's face. "I meant Sal, of course."

"Saul Merlini." Marek took a gamble, though it wasn't much of one. "Salvatore Marmo?"

As that registered, Karen straightened. "He changed his name."

"Yes, after all the bad publicity over Legrande's suicide, Saul was finished as a label. After I bought him out, he reinvented himself." Kuhl sighed and ran a hand through his silvered hair. "Look, I don't like the man. He's a sad sack. And he's turned into the kind of smarmy manager that makes our business look bad. But he's always had the ear—an uncanny knack to spot talent. I benefited from that, as I was able to do what he wasn't. Manage the talent."

"You recognized him right off," Karen said. "And you didn't say anything?"

"I believe I did indicate we knew each other, Sheriff. I didn't see that it was relevant."

Were they building to the finale? "Yet both of you came here, to the Big Jam, because you recognized that music in the video."

Kuhl's brows show up. "Very good, Detective."

Karen looked confused. "But no one had ever heard that music before. Right?"

"Not that specific song, no. But I knew it, Saul knew it, all the same." Kuhl's sun-kissed skin wrinkled around his eyes as he kept his gaze on Marek. "You're right—it's no coincidence that I came all the way out here from California to judge a rural music festival. I came for one reason, the same that Saul did. Because we both heard Legrande's musical signature in that boy's viral video. That had me really, really curious. Was it just a very good imitation as sometimes happens with young artists who ape their betters... or something more? Until I learned of the music's origins just now, I didn't know which."

Karen still looked baffled. "Signature?"

"Largely unconscious choices made in musical composition unique to the individual or the band. It's how you can tell Bach from Tchaikovsky or the Beatles from Bon Jovi."

"So the signature's like the genre of music?"

"More individual than that. Style, if you like, but so much more. Timbre, intonation—"

"I'll take your word for it." Karen leaned forward. "Do you know where Marmo is?"

That wry twist appeared again. "I imagine he's getting

drunk, is drunk, or is recovering from same. All he cares about, I'm sure, is showing up for Josh Bolvin's concert and convincing him—or his family as they presumably have money that he doesn't—that he has the connections to make him a star."

Marek felt the day slip away in a wild-goose chase. "You don't know where Marmo's staying?"

"I believe he has a hotel in Sioux Falls, as do I. However, I suspect not at such a high-quality establishment. I'm afraid that's all I can tell you. As you might have gathered, we are not copacetic."

Marek frowned. "Just why is that? You paid off his debts, right?"

"I believe it's called biting the hand that feeds you." Kuhl rose to his feet. "I don't know that any of this helps your investigation, but I did feel you should know."

"Thanks," Karen said. "It's been helpful."

With a wince, Kuhl sauntered off toward the restrooms as the festival organizers announced the beginning of a Name That Tune contest.

"The tune is murder." Karen smiled. "And it's got Marmo's signature prints all over it." Karen checked her watch. "Hopefully, it won't take us long to find out where Marmo is holed up. Maybe we'll get this wrapped up tonight."

Recognizing the song blasting out of the speakers on the stage, Marek grinned. "'It's All Good.'"

"MC Hammer." She grinned back at him. "Let's go hammer the hammered."

But when they got back to the office after retrieving the Sub from Gotsch's garage, Karen was the one to get hammered. A woman sat in Karen's office chair, her grey hair stringy, her face gaunt, her thin arms tattooed with guns and roses.

None of the deputies had removed her from the room, much less the Okerlund seat of power, and that sent alarms clanging. Marek stayed standing nearby, waiting to see if he'd be needed.

"About time." The woman jumped up, sending the chair back into the bookcase, where the radio wobbled. Marek reached out and caught it.

Hands on hips, the woman demanded, "Where the hell is she, and why the hell didn't you notify me? It's my *right*."

Looking down at the woman, Karen hooked her thumbs into her belt. "I don't know who the hell you are or who *she* is. But if you don't get out of my face, out of my office, I'll throw you in jail for loitering."

"I don't think so. Maybe I should introduce myself." The woman not only didn't back down, she stepped into the small space still remaining between them. She smiled, hard. "I'm your mother-in-law."

CHAPTER 24

R EADY FOR JUST ABOUT ANYTHING, from some old fling of Legrande's to an aging hippie groupie with an agenda, Karen dropped hard into her chair.

"Yeah, bet you weren't counting on me showing up, were you?" Lianne Mehaffey crossed her thin arms over a nearly concave chest covered with a minimum of fabric. "But I got rights. I lost my little girl, and no one even bothers to tell me she's found. I have to hear on the news in the shelter."

How Karen hated the media, even as she used it. Lianne Mehaffey could put a wrench in the emancipation hearing on Monday. But why? Just to be ornery? "How did you get here?"

"Hitched. How else? Not like I got money."

Now Karen understood. Lianne's little girl was coming into money as Legrande's beneficiary. Karen slowly uncoiled from the chair. "Maybe you didn't hear, Lianne, but I was named as the trustee of Legrande's estate. Nothing goes out of the trust without my blessing."

"I'll get a lawyer. Contest the will. I got *rights*." A fire—and maybe even a bit of real feeling—stirred deep in that ravaged face. "Hal was my *brother*. He was *blood*. You're just..."

"Just your son's wife. The one who sat by him, day after day, month after month, year after year, waiting for him to wake up. Where were you?" Seeing just a blank look,

Karen let out a breath of disgust. "You don't even know what happened to him, do you?"

"He ran away. Just like Hal. Ran away. Everybody runs away. Never saw neither of 'em again." The woman hesitated, bit her lip, and actually asked, "Was Patrick in an accident?"

Karen didn't know if Lianne really cared or was just trying a different angle. Addicts were geniuses of manipulation. "He was a medic during the Bosnian War and drove over a land mine. The doctors told me to pull the plug, but I didn't want to let him go." She'd believed her husband would beat the odds, just as he had coming from this woman. "He never woke up again and... died..." Was murdered—really a mercy killing—by another soldier. "A few years ago."

"Huh. Another soldier in the family. Wouldn't've guessed that. Hal ran away to the Navy, I heard. Sailed far away as he could and left me in the lurch." Her fire died out. "I want to see him."

"See who? I can take you to Patrick's grave, but—"

"Hal. They said he was murdered. On the news, they said. My brother. Left me without a by-your-leave. Never forgave him for that. Maybe now's the time."

Karen tried to figure an angle and couldn't find one. "You want to see your brother's body?"

"That's what I said. Can't you hear?"

Before Karen could reply, the doors opened, and Harlan and Danielle came in. Or rather, Harlan came in, and Danielle stopped abruptly just inside the doors as she saw Lianne, whose back was half turned to her.

"You gotta do something," Harlan told Karen. "Those vultures are hanging around the diner."

"Take your turn." Lianne actually shoved the old man. "I'm talking to the sheriff about way more important stuff than some hick diner."

That had Danielle moving in. Fast. "Don't you touch him, Lianne."

Lianne whirled. "Who the hell are... oh, that you, Danny?"

Changing her tack, she tried to hug her daughter, and when that didn't work, Lianne cupped her face. "My poor baby. Are you all right? Such terrible goings-on. I'll take you back to Omaha. It ain't safe here."

Danielle recoiled. "Get your hands off me."

Those hands fell and fisted on nonexistent hips. "Now, that ain't no way to talk to your mother."

"Mother?" Harlan, his grizzled brows furrowed, looked to Karen for confirmation. She nodded.

Danielle backed away. "No mother to me. All you ever did was screw up my life. And I won't let you screw it up again." Danielle allied herself with Harlan, who put an arm around her. "I'm not going to Omaha. I'm staying right here. And after tomorrow, I'll be free of you forever."

"What're you talking about? You're going back. You're still underage. You can go with me, or she'll send you back. She's the law. A friggin' cop." A sly look came. "Might lose her badge if I let Social Services know that she knew you was underage and didn't send you back."

Danielle didn't look at Karen. No forgiveness there. Karen didn't really expect it.

Harlan spoke before Karen could. "No, Sheriff Mehaffey wouldn't do that. She's the one who got everything set up for the hearing."

Karen turned on Lianne. "And before you start throwing around accusations, I've been working with Danielle's case worker."

"Shoulda contacted me." Lianne pounded her hollow chest with a fist. The sound was like hitting a melon—squishy, soft, and ripe. "I got *rights*."

A broken record. Just how badly fried was the woman's brain? Frankly, until recently, Karen had believed the heroin addict long dead. But somehow, through sheer cussedness, Lianne Mehaffey had managed to survive—and even go clean for stretches of time. Too bad she hadn't used that drive to better herself, as her son had and as her daughter was doing.

"What's the problem at the diner?" Marek asked. Karen didn't jump, but Lianne did and gave him a nasty look—from a safe distance.

"Mmm. Vultures."

"Has to be the press."

The deputies from Outer Mongolia finally made their presence known. Bork and Two Fingers leaned against the pillars. Kurt remained alert but silent at the chalkboard.

A frisson of fear coursed down Karen's spine. The woman could make a stink at the hearing. And Judge Rudy was never predictable. Then she shook it off. Even if by some miracle Lianne won back custody, she would never wrest away the trust. And that had to be the woman's real aim.

Stymied for the moment, Lianne reverted to her earlier demand. "I want to see my brother."

Karen stifled a primal scream. The woman was determined to be a pain in the ass. "Look, I'm kind of busy right now, trying to find his killer. Maybe on Monday..."

"No. Now. I'll lose my nerve, otherwise. It's important to me."

Karen wanted no part of it, but they were headed for Sioux Falls anyway. She sighed. "Let me see if it's even possible. It's Sunday."

Unfortunately, Dr. White was happy to oblige. After Kurt tracked down Marmo's hotel via his credit card, they loaded into the Sub. Marek took the passenger seat, and mother and daughter sat in the cage. Harlan had wanted to take Danielle home with him, but she'd unexpectedly decided that she also wanted to see the uncle she'd known but never as blood.

The tension in the enclosed space grew until Marek finally broke it. "Tell us about Hal."

"What do you want to know?" Lianne shot out. "He was my brother. Now he's dead."

"You never talked about him before," Danielle muttered.

Glancing up at the rearview mirror, Karen saw Lianne look at the daughter she'd birthed—and who was now plastered against the door, as far away as she could get. For a moment, Karen felt sorry for the woman. She herself had lost a daughter, even if by choice, and they'd had ups and downs in reconnecting.

Lianne finally said, "It hurt. Buried it deep as I could." Her lips trembled as she shot a look at her daughter. "Your father, that damned shrink who shafted us both and fled the state with that bimbo of a case worker, he said it was a 'coping mechanism.' That the drugs I got hooked on when I was younger than you, they were to cover the pain of losing him. I loved him, and he just up and left me. Not a single word. No one wants to hurt that bad. Being abandoned."

She hummed something under her breath that made Marek sit straighter in his seat.

"'Abandoned,'" he muttered. "On Legrande's original Wild Abandon album."

A common thread to many of the players. Karen glanced into the cage again. "You do know, Lianne, that your brother was given a choice: jail or military?"

The sunken mouth dropped open. "What? What for? He weren't no criminal. Kept outta the street gangs and told me to keep my nose clean, too. And I did. Until... after. After he left. What'd he do? Rip off a guitar or something?"

Karen slowed for construction. "He got caught smoking pot."

"Pot?" Now Danielle looked shocked. "*Jail?*"

"Times have changed," Karen said mildly. Though they hadn't changed much in South Dakota, where even medicinal CBD oil was still a crime.

"You mean to tell me, my life got screwed just for a *toke*?" Lianne surged against the cage, gripping at the mesh. "Are you kidding me?" She slammed back in the seat. "Why the hell didn't he just say so?"

"He was your big brother," Marek answered after they'd gone a slow mile. "Probably too embarrassed. Especially if he'd told you to stay off the drugs."

"Freaking idiot. Why didn't he keep in touch? Instead, I'm left with a spineless mother and a maniac for a stepdad. Now he's the one shoulda been in jail."

Karen frowned. "Stepdad?"

"Don't you know nothin'? My dad lit out when I was a tyke. Mom took up with Richard Wadleigh—we called him Dickwad—on the rebound. Never married him, but she pretended like it. He knocked her around, knocked us all around, and I think... I think he messed with Hal. Not me. I don't think he liked women, just used 'em for cover. He got himself killed at the grain elevator he worked at. Red-letter day that was, but that wasn't 'til years after Hal left."

"Why didn't you ever tell me any of this stuff before?" Danielle sounded subdued. "You never said anything about Hal, about a stepdad, about any of it."

"Old news. Long buried. You have to live for the day." Her mouth sank in further. "Just another of those holier-than-thou sayings your dad used to throw around. To think I believed him. Maybe I'm just as much of a loser as my mother, chasing after rotten apples."

The only sound was jackhammers and the rhythmic thump of tires over tar. A grating sound of summer Karen could do without.

Finally, Marek asked, "What about Hal's music?"

When Karen glanced back, she saw a jerk of the shoulder from Lianne. "He had a garage band with some of his buddies. 'Bout drove our mother crazy. Playing his guitar, playing his boom box, playing his drums. Worked hard to get 'em, too. Got us thrown out of one rental 'cause of the racket, and Dickwad was royally pissed. Beat everything to hell. That about killed Hal."

Marek turned his head around. "He beat him that badly?"

"No, never enough to put nobody in the hospital. No one

cared back then about bumps and bruises. You know, 'Spare the rod, spoil the child.' You can be grateful I never lifted a hand to neither of my kids. If they say otherwise, it's a lie." When Danielle didn't contradict her, she went on, "I meant the music stuff. Beat all of it to crap and threw what was left in the dumpster. Told Hal if he brought anything else into the house, it'd end up the same way. Mom even bought Hal another boom box on the sly, but Dickwad took a hammer to it. Like I said, 'bout killed Hal."

When everyone fell silent, Karen turned on the radio. The news of the newly recovered Legrande music must have spurred a bump in Wild Abandon playbacks. "Rock On" washed over the Sub and into the cage as they approached Sioux Falls.

"You know who I named Patrick after?"

Karen glanced back. "No, I assumed he was named for the saint."

Lianne clutched her thin arms around herself and laughed until she coughed. "That'll be the day. The church was never no help to us. Priests just spouted, 'Honor thy father and thy mother that your days will be long.' Yeah, right. Buncha crock. Nah, I named Patrick after Trick Legrande. Hal and me, we loved that music. I even got a tattoo."

Karen pulled into the parking lot at the Sioux Falls hospital that housed the morgue. When she glanced back into the cage, she could see one thin arm raised. Above the guns and roses was a circle of words: Wild Abandon. It looked old, fainter than the rest, and very basic. Probably done as a teenager on her own dime—or for some other compensation.

It was a long walk to the morgue. By the time they reached the swinging double doors, Lianne was shivering. "Damned cold in here."

"You don't have to do this," Karen told her.

"No, I gotta. Only thing I can do." She straightened. "Wish I could get him a stone."

"He'll get one." Danielle lifted her chin as she glanced at

Karen, as if expecting to be told that was not a reasonable request to make of a trustee.

"He'll get one," Karen agreed evenly.

"Will I?" Lianne muttered under her breath as she passed under Marek's arm through the swinging doors. Karen didn't think Danielle heard. Maybe she wasn't meant to.

Dr. White awaited them in a pristine white coat and a somber black-and-gray bow tie. Lianne hitched her step, but Karen wasn't sure if it was the body draped on the gurney—or the African-American pathologist whose hand rested there. Whichever it was, Lianne got over it and walked to the gurney.

"I am sorry for your loss, Ms. Mehaffey." Dr. White paused, looking past Lianne to Danielle. "And..."

Hanging back near Marek, Danielle dug her hands into the pockets of her skin-tight capris. Her mouth twisted. "Ms. Mehaffey."

When the pathologist lifted his brows at Karen, she pointed from Lianne to Danielle, and he nodded. Mother and daughter. He knew, of course, that Patrick had been her husband. A trio of dysfunctional family dynamics. He opened his mouth, perhaps to refer to her as Ms. Mehaffey, as well, but closed it. Good choice. Levity was always iffy with family under these circumstances.

"Are you ready?" Dr. White asked Lianne when she wrapped her arms around herself.

Lianne nodded. The pathologist pulled the sheet down to Birchard's chest.

As if forgetting that Karen was now the enemy, Danielle edged closer to her. "I've never seen anybody dead before."

"If you'd rather not stay, Marek can..."

"No, I'm good." Danielle lifted her chin and edged back away. "I can take pretty much anything." Including being accused of murder by a shirttail relation.

Karen sighed inwardly. At least the girl was talking to her. A bit.

Lianne frowned down at the bearded, bald man. "Boy, he's changed." Then she gave a humorless cackle. "Guess I have, too."

"When did you last see him?" Dr. White asked.

Her eyes lidded. "He was eighteen... no, maybe just nineteen. I was sixteen, same age as my daughter there."

A faint smile crossed the dark face. "In my experience, men tend to change more than women between that age and middle age."

Lianne tugged on strands of her hair. "Don't know 'bout that. I don't much look like I did then, neither. Had bright-red hair. Looked pretty good. All gone now." Lianne hesitated. "Not much I can hang on to, to recognize. 'Cept he had a scar right here." She tapped her upper left arm. "When I was seven, I stuck him with a screwdriver for taking my doll. Hal had to go get a shot and everything and passed out flat over the needle. So you don't get that locked jaw, you know?"

The pathologist took a stab. "Tetanus?"

"Yeah, that. Dickwad made fun of him for that. Called him a sissy. Sissy Birchard. That's what stuck, and Hal hated him for that as much as the beatings."

Dr. White's mouth tightened. He pulled the sheet away from the beefy left arm.

Lianne stared down, frowning, as did Karen, when there was no scar.

"Maybe it was the right?" Danielle suggested.

But other than some sun spots, that arm was also unblemished.

"This ain't my..." After a quick glance at Karen, Lianne shrugged. "Must be I misremembered. Or the scar just faded away. Seemed like a big deal when I was a kid."

Frowning, Karen asked, "Any other scars or identifying characteristics?"

"Well, there was... No, no, he didn't."

"Lianne, this is a murder investigation. Don't lie to me."

Karen nodded toward the body. "We can find out eventually with DNA, anyway."

Lianne backed away. "You're not gettin' my DNA."

"You can have mine." Danielle sounded more curious than upset. "That'll work, won't it?"

"Yes, it will." Karen stepped closer. "Give it up, Lianne."

The woman bit her lip almost off before she spoke. "All right. He wanted to prove Dickwad wrong, y'know? That he could face a needle. He got a tattoo, same time I did, that says Wild Abandon." She held out her arm again.

"Where was it?" Dr. White asked.

Grudgingly, she tapped over her heart. "Said he took that music to heart."

The pathologist moved the sheet to reveal the chest. Burly, hairy... and after Dr. White took a shaver to it, completely tattoo-free.

"Could he have removed it?" Marek asked.

"Yes, but not without leaving at least minor scarring." The pathologist took a magnifying glass from a drawer and held it over the dead man's chest. After several moments of millimeter-by-millimeter perusal, the pathologist straightened.

"Well?" Karen asked.

"I find no evidence of a previous tattoo."

"Then that ain't my brother."

And Lianne cried.

CHAPTER 25

AT THE SEEDY MOTOR-IN NEAR an abandoned strip mall, Karen knocked sharply on the door of Room 213. Marek waited out of view, his Glock 21 at his side. Neither of them expected the man to put up a fight, but many a dead cop had assumed that. Better to be safe.

Karen heard footsteps. Then a pause and a creak near the door. Marmo was looking through the peephole, no doubt. Would Marek have to break the door down? It wouldn't take much. The doors were as thin as the walls in this place, and more than a few of the doors looked like they'd been treated to the sole of a cop's boot.

The floorboards creaked again, and Karen started to move back to give Marek access. Then the door was jerked open, and a slurred voice emerged from the dim interior. "Welcome to my humble abode, Sheriff... Detective."

Marek had moved into the doorway and slowly reseated his Glock in the small of his back. As her own eyes adjusted a fraction later, Karen spotted the open suitcase on the rumpled bed. "Skipping town, Mr.... Marmo?"

He didn't appear to notice her hesitation on his name. "Getting run out. Credit card denied. Ain't that a kick. Thought I'd try to find a camping spot in the festival park for the next coupla nights."

Good luck with that. Besides, she had a better room for

him, complete with three meals a day. "You try to drive in your current state, I'll arrest you for DWI."

Marmo put up his hands. "Still here. Going later. Rental car's a beater, but it'll..." He trailed off as a tow truck pulled up below.

The owner got out and looked up. "One of you up there Salvatore Marmo?"

The ex-label CEO just shut his eyes, and the young man fastened on him.

"I got an order to take back this rental. Got a problem with that?" The gum-chewing young man with a Post Malone T-shirt looked like he'd prefer Marmo put up a fight.

Karen leaned over the rickety railing. "Go ahead and tow it."

The guy chewed his gum and sighed. "Figures."

"Just how'm I supposed to get anywhere?" Marmo asked.

Marek hefted the man's suitcase. "You're coming back with us."

He didn't seem particularly upset. "Am I? Why's that?"

"We've got some questions for you." Karen was itching to start asking them right here and now, but they still had the Mehaffeys in the Sub. Lianne hadn't said a word after they left the morgue. But at least she'd stopped crying. Though the rocking silence was almost worse.

As Karen escorted Marmo into the cage, though, Lianne slid out. Her eyes weren't on Marmo, but a man standing nonchalantly against a streetlamp at the corner. Drug dealer, Karen suspected. Lianne must be jonesing for her next fix.

"You can leave me here," Lianne said.

Karen didn't like the woman. But she did feel some responsibility for her. "Lianne..."

"I'll take that guy's room. I know how it works in places like this. They won't be able to clean it up and let it out until tomorrow."

Karen caught the woman's tattooed arm before she

marched up the rickety stairs to the open hotel room. "So that's it? Hello, goodbye? What about your daughter?"

Lianne glanced back, a flicker of longing in the eyes that she'd passed on to her son. Then she zeroed back in on the dealer. She shrugged off Karen's hand with a jerk. "I'll hitch down tomorrow. Gotta get something outta it."

"Out of what?" When the woman didn't answer, Karen got it. Out of the will of Hal Birchard—or whoever the hell he was. That was all up in the air now. But Karen grabbed Lianne's arm again, spinning her around. "Until we know who that man back there really is, there may not be any money. Zip. But if there is, I can tell you now, you won't get through me to squeeze Danielle for money. Not a cent. You stayed clean when you had her. And Patrick. I can thank you for that, for both of them, but you know as well as I do, your addiction runs the show."

Lianne didn't deny it. "You don't know what it's like. I've tried. God, I've tried."

"No, I don't know. I didn't travel that road. Neither, thank God, did Patrick or Danielle."

Tears welled. "I love Danny. I do. But..."

Maybe some small part of her did. Karen couldn't say. "Then let her go. Finally. Let her go."

"Let *me* go."

Reluctantly, Karen did so. After a short internal debate, she took some money out of her wallet and handed it over.

Clutching it like a lifeline, Lianne skipped up the stairs toward the vacated room, humming "Rock On."

Her stomach roiling—or perhaps rumbling, as it was dinnertime—Karen stalked over to the Sub. She felt a furious mix of pity, disgust, and anger for a woman who'd managed to birth two of the most amazingly resilient people she'd ever known.

When Karen slid into the Sub's driver's seat, she found Danielle in the passenger seat, with Marek and Marmo in the cage. Should be a fun ride back to Reunion. What she really wanted to do was talk to Marek about their mystery man. None of it made any sense. Could Dr. White be mistaken? Or was Lianne's brain so fried that she remembered things that had never happened? It was clear that Lianne believed the man wasn't her brother, despite the clear benefits—or so Lianne hoped—of believing otherwise.

As Karen drove by the Aleford truck stop to the beat of Asia's "Sole Survivor," Marmo snored in the back. Obviously, he wasn't terribly concerned about what awaited him in Reunion. Perhaps he preferred the fire to the frying pan he'd just escaped. Or he was just too drunk to think straight.

"Why'd you give her money? She'll only get high."

At last. "She speaks." Before Danielle could take offense, Karen answered, "Because I didn't particularly want to bring her back to Reunion. Maybe she'll stay lost."

Danielle threw her a cynical look. "Not if it means money. Whenever I was with her, she'd spend the money on drugs that was meant for taking care of me. Use it, lose it. Then lose me. Over and over again." Danielle's head hit the back of the headrest. "Oh, wait. I forgot. Hal's not Hal. So much for my so-called fortune. Oh, well. Easy come, easy go."

Far too easily, this girl had come and gone in the lives of the adults around her. Karen ached for her and wished things were different. But few adults, much less teens, would forgive what Karen had put Danielle through.

As if tracking the same line, Danielle burst out, "You treated me like I was a killer!"

Signaling her turn to discourage the pickup on her tail, Karen slowed for the Reunion exit. "It's my job to push buttons. To make people lose their control. I could have let Marek do that interview, but I didn't want to take the coward's way out."

Danielle threw a look back into the cage.

Marek nodded at her. "I offered."

The girl turned back. "Your job sucks."

"Sometimes, it does. But it didn't when we found you

back in May. And it won't when we find Hal Birchard's... or whoever's... killer. It will have been worth it. Almost." She drove down Main Street. "Because it won't be worth it if I lose you."

That was greeted with silence.

All that awaited her at the office was a huddle of media trucks. Dammit. She wasn't driving into that with Marmo and Danielle in tow. She took a side street and pulled into her parking spot behind the courthouse. She hoped the cameras would take a minute to come around. "Marek, take Marmo into interview. If the press... well, presses you... tell them I'll give them a statement after I take care of some business."

Marek hurried a blinking and stumbling Marmo into the back of the courthouse.

Karen put the Sub back in gear. "Danielle, I can take you back to the diner or my place. Take your pick."

"Your place?"

A question, not a direction. "My daughter, Eyre, lives there, but she'll be fine with it." At least, Karen hoped so. "I've got an empty room in the basement. I can't promise the press won't figure out where you're at, but it'll take them a while, and as it's my place, that might give them pause." Seeing a camera rounding the corner, Karen backed up and headed randomly down a road. "Just pick one."

Karen was almost to the fork where she'd have to head one way or the other before she got an answer.

"Your place. I don't want to cause trouble at the diner. I'll let Cookie and Harlan know that I'll be back as soon as... well, everything gets settled." Danielle slumped in the seat. "I just want everything to go back to the way it was. Smooth. Should've known better."

"It will blow over, Danielle. The press won't stay. They don't want to be here any more than we want them to be. For one, they don't have any place to stay. Unlike you. You can use any of my T-shirts as a nightshirt. Tomorrow, Harlan or Cookie can bring some of your stuff if this drags on."

Karen pulled to the curb at her bungalow and saw Eyre on the porch swing. Her daughter was lazily pushing the swing with a bare foot as she read a book and sipped on a glass of lemonade. Oh, to have an eight-to-five job again with her weekends free.

Karen beckoned Danielle and walked up onto the porch. "Hi, Eyre. We've got a temporary guest."

Her daughter looked up, her lips parting as she saw Danielle. Surprise widened her Okerlund eyes at the nose stud, and Danielle hunched her shoulders. But then Eyre smiled. "You must be Danielle. I've been so curious about you. I almost stopped in Fink once on my way back from Eder just to meet you, but I wasn't sure what to say."

The idea that an adult was uncertain about how to approach a teenager was obviously alien to Danielle. "Why would you want to meet me?"

"Oh. Well, you've led such an exciting life. Me?" Eyre lifted the tattered paperback. Obviously a comfort read. Her namesake. *Jane Eyre.* "I live in books, mostly."

"I like books," Danielle said. "I did well in school. Before, I mean."

"No reason you have to stop. What do you like?"

"Mostly fantasy. Like *Hunger Games.*"

"A bit dark, but I liked it. Did you see the movie?"

"Not yet. No cinema in this burg."

Satisfied her vastly different relations wouldn't stiff-arm each other, Karen left them to discuss their favorite books. Who knew? Karen herself preferred movies to reading. Though by the time she returned to the courthouse and gave a patently false there's-nothing-new statement to the press, she wished herself back to the bungalow, talking books, instead of heading for the interview room to talk murder.

CHAPTER 26

MAREK HAD INTERVIEWED A NUMBER of killers over the years, stretching back to his time on the Albuquerque homicide unit. And it always surprised him when all the suspect wanted to do was sleep.

Sal Marmo—or Saul Merlini—didn't even look up when he and Karen came into the interview room. Marek had to shake him awake.

"Wha...? Oh." He rubbed his eyes. "You got any coffee in this joint, Sheriff?"

Karen made a whistling sound through her teeth, probably keeping choice words about misogynist jerks from leaking out. But she went out while Marek read the man his rights.

"Yeah, I understand. Whatever." When Karen came back in, he actually thanked her.

She gave him a tight smile. "It's called Sisters' Blend."

"Trying to emasculate me? Sorry. Already been done." He sipped, and his eyes flew open. "Wow. That's got a kick. Good stuff." He saluted her with the South Dakota Sheriff's Association mug. Ironically or not, it did get Karen to relax enough to sit down. Usually, she liked to stand. But rapport was rapport, even if it was over a cup of coffee.

After one last appreciative sip, Marmo put down the mug with a click that sounded like someone chambering a bullet. "So... what questions you got for me?"

Marek eased into the questioning. "You've heard, I'm guessing, about Legrande's music?"

Blinking rapidly, Marmo straightened from his slumped position on the hardwood chair. "What about it?"

That's what Marek would like to know. The man had gone from almost comatose to a jangling quiver. Just how did Marek handle that? "You tell me."

After a long moment, Marmo said, "No, I think you'd better tell me."

So much for getting Marmo to spill the beans. "I take it you haven't listened to the news."

"In that fleabag motel? Only thing I cared about was the liquor store on the corner."

Marek decided that, despite his hard fall, Marmo wasn't going to be an easy out. After a faint nod from Karen, he played his hand. "Josh Bolvin's viral hit."

"Yeah? Decent voice."

"And the music?"

Marmo hesitated then shrugged. "Phenomenal."

The man wasn't giving them anything—yet. Fortunately, they had evidence on their side.

Karen took her stab. "Why did you go into the instrument tent?"

Once again, Marmo answered the question with another question. "Why would I do that?"

"You tell me," she returned.

Smiling faintly, Marmo just picked up his coffee. But at least Marek could see a fine quiver in the fingers that wrapped around the mug.

Unfortunately, when the silence strung out, Marek had to try another tack. "Why did you change your name, Mr. Merlini?"

Slowly, Marmo put down the coffee. "So you did a Google search. Whoopee. I changed it because Merlini was washed up." He snorted. "So I reinvented myself. What of it?"

So Marmo didn't want to be direct. He'd go indirect. "You and Anton Kuhl have some history."

"History?" As if deciding there was no point denying that, given they'd pegged his previous incarnation as Saul Merlini of S&M, he leaned back. "I call it a crime. Damn shark, that's what he is. Kuhl ripped me off, big-time. Had me over a barrel. Creditors not only nipping at my heels but gnawing at the stubs." He took a last drag on the coffee. "I used to have legs. Just the name S&M would open doors. Now I can't even get the bellboys to do that for me. Music is a brutal business. Don't let anyone tell you different." Marmo stared down into the empty mug. "Can I have more... sister?"

Marek heard Karen's teeth grind. But she took the mug and went. When she came back, she set it down hard enough that it sloshed. And she stayed up. No more rapport.

"Thanks. Look, I can do the dance. My father was a lawyer. But why don't we just get down to it. You tell me what the news was that I missed, and I'll tell you what you want to know."

Marek pursed his lips. "Bargaining, Marmo?"

"Don't take that deal." Karen crossed her arms as she leaned against the closed door. "He's got a lengthy entry with the Better Business Bureau. And it isn't good. He promises the stars and delivers... nada. Zip."

"I deliver dreams." But he didn't meet Marek's steady gaze. "And I've made some stars."

"A long time ago. Like... Trick Legrande." Another jolt. Marek pressed harder. "You don't need me to tell you what the news is, Marmo. You already know it. You've known it from the beginning. It's why you came here."

As if suddenly cold, Marmo cupped his hands around the cup, despite the warmth in the room. The air conditioner in the old building was temperamental at the best of times.

"I should've never come. Been a disaster from day one." He played with the mug a while longer, looking sober for the first time. "All right. I may have lost my shirt, but I haven't lost my ear. I worked with Trick Legrande for a long, long time. I knew his habits, his stage persona, his damn shirt size. And I damn well knew his music. So I came, I saw, but... I didn't conquer. Bastard. Legrande owed me. Because of him, I lost everything. So... when I picked him out of the crowd at the festival, we had words."

Though Marek had half expected it, Marmo's words still gave him a jolt.

"What!?" Karen stared at Marmo, then at Marek. "That's not possible. The autopsy..."

"Obviously flawed. It's really the only thing that makes sense." That was what Marek had come back to, again and again, during the trip back from Sioux Falls. If Karen hadn't had so much on her mind with Danielle and Lianne, she'd have come to the same conclusion, he was sure.

Surprise parted Marmo's lips as he stared first at Karen then Marek. "The news..."

"Was that the music Josh Bolvin played was Legrande's. Not that Legrande was, until Friday evening, alive and kicking." Now that they'd come to it, Marek was willing to throw Marmo a bone. "We found out earlier today that the body in the morgue didn't belong to the real Hal Birchard."

With a half laugh, Marmo lifted his mug in salute. "Well played, Eda County. Well played."

"It was going to come out soon anyway," Marek said. "One way or the other."

Still looking gobsmacked, Karen leaned back against the door. "You had words with Birchard... I mean, Legrande?"

"You bet I did. And I had his words—his songs, his music—locked down, right and tight. Legrande signed a contract that gave me a thirty-five-percent cut of all future work."

Sounded like highway robbery to Marek. "Even though you'd dropped him from your label?" Marek shook his head. "How is that even legal?"

Marmo snorted. "It's not about what's legal. It's about

what's precedent. Have to take it to court to do that. You want to challenge a contract, you need deep pockets. Sure, he'd likely have won if he went that route. Eventually. But the goal is to settle. Give a little, get a little. But he took it personally back then. And I got pissy. All around, that's all it was, start to finish. Just a pissing contest that got out of hand."

Marek had heard that before. From killers. "So you confronted Legrande before the Jam Off."

"Yeah, I recognized his walk, sort of a rolling walk, on the balls of his feet. Boy, he looked different, though. No hair, that big beard, a lot beefier. But I knew. So I went over, yanked on his arm, and said, 'You're not getting away from me again, Legrande.' He started to deny it, said I had him mixed up with somebody, but when he couldn't shake me off, he pulled me down the trail. Said he needed time to think. And if I blew his cover, he'd blow mine. I didn't care about my cover, but I gave him time. Let him fiddle on the roof."

Marek frowned. "But you didn't vote for him in the Jam Off."

Both Karen and Marmo blinked at him. That *was* off topic.

"Thought he'd be the winner, and I didn't want to give him the satisfaction. But that Axel Knutsen of yours got pissed that Birchard... Legrande... didn't follow the rules. Went on and on about traditional Norwegian Hardanger fiddle music. Fancies himself an expert. Just to annoy him, I voted for that heavy metal gal that he hated."

The man had relaxed into the flow. Marek said offhandedly, "You said after the judges broke, you waited in line for a drink, then you went back to the judges' tent."

Marmo tilted his head then nodded. "Right."

Karen went back on the attack. "We talked to the server. He says you cut into the front of the line. Judge's privilege."

"Okay, so maybe I did. Gotta get something out of

listening to a bunch of hicks who couldn't hit a true pitch on the broad side of a barn."

As Karen bristled, Marek eased out the copy of a credit card receipt. "You didn't get your drink until 6:41, but the judges broke at 6:30. The concession stand was right there. What did you do for those ten minutes?"

Marmo pulled on his lip. "So I sat in the judges' tent longer than I thought. So what?"

"So we've got you cold in the instrument tent."

"What do you mean? I wasn't ever in..." He snapped his mouth shut.

Marek opened the folder and took out the fax. "Fingerprint match on the mic stand."

Marmo knocked over the coffee cup, and dark-brown liquid flooded the table, rivulets running into the cracks, trying to find a way out.

"When did you decide to tamper with the amp?" Marek pressed. The man was off-balance. He needed to push him off his lawyerly caution. "After you had words with him?"

"Was that the plan you made while you were twiddling your thumbs during the judging?" Karen put her hands on the table and leaned into Marmo's space. "To make it look like an accident? But then when the shock didn't finish Legrande off, you garroted him, making it look like one of the contestants killed him?"

Marmo lifted his hands to ward them off. "Whoa. Wait a minute. I didn't tamper with the amp."

Marek tapped the fax. "Your prints are also on the amp cord."

"But that was after... dammit." Marmo put his hands on his face. "My father always said my big mouth would get me in trouble someday."

"You killed him. Because he wouldn't dance to your tune."

Marmo's hands slipped, and bloodshot eyes looked straight into Marek's. "No, I didn't." He sounded more weary than defensive.

"Just tell us, Marmo." Karen backed up out of his space. "No more posturing."

"Don't know if that's possible. But I'll try. Can I have more coffee?"

When Karen simply glared at the man, Marek corralled the mug, went to the breakroom, filled it up with the last of the Sisters' Blend, and came back with wipes. Karen took them, cleaned up the table, and ditched the remains in the trash can. "There. Talk, Marmo."

After another long drag on the coffee, Marmo sighed. "All right. Yes, I went into the instrument tent after Kuhl and Axel left the judges' tent. Axel dragged his feet, arguing with me, and I finally flicked him off by saying I'd reconsider my vote for Rad Wilson in favor of your deputy if he just gave me some space."

Interesting that Seoul had come so close to winning the Jam Off. Marek would have to find an opportunity to hear her sing sometime. "After that, you went into the tent to confront Legrande."

"Just to talk. When I walked in, Legrande was slinging on that guitar, like he was trying it on for size. Splayed his hands over it like it was a woman under his hands. A caress, that's what it was. And I knew then that he'd decided to blow his own cover. He'd told me, back in the day, that he wouldn't touch another guitar or sing another song. Rather not play at all than let me get a slice of his music." He shook his head morosely. "To think, if we'd just worked it out back then, we'd both be sitting pretty today."

Marek led him back. "What happened, in the tent?"

Marmo let out a breath. "Legrande flicked me a glance then leaned down to turn on the amp. I thought he was dismissing me again, and I said, 'Listen to me, goddammit,' and I shoved the mic at him just as he turned on the amp... and he dropped. God as my witness, that's all I did. And he just... dropped. I'll see it for the rest of my life. He jolted and dropped."

The ultimate mic drop. "What did you do then?"

"For a few seconds, I just stared at him. Then I realized what happened. It's not unheard of in the business. Electrocution, I mean. I pulled the plug on the amp. And..."

And... that was the kicker. "You left him there."

"He was breathing. I thought he'd be okay." Marmo swirled his cup. "But I felt he deserved the shock, for what he did to me."

"To you? What about what you'd done to him?" Karen demanded.

"What did I do but catapult him and his castaway crew into stardom? Who do you think took a gamble on him? Got him top-drawer backing, fantastic venues, whatever. And what does he do when I ask for what's mine? For what he signed of his own free will? Pulls a fast one on me, on everybody."

Karen leaned back into his space. "You wanted him dead for that."

But Marek already saw the answer in the man's shaking head.

"That's the last thing I wanted. Don't you get it? The reason I was on such a bender the last couple days was because he *was* dead. If he was alive, I still had a chance to settle with him. Dead? Iffy and messy suing the estate. More bad publicity. Better for both of us to come to a quiet settlement."

Unfortunately, Marek thought, the man was right.

Karen wasn't ready to give up. "But you gave up all your rights to Kuhl, right?"

"All but the future-work clause. Kuhl didn't care about that, with Legrande officially declared dead. I kept those rights more out of spite, truth to tell, than any inkling of Legrande rising from the dead." Marmo rubbed his head. "All I want is to retire. You think I like what I do? You'd be wrong. The business is changing. Just look at the brouhaha over Taylor Swift. Guy made her a star, and she complains when he takes what he's due. But she may have the last laugh."

Marek frowned. He'd heard some of the story on NPR. The young country star's songs had been bought out by a man she felt had cheated her. "How's that?"

"She can re-record the old songs and direct her fans to the new ones. She can go independent, make her own contracts, and snag all the money herself. Poor sod will be cheated out of his slice of the pie he baked, just like me." He held his head. "I don't even have enough on me to pay for a bed. I've got a ticket home. After that, the only job offer I've got is to work in Lyman Skinner's mortuary. Don't think I can work with stiffs."

"We could hold you pending inquiries." Karen tapped her fingers on the filing cabinet next to her. "Or..."

The man looked up without much hope. "Or?"

"You can take a bed in the jail. Cell unlocked. Three meals a day. As long as you keep your mouth shut about Legrande being alive. We don't want that to leak to the press yet."

"Glad my father never saw the day." Marmo heaved out a big sigh. "Deal."

CHAPTER 27

ONCE SHE'D GOTTEN THINGS SQUARED with her jailers and ordered Marmo's supper from The Café, Karen stalked back up into the office and headed for Marek. "You *knew.*"

He didn't play dumb. "I suspected."

The rest of her roster, in varying states of sugar overload from Eva Bechtold's pannekuchen, roused themselves to watch.

Walrus licked a bit of peach from his thumb. "What's up?" He jerked his thumb toward Marek. "The Silent Man hasn't said a word since he came out from interview. But you took Marmo down to lockup, right? We've got our man?" Walrus glared over at the chalkboard with Kurt's neat handwriting. "We're done with that?"

"No, we're not done with the timeline," Karen said.

"Mmm. I'm glad," Bork said. When Walrus turned on him, he raised his hands. "We put that much work into it, I want the payoff."

"I just want to see the inside of my eyelids." Seoul stretched behind her computer, which showed a photo of Rad Wilson peering behind a tent flap. If Karen wasn't mistaken, the rocker had something long and dark in her hand.

Distracted, Karen asked, "Is that a laser pointer?"

Seoul huffed her knuckles and burnished them on her tan duty shirt. "That it is. She's toast."

"Showoff," Walrus grumbled. "What's the deal on Marmo?"

Karen glanced out the windows. The press either had taken her at her word that there was nothing new, or they'd found something else to pursue. Or they'd gone to supper. "All this is for your ears only." She got all ears. "Hal Birchard wasn't Hal Birchard."

All sounds, even of Walrus chewing on another peach pannekuchen, stopped.

Two Fingers broke the silence. "Legrande."

Was she the only idiot? Karen hated being behind the eight ball.

"Nah, he's dead." Walrus wiped crumbs off his shirt then, at Kurt's glare, got a paper towel and scooped them up and into the trash. "Autopsy confirmed."

Karen riffled through her desk until she had the folder Eyre had left with her. "The body wasn't in the best shape after being in the water for six weeks." She scanned down and saw no dental records, only a notation that they'd been lost in a fire in California. The remaining clothing, however, had been identified as being the same that Legrande had last been seen wearing at a mooring off San Juan. And the clincher, per the doctor who'd performed the autopsy, was... "A small tattoo over the heart."

"Wild Abandon," Marek murmured. "Hal Birchard's tattoo. In honor of Legrande's music."

"Geez, talk about ironic. So I was right, just switched." Walrus raised his hands in a championship clasp. "Legrande killed Birchard."

"I don't think so." Marek played with a pen in his fingers. "Birchard had advanced cancer. I'd guess he died of it. VA records could confirm if it was terminal. And Tricia Cantor said Legrande asked whether a layman giving last rites would be valid."

"Did I know that?" Karen asked, turning on him.

"It's on record. But Josephine hasn't typed it up yet."

That made her feel a tad better. She caught her roster up

on the latest. "We don't have a print match yet for the inside of the amp. That might change things. But for now, Marmo's stashed but not at the top of our list. He lacks motive, other than being a jerk."

The phone rang. Karen reached out to pull the cord, but then she recognized the number. She'd been calling it enough. She picked up. "Mr. Link, good of you to return my call."

The intellectual property attorney from Los Angeles said, "I'm sorry," sounding not at all sorry. "I was away for the weekend and instructed my admin to deflect any and all calls. Regrettably, I did not foresee a call from law enforcement. How can I help a sheriff in...where was it? Fargo?"

Karen ground her teeth. "Reunion, South Dakota."

"I won't pretend I know where that is. But I'll bet it gets cold there. I enjoyed the movie, by the way. *Fargo*, I mean. Are female sheriffs a thing there?" He went on before she could answer. "Why are you calling me? I'm not in criminal law."

"We are investigating a homicide. Our victim called you last Friday at 4:37. He was on the phone for a couple minutes, so he must have left a message."

"I normally delete messages as I go, Sheriff."

Dammit. Karen sighed. "Do you recall any messages from a Hal Birchard?"

"No, none from a Birchard."

Karen rubbed her temple with her free hand. "Okay. Thanks for your time."

"Hold on. I did get a message. And I think... yes, it was the right time." Link waited a beat. "I kept that one so I could replay it for kicks. A real kook. Here, just a second, and I can replay it."

As he did his thing on his end, Karen transferred to speakerphone on her end. And Marek took out his mini-recorder so they'd have the message as evidence.

Once Link got everything connected, he replayed the

message. The deep voice that came on the line reminded Karen somewhat of Marek's, except Legrande's had more gravel in it.

Mr. Link, you don't know me from Adam, but I got your name from my lawyer. I need a good IP attorney who's not afraid to go head-to-head with the big guys in the music business. I'm caught in an old contract that takes a significant percentage of any future work. I've been told that won't hold up in court.

Karen saw nothing kooky about any of that. But she was glad to have it, as it helped confirm that their victim was indeed Legrande.

You're probably a busy man and don't have time for peons. I'm not. Old, yes, but not dead. I know you'll find it hard to believe, but I'm Trick Legrande of Wild Abandon.

In the background, Karen could hear a stifled laugh from Link. He'd eventually discover the laugh was on him. He might have made his name, and a killing on attorney fees, representing Legrande.

I've decided to come out of hiding and fight for my rights. And before you turn me down, I've got several million in the bank. Offshore. I'll wire you a retainer once you get back to me and we agree to terms. I also want to work out some arrangement with a young musician who wants to tour my music so that I retain the rights but he gets suitable compensation. He's also a decent songwriter and will get better with time, as long as I can keep the sharks off his back. Unlike others, I don't take advantage of the naïve. I've been there. I'll give you until Monday to say nay or yea before I go to your competition.

The click ended Hal's... Legrande's... call. Karen's mind hadn't fully made the switch from one to the other. Link came back on with a full laugh. "Offshore accounts? Get real. I'll give the guy this, he's got balls. Or had. Sorry he's dead and all, but he's clearly off his rocker."

Walrus coughed to cover his laughter as Karen shot him

a warning look. "That may well be. Thank you, Mr. Link, for your time."

"I'd say anytime, but time's precious. I've got some important calls to return." He clicked off.

Walrus let loose his laughter. "Oh boy, is he going to be livid when he finds out."

Marek said, "Interesting that Legrande was looking to compensate Josh Bolvin."

"Yeah, a good egg," Walrus agreed.

"And the music Legrande was sitting on is going to net Danielle a golden egg," Seoul told Karen. "You're going to have to find yourself a good IP attorney."

A daunting thought. But not one for today. Karen looked at her watch. Well past suppertime, and even Kurt was drooping at his chalkboard. "Okay, we're done for the night unless something breaks." That got cheers. "You can continue the timeline in the morning while Marek and I head for Vermillion to visit the Shrine." Karen gave Seoul a pointed look before the deputy could contradict her with the National Music Museum. "In the Dakotas, name changes take eons to stick."

But would the Shrine take second fiddle—or a Hardanger fiddle—to a murder?

CHAPTER 28

WHEN MAREK STEPPED OUT OF the Sub on a softly misting morning in the sleepy college town of Vermillion, he had to blink several times to make sure he was correctly reading the carved letters on the imposing limestone building. "Library? I thought it was a museum."

Karen glanced up from where she'd been studying the statues of bronzed children frolicking in a fountain in the courtyard to the tune of a bearded man with a violin—or a fiddle. "Weird. I never noticed that before. It's always been the Shrine to me. I'm guessing it was the original campus library."

It was likely one of the many Carnegie libraries that dotted the Midwestern landscape, bringing civilization on the broken backs of the coal miners who'd toiled for Andrew Carnegie.

Marek pulled open one of the heavy doors and let Karen go ahead of him. A large sign said the museum was closed for renovations until further notice. But the foyer had a buzzer, which she pushed. When no one appeared after a number of minutes, she buzzed again. Same result.

"I'm going to be royally pissed if we came all the way down here for nothing." Karen pulled out her phone. "Maybe Seoul can rouse the man from whatever hole he's hiding in. Or Judge Rudy will get me a warrant for the man's head."

"Good luck with that." But Marek had spotted movement. "Hold on."

Karen looked up, her finger hovering over the contact number for Deputy Durr. "About time." She pocketed the phone and pulled open the door as it was released from the other side by what appeared to be a gnome—a hunchbacked gnome in a rumpled gray suit and... slippers.

"About time," the man growled, in an unconscious echo of his visitor. "Where's the fiddle?"

Marek stepped up, the fiddle cradled in his arms, where it'd been for the entire trip down from Reunion. He was deathly afraid he'd drop it.

Intent on a locked case in the middle of the two-story-high foyer, Karen skirted the man and was peering at the violin inside, which looked quite old. "Is that...?"

"A Stradivarius?" Lanski humphed. "All anyone wants to see." He gave it a dismissive wave as he peered up at the fiddle. "Now *this*... this is interesting." He glowered at Marek under bristly brows. "Where's the case?"

That was the question. "It's missing."

Lanski shook his head. "Criminal to haul it around like a football." He beckoned them up a sweeping staircase to the second level. "Bring it along and be careful."

Marek followed past galleries and exhibits full of both recognizable and completely foreign instruments: player pianos, gleaming horns and trumpets, guitars both ancient and electric, and Native American and African drums. Yet the only sound was their footfalls—and Lanski's shuffles—on the marble floor.

Given the parking lot had been empty but for an old maroon Volvo, Marek deduced that the rest of the staff had yet to arrive. When Marek passed an instrument that looked like an upended centipede with a gazillion metal legs stuck in a wooden reed-like base, he caught his foot on the cabinet's leg and nearly went down.

"I said be careful!" Lanski looked like he wanted to snatch the fiddle out of Marek's arms.

When Marek righted himself, the gnome glanced at the alien instrument and muttered, "Harmoni-cor." Then he continued down the hall. Finally, at an instrument that looked like a collision of two harps, Lanski made an abrupt turn through an open doorway. They entered a high-ceilinged room dominated by a large desk completely covered with paper, mostly music. A display case on one wall held a mishmash of instruments and their associated paraphernalia. On the other wall was an upright piano that looked more functional than artifactual. In the far corner, a couple of music stands stood guard in front of a broken exhibit case.

What Marek didn't see were any chairs. To discourage visitors?

"Put the fiddle down here." Lanski moved a stack of music off his desk.

Marek carefully removed the fiddle from the large evidence bag. Lanski took the instrument from him before he could put it down, leaving him the bag. No doubt the man was afraid that Marek's big hands were as clumsy as his feet.

"Hmm." One finger traced the geometric inlays. "Traditional decorated fingerboard and tailpiece. Fairly flat bridge profile." Lanski turned the fiddle over. "In excellent condition, no cracks or damage, not even blemishes to the finish. Maker's mark..." He peered then hummed. "Excellent. It's a Helland."

"I thought it was a Hardanger," Karen said, finally speaking after the put-down over the Strad. She appeared to be intimidated both by the man and all the musical instruments. Not her area of expertise. Even Marek, who had a nodding acquaintance with music, was intimidated.

"Yes, yes. Olvar Gunnarson Helland made this Hardanger fiddle."

Marek exchanged a wry look with Karen, who made a face over the gnome's head.

"Four melody, four sympathetic strings... or should be." Lanski made a sound of disgust. "Where's the fourth string?" Before either Marek or Karen could think of a polite way to tell the professor that it had been used as a murder weapon, Lanski had pulled out a drawer. He began hauling out packets of coiled strings until he found what he was looking for—a steel one stamped as 0.26 millimeters in thickness. Grumbling, he quickly and efficiently restrung the instrument.

Lanski resumed his catalog of the instrument, finally glancing above the tuning knobs. He plucked off the small protective sock—one of Becca's castoffs—that Marek had put over the finial "A traditional carved finial in the shape of..." As Lanski's brows shot up, Marek finally saw the man's eyes: a surprisingly youthful, even twinkling, hazel. "Oh my goodness gracious." He straightened out of gnome shape. "Do you know what you've got here?"

Karen got that one. "It's a devil."

"Not *a* devil. *The* devil."

Karen stared at him. "Excuse me?"

"This fiddle is called 'The Devil,' and it disappeared soon after it was made in 1896 at Helland's workshop in Telemark. We don't know who commissioned it, but it had a finial in the scroll of a devil with horns. Helland noted that the fiddler had been thrown out of church and his previous fiddle destroyed because he dared to play a tritone for the wedding procession."

Marek hazarded a question. "Tritone?"

"Or devil's triad." After handing the fiddle to Karen—Lanski apparently thought her less likely to drop it—Lanski went to the piano, moving a stack of sheet music off the stool. Splaying out surprisingly long fingers, he picked out a single chord. B and F. The resultant sound wasn't entirely pleasant but not particularly unpleasant, either. Nothing to warrant being sent to hell, so to speak.

"Where's the third?" Karen asked, and Marek winced.

"Third what?"

"Tone. Tritone, right? Three tones?"

Lanski swiveled on the stool. "You obviously know nothing about music."

"Obviously. Enlighten me."

"Very well. Do you know what an octave is?"

"Same note, but higher or lower?"

"That will do." Lanski swiveled around, and his right hand spanned to play middle and high C. An octave. Then he played consecutive white keys. Middle C and D. "The latter's a whole tone. A half would be a sharp or flat." He played from the white middle C to the black C# key. "A tritone splits the octave with three whole tones on either side." He gestured at the keys above and below. "Hence, tritone. Do you understand now?"

Marek wasn't sure that Karen really did, but she nodded. "Got it. But... why is it the devil's triad?"

"Because to the medieval choirs singing God's perfect praises, it was a jarring, imperfect interval compared to the perfect fourth or perfect fifth." Lanski demonstrated both the fourth and fifth, then went back to the devil's triad.

"That doesn't sound that bad to me. Though it does feel..." She hesitated. "Unfinished?"

"Unresolved. Yes, that's true. It builds a tension that seeks release." He resolved the tritone with a perfect fifth, and Marek felt something in him relax, though he hadn't realized he'd tensed.

Lanski rose from the stool but continued his lecture, almost as a natural reflex. "Our modern ear finds the tritone less dissonant than our predecessors did." He took Karen's measure, as if judging her level of musical taste. "It's found fairly often in rock, especially heavy metal. That started with Black Sabbath, who picked it up from Gustav Holst's

'Mars, Bringer of War.' Of course, Holst picked the tritone up from previous composers, and on back it goes. Nothing new under the sun."

Marek wondered how Rad Wilson would take the news that heavy metal owed its edge to classical music. What was old was new.

The lesson apparently over, Lanski retrieved the fiddle from Karen. Picking up the bow, he played something quick and lively, then slow and mellow, before nodding abruptly. "Very nice tone. One of Helland's better efforts. Yes, quite a find, this fiddle. I will forgive... what was her name? Jazz Annotations."

That Karen could answer with confidence. "Seoul Durr."

"Ah, yes. An apt name."

"How much is the fiddle worth?" Marek asked.

The brows bristled down. "Worth? It's priceless."

"Even a Strad isn't priceless," Karen told him.

"Culturally. Academically." His hazel eyes reappeared fleetingly. "Oh, yes. I can get quite a bit of traction with this instrument in the literature. You've just solved one of the greatest mysteries of Hardanger fiddle lore."

"Give us a ballpark," Karen said.

"Perhaps as high as a hundred thousand at auction, given its history. But more likely in the twenty to fifty thousand range."

Not exactly worth killing for. Unless someone believed it was worth more or wanted it for its cultural or academic value. Axel Knutsen?

Marek asked, "Could you play us something traditional? Norwegian, I mean?"

"Are you Norwegian? Look Slav to me." Lanski lifted his bow. "I can play you Dvorak's 'Slavonic Dances.'"

Karen saved Marek from himself. "I'm Norwegian. Part, anyway. Halvorsen."

With a big sigh, as if deprived from an anticipated pleasure, Lanski handed the fiddle back to Karen. Back at his desk, the professor started rooting through the stacks of music, one of which would have toppled if Marek hadn't caught it. Lanski snatched the stack back then stared at the top sheet with a humph. "There it is," he said, as if Marek had been hiding it from him in plain sight.

"Get me a stand," Lanski ordered.

Used to being the designated brawn, Marek brought over one of the music stands. The professor placed the untitled music on it and, raising the bow, began. The music seemed a bit odd to Marek's ear, as if it were stopping and starting, with trills and faintly Celtic-sounding music. No wonder Axel had been disapproving of Legrande's fiddling, if this was how it was supposed to be played. Marek moved a step closer, trying to concentrate on the music, and thought he'd caught up with the notes on the score.

He must've made some sound, because the bow suddenly stopped, and Marek found himself staring down into those hazel eyes—not at all twinkling. "Problem?"

"Probably just my ear is off." Marek tugged it apologetically. "Seems out of tune to me."

The bristly brows shot up. "Nice catch."

"Sounds fine to me," Karen said. "I mean, in tune."

"The music is in tune, relatively speaking, Sheriff." Lanski turned back to Marek with a reappraising air. "But the Hardanger is traditionally played up a whole tone from what's written. You have perfect pitch, Detective?"

Marek shrugged. "If so, it's the only perfect thing about me."

"It's a rare and precious gift." Lanski lifted his bow again and glared down it, looking disturbingly like the devil on the fiddle's finial. "Use it."

When the concert was over, Karen frowned. "It doesn't sound like a violin... exactly. It's... deeper?"

"What you hear is resonance coming from the sympathetic strings." He indicated the understrings that he hadn't touched at all with the bow. Apparently, they weren't meant to be played. "You may be familiar with the *Hardingfele* without knowing." He played them an instantly recognizable tune, with its soaring and melancholy soundtrack. "The theme for Rohan from *The Lord of the Rings*." He played another tune, equally haunting. "That's an arrangement of the traditional Norwegian tune 'The Lost Sheep' from *Fargo*."

Seeing Karen's surprise, Lanski gave her a sour smile. "As I still teach to earn my bread and butter, I do have to find something to relate to with my students."

Lanski placed the fiddle back in the bag. Carefully. "Yes, yes, an excellent instrument." He handed the fiddle back— to Marek. Apparently, perfect pitch redeemed all sins. "We would be very interested in acquiring this fiddle for the museum."

Karen told him, "Right now, it's part of a murder investigation."

"Is it now?" The eyes made a brief appearance again. Then he waved that away as if trivial. "Who is the owner? Is he dead? Perhaps his heirs will want to sell it?"

"That's also a mystery. Some of the instruments were bequeathed to various museums, but I don't know if this was one—or if our victim even owned it."

"You find out, you call me, night or day. That girl... Jazz Annotations... she has the number." After one last lingering look at the fiddle, he glanced up at Marek. "You break it, I'll break your fingers."

"Yes, sir."

CHAPTER 29

KAREN HATED THE SOUND OF silence.

Marek was thinking his own deep thoughts as she drove through the misting rain to the slow, almost mesmerizing ticktock of the wipers. Finally, she couldn't stand it any longer. She'd fall asleep at the wheel if the silence went on much longer. "So... did someone want the fiddle? I mean, twenty to a hundred thousand isn't peanuts to some people."

Marek roused and almost lost the fiddle in his lap. "What?"

Karen realized he'd been napping, not thinking. Hard to tell with Marek. But at least the tension of the long silence was gone. "The fiddle. Did someone covet it? Or are we looking at Axel, who was incensed that Legrande dared to challenge tradition. Pretty ironic, given the fiddle is the devil's instrument, right?"

"Right." Marek checked the fiddle as if to make sure he hadn't done any damage. Apparently not, as he let out a relieved breath. "And I'll be glad when it goes back to its owner, whoever that is."

Karen tapped on the wheel to break up the monotonous beat of the wipers. "Who would know? The Bolvins?"

Nodding, Marek took out his phone and made the call. "Hi, Nick. I have a question for you. Do you know who owned the Hardanger fiddle that Le—that Birchard used in his Jam Off act?"

Good catch, Karen thought. He'd almost let the cat out of the bag. She listened to Marek listen and wished he'd put it on speakerphone.

"All right. Thanks. What?" Marek pursed his lips. "Flattered but ... not happening. Bye."

Karen glanced over at him. "What?"

"Nick said Legrande had the fiddle on loan. He assumed from someone local."

That wasn't what Karen had meant. She wanted to know *what* wasn't happening that Marek had found flattering. But she let it pass. They needed to find their killer before the festival ended tonight. Though if it continued to rain, maybe the outdoor concert would be postponed, giving Karen a reprieve. At least Josh Bolvin was in the clear, and from what she'd heard, the concert would be very well attended given that he was playing "Plain Sight" with the Sioux Falls bandmates Legrande had handpicked—and paid, apparently. Larson had called her at daybreak with the financial angle.

Legrande had three-point-four million. Offshore account. From what Larson had relayed from the thrilled Wild Abandon fan who was the forensic accountant in Pierre, the money had been in that account stretching back as far as online records went. And Legrande had grown it from a mere quarter million in that time. Karen wondered just how much the seed money had been. She'd hire Legrande in a heartbeat to manage her meager investments if he were still among the living.

So the fiddle was on loan. "Could the fiddle belong to Axel? That would explain why he was so upset about what he'd see as a desecration of the traditional Hardanger music. And he was seen near the instrument tent, remember? Rad Wilson gave him the finger."

On the armrest on the door, Marek added a counter beat

to her tapping on the wheel. She had to smile. Was that desire to make music, or at least rhythm, unconscious?

"Axel seems like an unlikely suspect." Marek paused his counter beat. "Did anyone talk to Doc Hudson?"

"I did. Last night." Karen fought a smile and lost. "He confirmed that Axel had a prescription for Viagra that needed to be renewed ASAP."

"Lucky wife." Cheeks reddening, Marek stared straight out into a misted view of cornfields. Then he frowned. "It was a Friday, late afternoon, nearly suppertime, and he's a retired man. Why wait until then?"

She'd been too amused to be struck by that oddity. "You mean, was he trying to establish an alibi by tracking down Doc Hudson?" And amusing everyone in the bargain—a clever way to cover a very unamusing murder? "Axel said he turned around and didn't go into the instrument tent. But what if he was coming out of it, not going into it, when that picture was taken?"

"Only one way to find out. We need to take another look at the photo."

And at Axel Knutsen. She pulled off Interstate 29 and onto the county road toward Reunion. Country road. Take me home. She was relieved a few minutes later to see no sign of the press outside the courthouse. Their homicide was apparently no nine days' wonder. Not even a day, apparently.

Then she remembered the concert. The press were probably staked out at the Bolvins' or Grove Park. At least they were off her back. It was a relief to walk into the office and see her men working quietly on their computers, the blackboard now cramped with Kurt's neat handwriting. And once again, she found Seoul there off shift.

"Deputy Durr, do you not need sleep?"

"I'll get some later." Seoul waved that away as if it had little importance, just like Lanski had with the Strad. "Finding a killer is more important."

Oh, to be twenty-two again. Karen turned back to the

chalkboard and was looking for Axel's name when the double doors of the office opened.

"Uncle Sig." Karen smiled at the lanky man in his sixties who looked more like her father than her own did. "Back from the wilds of Boise, I see. Did you enjoy your cookout last night with Blake?"

"That I did."

"Is Lance covering for you at the shop?" The front store for Sig's small meatpacking operation that catered to the health-conscious grass-fed-beef crowd, both locally and in the tristate area, was just a short walk down the street.

"That he is." Sig stuck his hands into his jeans and beamed, as always, at the mention of the other of his twin sons. "You've been back in the news, Karen. I have to think you like the spotlight."

Though he smiled, she could see the sadness in his deep-fjord Halvorsen eyes. Gregarious as most Dakotans were not, he knew just about everyone in town. There weren't many vegans in Reunion. "You knew—" Karen almost said Legrande. Loose lips sink ships. "Birchard?"

"That I did."

She wondered why Sig had come, if he was going to suddenly become a Dakotan and save his syllables for a rainy day. Which it was. "Uncle Sig, I'm always glad to see you, but..."

"You're busy." He blew out a breath. "I know it's not the best time. I just wondered..." He blinked as Marek came in from the restroom and picked up the fiddle sitting on his desk. No doubt to return it to the evidence room.

With a few quick steps, Sig cut him off. "Oh, thank goodness. I didn't want to ask, but it *is* an heirloom."

All movement in the room ceased, from chalk on board to fingers on keyboard.

"Heirloom?" Karen stared at her father's cousin. She'd never seen that fiddle before in her life. Had it come from his mother's side? "Are you telling me that the fiddle belongs to you?"

Sig looked abashed. "To the family, yes. It came to me as the eldest son of the eldest son back to immigrant Sigurd Halvorsen. But I can't play it."

Karen shook her head to clear it. "It's a Halvorsen heirloom?"

"That's so cool," Seoul said when Sig nodded.

"More than you know." Marek hefted the bag. "According to Dr. Lanski, it's apparently been lost to history. The Shrine—"

"The National Music Museum," Seoul corrected.

"—wants to buy it for their collection."

"Oh. Well, I'm not sure. I'll have to think about that, talk to the family."

Walrus shook his head sadly. "It'd be a crying shame for it to just sit in a museum somewhere."

In a rare point of agreement, Kurt nodded. "Can't anybody in the family play it?"

"Not that I'm aware of," Sig said regretfully. "In fact, I don't think anyone other than old Sigurd played it."

"No wonder it's in such good condition," Seoul said.

"The tradition is, Sigurd's second wife banned it from their home."

How ironic. "Because it was the devil's instrument?"

"No, because she hated the sound. Said it was like cats screeching."

Karen stared at the fiddle. "Well, Eyre plays the violin. I wonder if she could play that."

Sig brightened. "She'd certainly get a kick out of the history."

"She's also in Vermillion a lot," Seoul mused. "Could be a win-win. Put it on loan at the museum with rights to play it or take it out as desired."

"You just want to keep on Lanski's good side... if he has one."

Seoul raised a hand. "Guilty as charged, your honor."

That reminded Karen of the emancipation hearing, the last thing on Judge Rudibaugh's docket for the day. She'd tried to get a warrant for the sealed codicil from him, but he'd rebuffed the request, saying that it was obviously the revelation she'd already discovered: that Birchard was Legrande. When she'd argued the codicil could influence the outcome of the hearing, depending on what Birchard-Legrande had said, the judge just stared at her. That stare had made killers piss. She'd backed off.

Marek asked Sig, "You met Hal at the shop?"

"Yep, he had a standing order for prime rib. Not a real talkative man, like ninety-nine percent of my customers." His eyes twinkled. "Except on one topic."

Not hard to guess. "Music."

"When I told Hal that I had an old Norwegian fiddle gathering dust in my closet, he told me he'd be interested in seeing it. So I brought it to work with me the next day, and when he next came in, I took him back to the office and showed it to him. You'd think I'd brought him the crown jewels. When he asked if he could buy it, I told him it was an heirloom. He didn't push. But I was happy to loan it to him. And I'm very sorry I didn't get to hear him play it. I thought I'd have more chances."

"We've got a video of the performance," Karen told him. "And Hal added another layer to the saga of the devil's instrument. I hope it's not cursed."

"Are you any closer to finding Hal's killer?" Sig asked.

Karen thought about Axel Knutsen. If the fiddle wasn't his, there went motive... unless they considered him outraged enough by mere violation of tradition. "Fiddlesticks. You may have just knocked a big gaping hole into my latest theory." Karen turned and looked at the chalkboard, noting the time Rad had given Axel the finger outside the instrument tent. 6:43 p.m. "Do we have a time for Axel Knutsen meeting up with Doc Hudson?"

Kurt looked abashed. "Sorry. No, I can—" He reached for a phone.

"I've got this." Karen pulled up the number on her recent contacts. "Hi, Doc. Sorry to pull you away from a patient. I just wondered if you might have noticed what time it was when Axel asked you for the prescription on Friday."

"Ah..."

She sighed inwardly. "That's okay. Just thought I'd check. Thanks for—"

"Hold on. I called it in for him right then and there. He and the wife are leaving for a Caribbean cruise right after the festival, and he hadn't realized he was low. Let me take a look." Doc Hudson must have lowered the phone to check his own recent contacts. Then he came back on the line. "I phoned the prescription in at 6:45 p.m. Does that help?"

Karen did the very easy math. "Yes, for Axel. It eliminates him." He must have gone straight from his encounter with Rad's finger right into the arms of the doctor.

There was a long silence on the line. "Surely you weren't looking at Axel? If so, I think you'd better come in."

Was he going to give her a break in the case? "How so?"

"To have your head examined." He clicked off.

"You were looking at Axel?" Sig stared at her. "You need your head—"

"Examined. Yes, I got that. And Axel can go off to the Caribbean with a clear conscience." He and his wife could even visit Legrande's gravesite on San Juan. No, not Legrande. Birchard. Wasn't that going to cause some issues? And they'd be her headache, Karen realized, after Sig took his leave.

All in all, this case had been a dead loss. The phone in her hand rang. Larson.

Without preamble, he said, "Print match. Rad Wilson. Inside amp."

CHAPTER 30

"TOLD YOU SO! RAD WILSON'S our killer!"

Marek watched, bemused, as Seoul jumped to her feet and did a little shimmy. He almost hated to ruin it for her. "Hold on."

As she stopped mid-shimmy, he exchanged a look with Karen.

She pointed out the flaw. "Rad had to have tampered with the amp *before* Marmo was there to push over the mic. That means Legrande was alive and kicking."

"Oh. Right." Seoul fell back to her chair.

Marek gave her a consolation prize. "But we have leverage now. And a reason to bring her in."

"But why even bother if she wasn't our killer?" Then Seoul straightened. "Oh, I see. She could've gone back later. I've got her sneaking around the judges' tent and it's only around the back and over to the instrument tent." Seoul jabbed a finger at the chalkboard. "And look, we have no sighting of her after she gave the finger to Axel at 6:44 p.m. until the judges reconvened at seven. So she could've done the dirty deed."

"All good points," Karen agreed. "But she's hardly the only one we can't account for. However, we do need to confront her about the tampering. Have you got any background on her? All I know is that she's got an attitude and more than enough heavy metal to sink a ship."

Seoul's mouth twisted as she flopped back in the chair. "You know how you really want to hate somebody, but then you find out stuff that makes you figure they've got a right to be the way they are?"

"Don't tell me." Karen shook her head sadly. "Another of the abandoned?"

"Got it in one." Seoul heaved out a sigh. "Single mom dumped her on the system at age nine and took off to God knows where. Owing to the 'tude, Rad—or Jenny as she was then—was never adopted. Aged out of the system last year."

So she'd be about nineteen, the same age as Josh Bolvin. Marek had been booted out of his home by the death of his mother at age eighteen and out of the county by his half-brother soon thereafter. And Marek had made it on his own. But he'd had a trade. "How does she survive?"

"Gigs. Couch surfing. Occasional waitressing."

Like Danielle, then. Except nothing like. Still. "What's the motive for murder?"

"Eliminating the competition," Seoul replied promptly. "Girl's got no impulse control. She wants a record deal. And she came to this bumfuck—her word—to get that. Full stop."

Marek thought about that, about the cat-got-the-canary look, but he still couldn't figure it.

"Mmm. But the judges were deadlocked when they broke," Bork said.

Two Fingers picked it up. "And all three championed a different musician—Kuhl was for Birchard-Legrande, Marmo for Rad, and Axel for..."

"Yours truly," Seoul said with a bright smile at the taciturn deputy. "Isn't that a kicker."

"Hey, have we eliminated *you*?" Walrus asked.

She rolled her eyes. "I'm incorruptible."

Ignoring the byplay, Marek turned that angle over in his mind. Not Seoul but Rad. Marmo had told Axel before the break that he would reconsider his vote for Seoul. That would give the majority vote to the deputy. Yet... Rad Wilson had seemed almost gloating. Why? "Killing Legrande wouldn't give Rad Wilson what she wanted. Unless Marmo lied when he told Axel he'd swing your way."

Obviously news to Seoul, that struck the deputy speechless while Walrus gave her a mock sneer. "Told you guys. She's our killer. Perfect Agatha Christie ending. The deputy did it."

"Maybe Rad Wilson knew Birchard was Legrande?" Two Fingers suggested. "A spot of bribery?"

Karen shook her head. "Bribery wouldn't work. Marmo's take was that Legrande was going to blow his own cover. So what was the payoff?" Karen yanked on her ponytail. "We're just going in circles."

"Round and round," Walrus agreed. "Like Frere Jacques."

"Let's bring her in." Karen glanced at Marek. "Maybe we can shake something loose."

Marek nodded. "Rad Wilson knows more than she's telling."

And Seoul took a point and a bow.

Half an hour later, Rad Wilson swaggered into the interview room, giving a finger to the stoic Two Fingers. She stopped just inside. "Like, I've seen johns with better 'ambience.'" Her fingernails slashed the quotes with black highlighted with yellow today instead of scarlet. "This place sucks."

"But it's home," Marek said mildly. He and Karen hadn't decided how to handle her. How did you handle the unpredictable? They'd play it by ear. Ad-lib it. "Have a seat."

Snickering, Rad whirled a chair around and straddled it. "Chief No-Funny-Business out there said you had more questions. So, shoot. Your last shot." She sneered at the dingy walls. "I'm not staying in this burg longer than I have to—first thing tomorrow, I'm out."

Marek wondered why she was even staying the night. Was something going to happen? "I'm surprised you haven't already left."

The girl shrugged, pulling on a black leather bra strap. "Boy Wonder's just blah, but the music?" Genuine excitement made her look younger, almost giddy. "Wild Abandon and Legrande, they rock."

Interesting. Another fan. Given her background, though, maybe that wasn't too surprising. Only that she knew who they were, given the generational difference. But did she know who Birchard really was? Or had she found out? Perhaps it wasn't so far-fetched that an idol turned "bad trad" was worth garroting. No impulse control, Seoul had said.

"You identify with Legrande?" he asked her.

"I-den-ti-fy?" She mocked his word. "If you mean, did we groove to the same tune in life, yeah. Legrande got gypped. So did I. But I'm not sunk yet."

Again, Marek caught a whiff of the gloat. For a girl living on the edge, both in her music and in her life, that didn't make much sense. Almost, he sensed a resolution.

But Karen broke his concentration as she leaned down. "You knew Legrande was there."

The girl only looked confused. "Birchard, you mean?"

"Sorry, slip of the tongue."

Marek didn't see what he'd hoped, what he'd seen with Marmo—the knowledge that the two men were one and the same, at least for the last couple of decades. "You gave Axel Knutsen the finger. Why was that?"

"Who? Oh, yeah. The old guy living in la-la land. He deserved the finger. He called my music a godawful racket."

"And you knew that because?"

Too caught up in her own head, the girl said, "Heard it." Then she straightened. "Around."

"Yeah, around the judges' tent." Karen set down a printout. The lightning-faced Rad was clearly visible, leaning with ear to the side of the canvas tent. "You're an eavesdropper, a snoop."

Rad stared at the printout then flicked it away, her

daggers-in-hearts bracelet jangling. "So? Not a crime. You grow up with other people making decisions about your life, you listen."

"And when the going gets tough, the tough take out the competition?" Karen slapped down the next printout. The one with the laser pointer. "Gotcha."

The girl's face slackened, then she sneered. "You never seen a stylus before?"

"Oh, you've got finger dexterity issues? Where is the stylus, *Jenny*?"

The girl actually came out of the chair. "Don't you call me that. My name's Rad. Legal."

Obviously a trigger. Karen held up her hands. "Your choice."

"Yeah, it was. First thing I did when I turned eighteen."

"And the stylus?"

"What? Oh." Rad sank back down. "Got bumped outta my hand in the crowd. Lost it." Her smirk dared them to prove her wrong.

Marek took his shot. "You went into the instrument tent during the Jam Off."

His soft words had the girl jolting. But she recovered swiftly. "Sure I did. Had to tune my guitar and wait my turn, didn't I?"

Karen slapped down their final card. "And tamper with Josh Bolvin's amp."

"I never—"

"Take a good look, Rad. Your bad. You *are* bad. It's a fingerprint match."

The girl stared at the faxed report.

"Not so easy to wiggle out of that, is it, Rad? I'm sensing a pattern here. And I'm guessing a jury will see the same. We've got you cold on the laser pointer—a federal crime. You're going to do some prison time for that. Do you realize you can blind somebody?"

"I didn't hit anybody in the eye!" Her lips snapped shut too late.

Now that they'd got her, what did they do with her? "Why did you tamper with Josh's amp?"

"Look, I only meant to give Boy Wonder a little zing when he warmed up for his solo act that night. Nothing serious. Everything fell into his hands. Birchard's backing. Legrande's music."

"You didn't know that at the time," Karen pointed out. "All you knew was that he was an obstacle to what you wanted. Just like you messed with my deputy with that laser pointer."

Rad hugged herself, disturbingly like Lianne Mehaffey. "Look, I know who really killed Birchard."

Karen gave a patting yawn. "You've cried wolf one too many times, Rad."

"No, I *mean* it." Real fear took off years—and most of the attitude. "You don't understand. I've got nothing else. No *one* else. The state kicked me out when I hit eighteen. No college, no tech school, no nothing. Don't let the door hit you on the ass. I can't even go to the military 'cause I had some hits. Weed. It's music or die. If you put me in prison, I'll lose my chance to—"

Marek finally got it. "When did you get the contract?"

Though Karen's head jerked around, Rad didn't appear to notice. Instead, she dropped her head into her hands. "Why does everything go south for me?"

"Just tell the truth," Marek said.

Easing out of the girl's space, Karen took a less contentious tack. "If what you give us leads to an arrest, then you might turn witness."

"And lose my chance at the same time?" Rad hooked onto Marek. "I was going to tell you guys..." Her eyes rose to Karen with sudden anger. "But you kept putting me off. And I... well, I took my chance. Made a deal with Kuhl."

And that explained the gloat. She had her music contract bagged. Marek leaned back. "In exchange for...?"

Her shoulders jerked. "I just said to Kuhl... that I knew he was the last to see Birchard before that girl found him. That I'd seen him coming out of the instrument tent."

Karen let out a disgusted breath. "Good try, but he'd already know you'd seen him, if that were the case. Which it isn't."

"He didn't see me. After that run-in with the old guy, I circled back behind the judges' tent to wait for them to come back. Besides, I'm good at hiding in plain sight." Her gaze hit on the printouts. "Usually. When I'm not all dolled up. Without all the face paint, I'm what my mother always said: ugly as a night crawler, wiggly and sick white."

Marek liked Kuhl. But who knew what anyone might do in the heat of the moment? Still, Rad had lied more than she'd told the truth. "Where did Kuhl go after he came out of the instrument tent?"

"Straight out and down a trail into the woods. I didn't see him again until he came back to the judges' tent maybe five minutes later."

Karen took a seat and looked at the girl straight on. "You have proof Kuhl offered you a contract in exchange for your silence? Anything in writing?"

Rad blinked. "Well, no, but—"

"If you really thought Kuhl killed Birchard, weren't you worried he'd kill you, too?"

"Without the contract, I *am* dead."

A humming silence greeted that. Then Karen shook her head. "Why would Kuhl kill Birchard?"

"I don't know. But he was the last out of the tent."

"Even if he was, that doesn't make him the killer. It only means that he didn't report it. And he may have given you the contract to keep *that* quiet."

Her head hit the table. "Then I'm sunk."

Not quite yet.

CHAPTER 31

THE CHALKBOARD TOLD KAREN NOTHING she wanted to see. Kuhl was absent from the time when the judges broke up at 6:30 p.m. until he'd set off the motion sensors at the footbridge at 6:56. The judges had reconvened when he returned four minutes later. Nothing said "gotcha." He'd told them he'd taken a walk to clear his head, wandering around the various trails, and he'd been caught doing just that. Big deal. She walked—or more often, played ball—to clear her head.

Rad Wilson's timeline, however, was much more complete, at least until she'd given Axel the finger at 6:43 p.m. And while there was a gap in sightings within the timeframe she'd claimed to have gone behind the judges' tent and seen Kuhl come out of the instrument tent, that proved nothing. They had Rad stashed down in the jail, pending further inquiries but not yet under arrest. Like Marmo, she had taken the deal of a bed and board with a measure of relief.

The girl had, as it turned out, been living in her beater.

Frustrated, Karen turned to look at her men—and one woman. "Even if by some miracle Rad told us the truth and Kuhl did kill Legrande, she's not going to hit a high note with a jury."

"Low note, that's for sure. She's just trying to weasel out. Again." Seoul stretched behind her computer. The timeline was complete—or as complete as they could make it. "Crying wolf."

"I agree." Kurt meticulously boxed up the chalk. "Anton Kuhl has no motive."

"But he's got a link to Legrande," Two Fingers said.

"To the music, not the man." Karen paced to the window. No vultures. Good. "We've got no indication that Kuhl knew Birchard was Legrande. He only recognized the music. Not surprising since he owns the rights."

"But not the future rights," Seoul pointed out. "And 'Plain Sight' and the rest of the music we found would qualify as future. So he doesn't profit."

"At least Kuhl must be rolling in it this week after the bump in interest in Legrande." Walrus patted his rumbling stomach. "And I could use a roll—or two or a dozen. Can we eat now?"

Karen saw Marek give the deputy a long, considering stare. What had just tripped in that unpredictable brain of his? "Marek?"

He blinked. "Lunch sounds good."

She deflated. So much for a break. At least of the investigative sort. "Okay. Let's take a break for lunch. A *long* lunch. We all need to clear our heads. Back at two."

That got a ragged cheer. Kurt flipped the chalkboard over, just in case the press got snoopy, and then headed for home to his sister. Karen envied him the in-house cook.

Her stomach rumbling, Karen drove the Sub home with the radio on and hummed along with ABBA's "Money, Money, Money."

All right, she got the message. Police work was mostly grunt work. After parking at the curb, she picked up her phone, called Larson, and got that ball rolling. Nothing she'd seen or heard had given her a sniff in Kuhl's direction. Unlike Marmo. But it was the details—and the patience— that closed cases.

When Karen walked into 22 Okerlund Road, the house

was empty. She'd expected Eyre to be at work, but where was Danielle? Had the press gotten to her? On the kitchen table, she found a note written in block letters on the table. No one knew cursive anymore.

VULTURES GONE. WENT BACK TO WORK. SEE YOU AT HEARING.

And then a p.s. in smaller print. HARLAN WILL DRIVE. CAN'T ARREST ME YET.

Yet? Karen hoped that was a stab at humor. The girl would need her own wheels if the hearing went as Karen hoped. Maybe even if it didn't, because if Judge Rudy named Harlan or, God forbid, even her as guardian, Danielle was past due for a ride. Many kids drove tractors long before they could get their driver's permit at fourteen.

Struck with a thought and an almost coincident pang, Karen paused in the middle of pulling leftover grilled brats out of the refrigerator. Could she? Well, why not? Times moved on in the wake of death, leaving things, sometimes valuable things, as Legrande had in his music.

Had Hal Birchard left anything? An identity for Legrande but not much else. Washed up. Still, he'd mostly stayed out of trouble and seen the world. Not a terrible epitaph.

By the time she'd finished off the brats—left by Sig with a note that he suspected she could use the extra protein—Karen was restless. Finally, she decided to go bug Marek—or at least talk to him. She needed a sounding board.

After walking across the street, Karen knocked on the solid oak door, and through the open windows, she heard Marek's rumble to come in. She pushed open the door and found him in her grandfather's rocker by the empty hearth, his head back, the room echoing with the sounds of an orchestra sliding out from his high-tech speakers. She'd never gotten beyond boom boxes, radios, and CD players, and now her phone, once LPs bit the dust.

Whatever the music was, it wasn't something she'd ever heard before, even in commercials. Sort of meandering but majestic. A rippling sound tickled her ears. Maybe a harp? The whole thing sounded faintly sad and deep, even opaque, with distant, distorted chords coming from afar, as if the composer was trying to reach for something long gone, or well hidden. Like trying to catch a cloud in a fog. She wasn't even sure what the instruments were. Brass and some of those reedy instruments. "What's that?"

Without opening his eyes, Marek said, "Alan Hovhaness. 'Mysterious Mountain.'"

She gave a soundless laugh and looked at her mysterious mountain of an uncle and detective. Very apt. "Music to think by?"

Marek opened his pale eyes, always a bit spooky. His skin wasn't dusky like his half Hispanic-Native daughter's, but the summer sun had still bronzed his skin. "My mother used to clean house to Herb Alpert, grade homework to Bach and Mozart, chill to Joan Baez and Cat Stevens, and think or brood to Hovhaness. Report card day had a lot of Hovhaness."

The wonder then was that Marek had ever played the music again. As if reading her mind, he said, "It calmed her down. A good thing."

Unlike the one time Janina Marek Okerlund had taken a belt and beat the crap out of him when he was ten, leaving a scar from the belt buckle. Karen had heard his screams all the way across the street in her attic room and called her grandfather. No matter it was done out of genuine fear for her son's future, Karen had never forgiven the woman for that. Unlike Marek. Despite wearing his murderous grandfather Marek's face and frame, he really did take after his father, the gentle Leif Okerlund.

What would her life be like, Karen wondered, if Marek had never lost his wife, never returned to Reunion? Different, that was for sure. She'd likely not be sheriff, as he'd saved her from herself more than once. Maybe he'd do it again.

She paced over to one of the speakers. The hardwood floor

creaked and groaned under her feet. It had been revarnished to within an inch of its long life, so she didn't know what it had to complain about. Unlike her own flooring. Once this case was over, she might get him to redo her own and the kitchen cabinetry to boot.

"So... Anton Kuhl." She did a precise about-turn. "How viable is he as a suspect, really?"

"The only scenario I can make work," Marek said, proving he had been in thinking mode, "would require that Kuhl knew that Birchard was Legrande."

"How so? Kuhl didn't have any claim on future rights."

"Walrus gave the best answer."

She thought back. "The bump in sales of Legrande's backlist? Given our ADHD culture, I don't see that as a great motive for a man as cerebral as Kuhl. Nor would it last. And he'd get that bump just from news of Legrande's music leaking. He's... well, cool and collected. He's stayed in the business and thrived. Or at least by appearances—I just put Larson on that to confirm. But he's basically the opposite of Marmo."

Marek opened his mouth, but Karen was distracted by a noise in the kitchen. "Nikki here?"

"No, Becca."

Karen peeked into the kitchen and saw her young cousin at the table. And boy, wasn't that a kick. Cousin. The generations in her family were all mixed up. Becca was, not to Karen's surprise, intent on a drawing as she sat at the table, a plate of congealing Spaghetti-O's nearby.

Marek must have retrieved her from the Bolvins' after he'd left the office. Karen knew that one of the reasons he'd come to Reunion, and stayed here, was because he didn't want Becca to play second fiddle to his work. Good for him. Though as father and daughter were each doing their own thing, separately, she wasn't entirely sure that it counted. For quiet types, maybe it did. Was she messing that up?

"A signature," Marek mumbled. Then he sat up abruptly. "Becca!"

After a moment, the artist came into the living room with colored pencil still in hand. She looked less than pleased at the interruption. "What?" Then she saw Karen and rushed over, non-pen hand raised. "Hi."

Karen gave her a high five. "Hey, kiddo."

Rising, her father drew her back. "Sweetpea, we'd like your help."

They would? That was a new one. A pint-sized detective in waiting?

Marek sat back in the rocker and patted his lap. "Come sit." Becca did, her brow quirked in a very familiar way. "I'd like you to listen to two videos and then tell us if anything about them... looks... the same."

Looks? Karen opened her mouth to ask if he meant *sounds*, but Marek held up a hand. Obviously, he wanted no tampering with whatever scheme he had in mind.

Taking out his phone, he played the viral video of "Plain Sight" from YouTube and the much less high-production video of Legrande's last fiddle performance. Becca listened to both with an intensity that was almost frightening in one so young.

"Well?" Marek asked as he lowered his phone. "Is anything the same?"

Becca shook her head. "The colors are all different. And the shapes."

His shoulders slumped. "Oh, well."

"'Cept one." Her pencil went up. But she couldn't draw on air.

Karen brought the sketchpad and handed it over. Tongue bit between her teeth, Becca started drawing. A weirdly bulbous shape took form, one that reminded her of drawings in a calculus book of a premed teammate in college.

When Becca finished, Marek took it. "Thanks. Can I have it?"

Becca nodded and went back into the kitchen.

"What was that all about?" Karen asked him.

"I found out this weekend that when Becca hears music, she sees shapes and colors. It's rare but not a bad thing, apparently. Nikki said she's something called a synesthete."

Somewhere, somehow, that pinged. "How do you spell that?"

Marek gave her a wry look. Right. She googled it. And the light bulb went on. She did another quick search and found the reference that had pinged. "Kuhl's a synesthete. It says on his bio."

"Yeah, I saw that, too. Not so rare, then."

"Selection bias," she said absently. "He's a music guy." She paused. "But what does it mean to our investigation?"

"A signature." Marek smiled. "Not much to hang our hat on, I'll admit. But I'm suddenly a lot more interested in the whereabouts of our cool Mr. Kuhl."

"In the woods."

"Do you still have the video of Kuhl at the creek from Connor's VHS tape?"

Karen nodded and queued it up on her phone then pulled over a footstool so he could see it play. The video was taken close enough to the trail that the picture was cut off just below Kuhl's waist. His hands were in his pockets, and he sauntered down the trail, looking cool and collected, as usual.

When he reached the creek, Kuhl dipped down. "Testing the water? Tying his shoes?"

"Or putting something down."

"Like what? He wasn't carrying anything."

But Marek took the phone and restarted the video. "Watch again. What don't you see?"

"His left hand. But it's on the other side. So..." Then she got it. "It's not swinging. You walk, you swing your arms. Hot diggity dog. He *is* carrying something. And when he stoops down, his shoulders are moving. Wait, moving forward, like he's shoving... or throwing?"

"And I think we both know what it was." Karen smiled fiercely at her uncle. He made a bang-up sounding board. "If we can find the case..."

"We'll make our case." Marek pursed his lips. "We didn't ask Rad if she saw him carrying anything."

Karen rose to her feet with her phone. "Easy enough to remedy."

"Yeah, what?" the girl asked sulkily when Tammy put her on. "I'm here. I'm staying put. Your jailer ain't bad. She likes Disturbed."

That was... disturbing. "Just love your can-do attitude, Ms. Wilson." When that got a snort, Karen eased into what she really needed: permission to record the conversation on her phone. She didn't want any hint of collusion or malfeasance in the chain of evidence they were building. After a few snide remarks, Rad granted her permission.

Karen crossed her fingers. For the first time, she was glad the girl was a snoop. Putting the call on speakerphone, Karen crossed her fingers and asked the burning question. "When you saw Kuhl leave the tent for the woods, was he carrying anything?"

A short pause. "Yeah, he was."

Karen rolled her eyes at Marek. "And that was?"

"A case."

And now *they* were rolling.

"In which hand?" Marek asked.

"Away from me." Another pause. "Left."

Thank all that was holy. That meshed with the video. "What did it look like? It's important, Rad. Be as specific as you can."

"Like a case," came the snippy answer then a considering pause. "Not big like a guitar, more like... well, I guess more like a violin case. It was old, kind of rag-tag. Had a piece torn off near the top and showed red underneath. Velvet or

felt or whatever. Colors reminded me of my nails that day."
She hesitated when she got silence. "That help?"

"Might. If it does, you're not washed up."

A voice without a hint of snide and full of a girl's sincere
relief came out. "Cool beans."

Or Kuhl beans. Were his cooked?

After hanging up, Karen said, "We need to drag the creek."

Marek nodded. "I'll drop Becca back at the Bolvins'."

"Yay!" came from the kitchen and a second later, Becca
followed.

"Yeah, you're sprung from house arrest. Dad-time sucks."
Marek picked her up and Eskimo-kissed her, much as Nick
Bolvin had Em. Karen couldn't imagine doing the same to
a grown Eyre. Or even a younger one. They hadn't had that
Mom-time. Through her choice. And circumstance. So it
goes.

But she snatched Becca, gave her a hug, then handed
her back. A bit of Karen-time. That would have to be enough.
Until the case was closed.

CHAPTER 32

MAREK KNEW THAT THIS INTERVIEW was going to be one of the most difficult he'd ever conducted. They had only a short time frame to work with and, so far, not much leverage against a man who was far too controlled, too intelligent, and too savvy to be drawn into giving an easy confession.

When Anton Kuhl was ushered into the cramped interview room, he didn't comment on the decor, or lack thereof, as Rad Wilson had. Instead, he seemed struck by the overflowing filing cabinets. "I never imagined you had so much crime in your bucolic county."

Stifling a yawn, Marek shuffled papers in a folder prominently labeled Statements. "We have our share. But that's also decades' worth."

"Ah... I see. I thought they were working files." His mouth twisted as he continued to survey the cabinets. "I'm not sure this is even a day's worth of working files in LA."

"Yet you want to get back there?"

"It's home." Kuhl checked his watch. "It's been something of a working holiday for me. But all good things must come to an end."

If Marek played his hand right, Kuhl's run would end here. He'd never get home. But Marek wasn't at all sure he could pull it off. One wrong step, and the man would walk.

Kuhl sat. "Your man said you wanted to re-interview me?"

Marek gave him a wry smile. "The festival is breaking up after tonight. We need official statements before everyone drives—or jets—home." Lazily, Marek switched on the recorder. "Let's get the formalities over with while we're waiting."

The man's eyes lidded. "Waiting?"

"For Sheriff Mehaffey. She got held up by the press."

"Ah, yes. I don't imagine she's happy in that role. It's not like you've got a media liaison."

Karen had more media experience than the man would guess. But Marek shrugged. When they'd completed the Miranda rights, Marek stretched then waited until, as he'd hoped, Kuhl pulled out his phone and began scrolling through messages.

After a few minutes of that, Marek cleared his throat. "I've got a daughter. She's eight." When the silver brows shot up in surprise at the non sequitur, Marek looked abashed. "She's one of those synes... you know, she can see music."

"Synesthetes? That's rare. Very rare. I should know."

"Yeah, I saw that in your bio. I just... Before the sheriff comes back..." Marek squirmed a bit. "I've got a bet going with my SO. She says you can't possibly tell the musician just by colors and shapes. That it's not evolutionary—that is, it doesn't dovetail with anyone else's perception. So I thought if I had a chance, I'd test it out." He unfolded the picture he'd tucked in his back pocket and splayed it out on the scarred table.

The brows shot up even further. "This is the work of an eight-year-old?"

Marek smiled. "Yeah. She's good."

"Better than." Kuhl studied it. "But I believe I can help you win that bet."

"Really? Who do you think that is?"

Kuhl's mouth twisted. "Is that a trick question?"

When a question was answered with a question, the lawyers had won. "Um..."

Then Kuhl smiled. "Trick Legrande."

"That's right." His gamble had paid off. But all he allowed to leak to his face was an eager curiosity. "So you *can* tell, just by listening to someone's music, who the artist is? Like... a signature?"

"Exactly like." Kuhl pulled out his phone and started to go through his messages again.

Marek kept his eyes on the drawing. "So the fiddle performance had that shape?"

"Yes, yes, quite distinctive. Not that I needed it. As I told you before, choices in musical composition, often unconscious, betray the artist." Kuhl checked his watch. "How long do you expect Sheriff Mehaffey will be?"

Kuhl didn't realize that he'd just betrayed himself. The unconscious mind did that, when distracted. Lying took conscious effort. "Oh, not too long." He hoped.

♪♫♪

On the bank of Connor Creek, Karen watched with growing frustration as her men dragged the tributary of the Big Jammer. To no avail. Much longer, and they'd be around the bend—literally and figuratively.

Without the case, they had no case. She knew that, Marek knew that.

Her phone rang. Had Marek finished with Kuhl already? Maybe she should have stayed behind to keep the man occupied, but Marek had wanted to try out his synesthete shtick.

Karen read the contact. DCI. Only a Pierre number, not Sioux Falls. "Sheriff Mehaffey here."

"Hello, Sheriff. Anna Delaney. Forensic accountant. Agent Larson put me on your Anton Kuhl after Marmo and Legrande. I must say, I haven't had this much fun in a long, long spell."

Karen watched as Two Fingers pulled up an old boot,

thick with the slime of mud. "Glad someone's having fun. Do you have anything for me?"

"Well, Kuhl hasn't cooked his books."

Karen heaved a sigh. Nothing was going right. "A pity."

"But he's cooked his company. At least to sunny-side down."

"Oh, really?" That was more like it.

"Overextended. And not enough inflow. He's got some solid backlisters that float his label but not enough new talent. Wild Abandon is his biggest moneymaker."

"So he's basically sunk, long-term?"

"Well, I wouldn't go that far. He's been busy working the licensing circuit and made some really nice deals, especially for commercials and sports venues. The latest bump with Legrande's music will give him some breathing space. I'd bet he can pull it off. He's been in the business a long time."

Karen smiled. "He's not going to have *any* breathing space, if things go our way."

"You're seriously looking at him?"

"He's on our radar." If only they had creek-penetrating radar to find one lost case before they lost another.

♪♫♪

Beginning to look bored, Kuhl slipped his phone into his pocket. "Did you ever find Saul... Sal?"

Marek flared his nose, as if he'd just stepped in a cow patty. "Yeah, we found him at a fleabag hotel in Sioux Falls. He's stashed down in the jail."

"Oh my. Do you suspect him?"

"Remains to be seen. Held pending inquiries." Marek looked up from the statements he'd been ostensibly reviewing. No boredom now on Kuhl's face. "He definitely played a part."

"How so?" Then Kuhl held up his hands. "Sorry. I know you can't say anything during an active investigation."

Marek had already picked up that the man considered

himself savvy when it came to police procedures. As did anyone with a TV remote these days. "You don't seem particularly surprised."

"Well, Saul did have words with the man, as you told me earlier. And the way he drinks... well, it does loosen inhibitions, does it not?"

Marek allowed genuine curiosity to leak through. "Why would he do it, though?"

"Because Legrande was..." Kuhl caught himself. "Legrande's *music* was the bone of contention. In hindsight, it's obvious what must have happened. They argued over the rights. As I said, we were both at the festival because of 'Plain Sight' and its striking resemblance to Legrande's signature style. Saul had a stake in any future work. Birchard had at least one piece." Kuhl warmed to the subject. "Who knows? Maybe more. Either way, Saul was desperate. Legal or not, in court, Saul had a case."

And Marek hoped Karen did, as well.

"What're you looking for?"

Nearly jumping out of her skin, Karen looked up from where she'd battled the underbrush so as to stay abreast of her increasingly despondent men as they ranged further down the creek. The boy perched in the fork of a cottonwood wore a baseball cap and an engaging, if inquisitive, smile.

Bobby Jensen was the park manager's new stepson. Smiling back, Karen told him, "A fiddle case that went into the water down by the footbridge."

"Oh, boy. That sucks. Maybe I can help." Bobby swung down. "Did that guy trip and lose his fiddle?"

About to tell the boy to move on, Karen stopped. "What guy?"

"The guy on the trail the other day. He was kinda old."

Karen took a deep breath. Maybe without a case, they still had a case. "Bobby, this is really important. I want you to call your mom and get her okay to make a statement for me."

His nose wrinkled. "A statement? I thought I'd help you with the case."

"You are. Kind of like when your mom helped us with the case a while back."

"No, I mean the fiddle case." He pointed down the creek. "When I put a stick in the water, it always fetches up at the beaver dam at the bend."

CHAPTER 33

J UST WHEN MAREK THOUGHT THERE'D be a revolt, as Kuhl rose to his feet, words of undoubted dismissal on his tongue, the door opened, and Karen strode in.

"I'm so sorry, Mr. Kuhl." She looked harried and grim. Marek's hopes went splat. "I got held up longer than I'd hoped."

Kuhl slowly sat. "Very well. I'll give anyone a break after dealing with the press."

She turned to Marek and gave him nothing. "Let's get this done. Have you gone over his previous statements with him? No? All right, let's do it."

As if sensing their despondency, Kuhl's own mood—or at least his boredom—seemed to lift. "I'm at your disposal."

They went through the statements, and nothing differed appreciably, except perhaps in wording. "So, to wrap up, you neither knew Birchard, nor had any contact with him, other than listening to his performance, much less had any reason to kill him?"

"That is correct."

"All right. We've got some follow-up questions." Karen looked apologetic. "In the course of our investigation, we have to ask some uncomfortable ones. Such as... finances."

He looked amused. "Mine are fine, thanks. If you're looking for desperation, try Saul, who your detective tells me is in your jail."

"He is. But only pending inquiries. Which is what we're doing here. So... profit. You profited from tipping the media to Legrande's music."

That hitched the cool smile. "Did I?"

"Phone records are not a difficult thing to access, Mr. Kuhl," Karen said wearily. "Please just answer the question. I've had enough questions thrown in my face lately."

"My apologies. Very well. I admit I left a tip for your local newshound. I found his broadcasts rather amusing in a sort of Prairie Home Companion way."

Marek pursed his lips. "You can't get his broadcast in the park. How did you learn of it?"

Kuhl shrugged elegantly. "I mentioned to one of the workshop attendees that I was curious about the a cappella group that Birchard sang in. The one that was supposed to open Friday night. Someone tipped me that YRUN was running around-the-clock reruns of some of their performances as a tribute. So I drove into Reunion and picked up some butterhorns at a place called Milstead's Bakery and listened. They are... were... quite good. Excellent, even. The group, as well as the butterhorns."

Marek eased into the next question with nonchalance. "How long have you known that Birchard was Legrande?"

The long face went blank. But not before Marek saw the truth. Unfortunately, a recognition deep in someone's eyes wasn't admissible in court.

"Pardon?" Kuhl pulled his ear. "Did you say... Hal Birchard was really... Trick Legrande?" When he got a nod, he shook his head. "I find that impossible to believe. Are you trying for some kind of Plains humor I'm not aware of? Because I don't get the punchline."

Karen gave Marek an inquiring look.

"You already admitted you knew." Marek tapped the drawing on the table. "You said it was easy. Same shape. And that you didn't even need that to confirm. Same musical signature."

Kuhl's eyes darted back and forth, searching for a way out. Though the man didn't know it, he was being videotaped, as well as recorded—by the little eye Blake Halvorsen had rigged for them a while back with another killer who'd expected nothing out of rural policing but bumbling.

"Did I? Obviously, I meant the song 'Plain Sight' triggered that shape, not Birchard's fiddle. A slip of the tongue... I believe I was distracted by a text message when you asked." He gave a wry smile. "And I don't believe synesthesia is admissible evidence in court. What could I possibly have as a motive to kill Birchard... or even Legrande, if indeed he rose from the dead?"

Marek knew that this was crucial. "Because you needed him to stay dead. Alive, he could re-record those old songs you own the rights to—with better equipment, better talent."

Karen pressed the point. "And with all your new licensing deals to the old music, you're sunk."

Shock melted into blankness then a careless shrug. "I've weathered many storms, Sheriff."

"Not this one," Karen said. "I talked to a few in the business. They all said that independent musicians are eating into the profit margins."

Kuhl's eyes flashed. "No independent can sustain a career without already being boosted by a label, by distribution, by backing."

"That's an old tune, a dead tune," Marek said and saw the flicker. "It may not be immediate, but it's already started. I've seen the stats."

"There will always be those who line up to sign a label. Just ask Rad Wilson." That hint of anger slipped out, just as it had with Marmo. "And I could sign that boy, Josh Bolvin, in a heartbeat."

"But could you keep him?" Marek asked mildly. "Because Legrande was warning him off."

"Of Saul," he corrected then bit his lip. "Or so I would assume. Any would do the same." Kuhl made a show of looking at his watch. "Look, you've asked your uncomfortable questions, but you have no case."

With a glance, Marek passed the baton back to Karen.

"Actually..." Karen opened the door and held out a hand, waiting, Two Fingers handed over a large evidence bag. She took it, closed the door, and set it on the table. "We do."

After pulling on gloves from her back pocket, she opened the bag. And she pulled out a case—not just any damp and mud-smeared case, which Marek had half expected, but clearly *the* case, complete with scarlet velvet from the torn top.

Almost, Marek missed the utter shock on the man's face. But the video would show it.

"And this is...?" he asked as it was laid out.

"I would think you'd recognize a fiddle case," Karen said. "Especially this one, which you carried down the trail to dispose of in the creek after you killed Legrande."

Kuhl just shook his head sadly. "I don't understand your obsession with me, Sheriff, when you've got Saul down in lockup. If anyone disposed of the case, it was him."

"You don't ask why a fiddle case is significant," Marek murmured and was gratified to see the man actually close his eyes for a moment.

But when Kuhl opened them, he'd recovered once more. "I may not be a detective, but I'm not stupid. All the news reports agree that Legrande was garroted with a steel string. While I had not heard the case was missing, that it was found... Well, that's its own story."

And once again, Kuhl had said Legrande, not Birchard. Not significant in itself. Add it up?

Karen smiled at him. "We have two witnesses who saw you with the case."

"They couldn't have, since I didn't have it." He spoke smoothly, no doubt thinking they were lying to him. For all Marek knew, Karen was lying about one witness, as he only knew about Rad, but he didn't think she was. No reason to.

"First, Rad Wilson saw you. Ah, that hits, doesn't it. She's told us you offered her a contract in exchange for keeping quiet."

"That girl is delusional. And if you can produce said contract, I'll eat my hat."

"In addition," Karen went on, "a boy saw you with a case, walking on the trail."

"I didn't..." He bit his lip.

"Didn't see him? He was up a tree, a favorite spot of his, by the creek. At the time, he didn't think anything of it, because of the festival. Only when he saw my officers dragging the creek did he tell them what he'd seen. He picked you out cold." Karen waved at the case. "My officers found the case washed up against a beaver dam. The rock you put in there from the footings of the bridge wasn't heavy enough to sink the case for long. There was enough of an air pocket that it floated down."

With what looked like a lot of control, Kuhl stayed cool. "Lying to a suspect is a well-tried technique, but it does get old, Sheriff. Please, move on."

"Certainly. Being from the big bad city where they often use video, perhaps you are unaware that it is also common in rural areas... to mount trail cameras that are triggered by motion. There's one by the footbridge. We have video of you leaning down to the creek and pushing the case in."

Now he looked wry again. "If you actually had such a video, I'd be sitting in your jail instead of Saul. And I would have been there since day one. Nice try, though."

Karen shook her head, and with her gloved hand, she opened the case. "As you can see, there's an empty packet that held a metal string of the same exact thickness as the one used in the murder. You'll notice the bloodstained gloves you used are gone. They're on their way to DCI. You'd know to wear gloves, of course, as does anyone with half a brain. It's amazing what they can do these days, though, making a

DNA signature out of a few skin cells." She paused, a silent beat with a kicker resolution. "From *inside* the gloves."

Almost, Marek felt sorry for the man as that sank in. Though it might not pan out, there was a good chance it would. Marek leaned forward. "It's not about just one thing, Mr. Kuhl. It's a signature." Now Marek gave the man a wry smile. "A sum made up of choices, conscious and unconscious, that betray the killer—and they all point one way."

Kuhl gave the very faintest of nods. "I think I'm done."

"I think you are, too." Karen closed the case with a snap. "You're sunk."

"I meant," Kuhl said with a twist of his mouth that showed no humor, "that I will now invoke my right to silence—and an attorney."

So they'd get no confession. Marek hadn't really expected one.

No real reason for the man *not* to take his case to trial. Convictions for both first- and second-degree murder carried life terms in South Dakota. Only difference was that first degree could carry the death penalty, and Marek didn't think Kuhl premeditated the murder, just yielded to temptation. Everything he'd worked for could be lost if Legrande didn't stay dead. So why not make sure?

If Marek were in Kuhl's shoes, he'd take the mercy killing tack. The grateful dead. He'd thought Legrande was dead after the electrocution, or as close to it as made no difference to a musician—maybe incapable of playing music, of hearing it. Maybe that spin would even work, and he'd end up doing time for manslaughter. Or maybe they'd persuade everyone that Marmo was the real killer, and Kuhl would get off altogether, but Marek doubted that.

Despite the meandering chords, they'd found the melody, and a Dakota jury would, too. The only dead tune was an old tune that never died—murder never paid.

CHAPTER 34

A FTER SENDING OUT A MEDIA alert that she was holding a press conference on the Birchard homicide at four o'clock sharp, Karen called Blake Halvorsen.

"You'll want to make sure you're at my press conference," she told him without preamble. She was picking up Larson's habits. Though at least she spoke in semi-complete sentences. "With bells on—and all the whistles. It's going to be big. Bring down a full crew."

Blake hummed. "They'll spring me for a local scoop, but I'm not sure about the full crew. There's an active-shooter situation going down here in Sioux Falls at the metal-fabrication plant. Can you give me a hint?"

"Let's just say that you'd better get your tickets to the Big Jammer Music Festival finale tonight. They'll be scarce. Very."

"More music from Legrande?" That spiked his voice. "Not just that 'Plain Sight'?"

Karen wasn't going to give him the lead. "Just be there. Both places. Bye."

And she clicked off. She debated whether to give Nails a heads-up and finally did text him to make sure he had his digital ears tuned to the courthouse steps. But she did not text the same to the Twin Cities newspaper reporter Bates McLean. Let his arrogant affiliate TV reporter, who'd departed in disgust over the slow pace of rural *everything,* stew in his missed scoop.

The wonder was that somehow, some way, they'd kept Hal Birchard's true identity under wraps for so long. Of course, she still had Marmo and Rad Wilson stashed in the jail, though as much to protect them from the press as anything else. Though their stay was entirely voluntary, she'd let both of them know that charges would be pending before any immunity deals were on offer. But they'd bonded during a joint jam session of gloating while a silent and stoic Kuhl had been booked.

A trio of dissonance. The devil's triad. If Rad Wilson hadn't tampered with the amp, if Marmo hadn't pushed the mic and left Legrande lying on the ground, and if Kuhl hadn't yielded to impulse to make a problem go away... Legrande would be making his bow for himself tonight, instead of Josh Bolvin in his stead.

Karen took a call from The Seasons then made a few more calls of her own. She'd sent Marek off to retrieve his daughter for more Dad-time. No point in making him or the rest of her roster, other than those needed on shift, stay. She'd given Seoul, in particular, stern orders to hit the sheets before the concert tonight, when all of her deputies were slated to help with crowd control.

For the press conference itself, Karen didn't need backup. In fact, she just might enjoy playing on center stage, for once.

At four o'clock sharp, she walked out into the sunshine, glad for the wind to stir the air that edged toward humid from the earlier drizzle. She nodded at the small cache of press. Mostly second-stringers. Let them have their day. She didn't need the bigs of the business to get the word out. Fewer had come than earlier—when the big news hadn't been the death but the music. Now it was going to be the death of the musician. But there was Blake... with a bell on and a whistle on the camera. A big satellite van backed him. Full crew. He looked worried.

Barely, she kept her face bland. "Thank you for coming on this fine afternoon," she told them. "As you know, we have had a recent homicide under my jurisdiction at Grove Park's Big Jammer Music Festival. I'm here to announce we have made an arrest in that case." She paused, waited until they unconsciously strained forward. Kuhl really did know his stuff—too bad he'd had the bad taste to snuff the golden egg. "We have taken into custody Anton Kuhl of Kuhl Records in Los Angeles, California."

That brought surprised murmurs and a shouted question from a shiny new reporter from Sioux City, which she ignored. She waited for the hubbub to subside before leaning back into the mic. She wanted this as clear as a bell: "For the unlawful and willful murder of Trick Legrande."

At the awkward silence that greeted that, Blake actually looked sorry for her. He lifted his hand—and his voice—apologetically. "Um... you mean, Sheriff Mehaffey, for the murder of Hal Birchard?"

Karen looked straight into the cameras held by the crew at his side. "No, Mr. Halvorsen, I mean music legend Patrick 'Trick' Legrande..." Once again, she paused. "...who assumed the identity of Hal Birchard after the latter died on his boat in the Caribbean decades ago."

Oh, how fun it was, seeing the press scramble, frantically texting and calling in to their media hubs. Predictably, Kuhl was lost in the firestorm that followed. As was Birchard.

She outlined the case and the conclusions as succinctly as she could.

The Sioux City reporter still looked skeptical. "But there was an autopsy on Legrande, correct?"

"There was, but not up to today's standard." She gave him a tight smile. "I'm sure that any conspiracy theorist worth his salt today would have shredded it in mere milliseconds. No dental, no prints as the fingertips were too bloated, mostly just circumstance and a tattoo of Wild Abandon over his heart. One that Hal Birchard was known to carry as attested to—very reluctantly, I might add—by Birchard's sister. Not to mention, Veterans Affairs confirms that Hal Birchard was diagnosed with terminal liver cancer and given six months to a year to live. He refused all treatment. Apparently, he and Legrande hooked up in San Juan and, though it has yet to be confirmed, concocted the scheme so that Legrande, who was a hero of Birchard's, could live life again on his own terms."

The reporter pursed his lips, nodded. "Did Kuhl confess to the murder?"

"No, he has not confessed, but we have solid evidence, including forensic, witness, and video that ties him to the murder." Once again, she summarized the case.

"What was the motive?" asked a pimply-faced reporter from Omaha.

"In Kuhl's mind—and his pocketbook—Legrande was better off dead." Briefly, she discussed the licensing deals and the somewhat-precarious nature of Kuhl's finances.

Blake stepped forward as the usual, and expected, questions ebbed. "As Legrande lived for decades after his supposed death, does this mean that there is more music?"

The other reporters looked at him like, *Why didn't I think to ask that?* Blake was a natural.

"I can only speak to music written before his supposed death. And yes, there is a stack of it, found in a locked cabinet in his home. I imagine there is more, but I can't confirm at this time. As he had his own studio in his basement, he may have done solo recordings. I can tell you that he arranged and sang with a local a cappella group." She glanced up kitty-corner at Nails's hideout. "Our local newsman, Nails 'Rusty Nails' Nelson of YRUN has recordings of those. I'm sure he'd be happy to hear from you. Also..." She paused again. "A selection of the pre-Birchard music, including

'Plain Sight,' will be played live by Josh Bolvin and his band at tonight's finale."

She started to move back from the mic.

"Is Danielle Mehaffey still the heir to all this wealth of music?" Once again, Blake beat the others to a question they hadn't thought of yet. "And what will you, as trustee, do about the rights to that music going forward?"

Very good questions. "Yet to be resolved." She checked her watch. My, time flew when she'd been having fun. Looking back up, she said, "But I will tell you this. I will do everything in my power to make sure that Legrande's music, both old and new, hits the airwaves." She paused to smile. "Rock on."

When other reporters began to pepper her with follow-up questions that she couldn't answer, she held up a hand. "Sorry, it's been fun, but I have to wrap it up. I'm due in court at five. If you know Judge Rudibaugh at all, you'll know that it's my life—or at least my badge—if I'm late."

She caught Blake's grin as she turned. She gave him a subtle thumbs-up before he began his own live summary of events, suitably solemn and sans bell as he nailed his big break—a broadcast that would undoubtedly go not just national but international.

As she walked back into her empty office, her phone pinged.

Knew something was off-key in Eda. Dickwad TV reporter. Hat tip to Halvorsen. He want a job?

She texted Bates McLean back: *You can't have him. Yet.*

Then Karen powered off and pocketed the phone as she sprinted up the stairs to the courtroom.

Was Lianne Mehaffey going to show?

CHAPTER 35

THE FIRST THING KAREN SAW as she entered the courtroom was the judge, staring pointedly at the large wall clock on the wall just above her head.

She craned her head back to read it—and hoped it wouldn't hit her on the head if she was late. As the second hand had just clicked over the hour, she didn't think that his pointed look was fair. But she sucked up the sulk. "Sorry, Judge. I would have been here earlier, but I had to fill in the press on our arrest in the Legrande matter."

That shot up the patrician brow over the incongruous bulbous red nose that had given him the nickname Judge Rudy—though never, *ever* in his presence. "I am surprised they let you go."

"I insisted." Karen finally took in the occupants. She thought the entire Fill-er-Up clientele—and its chief cook and bottle washer, Cookie—had made the trek into Reunion. By the number of crossed arms and jutted chins, Karen had some fences to mend, because they looked like a mean jury.

Aptly, Danielle and Harlan were seated at the table for the prosecution. The judge nodded to the defendant's table. "Sheriff."

Karen took it, but she hoped this wasn't going to be an adversarial proceeding. What she didn't see was Lianne Mehaffey, which would have guaranteed to make it one.

She let herself relax until the judge asked, "Where is the mother?"

Everyone looked around, as if expecting to see her hidden somewhere in the woodwork. Karen hoped that the judge wasn't going to suspend the hearing.

To prevent that, Karen spoke up. "I know where Lianne Mehaffey was last seen, but I need to confirm she's still there. With your permission?" Karen held up her turned-off phone. He eyed it with distaste but nodded.

As quickly as she could, Karen brought up the number of the Motor-In and got a gum-smacking receptionist. "Room 213? Oh, yeah. Checked out. Actually, she never checked in, turns out. But she's gone."

Dammit. That meant Lianne could still show. Though by arriving late, she'd tick off the judge, so there was that, at least. "Did she happen to say where she was going?"

That received a laugh that turned into a cough. Hopefully, the woman hadn't just swallowed her gum. "Yeah, she got herself checked into real plush digs downtown."

God looked after fools, apparently. "She hooked up with somebody?"

"Somebody got her hooked up—or should I say, cuffed."

Karen sat up straighter. "Arrested?"

At the other table, Danielle put her head in her hands, while Harlan patted her on the back. Karen wasn't sure if it was in sympathy or congratulation.

"Oh, yeah. Big doings last night." The woman apparently blew a bubble, as it popped with a loud smack. "A sting. Cop cars all over the place. They hauled off a paddy wagon full. Your Room 213 was dragged off kicking and screaming, saying she had 'rights.'"

"That's her. Thanks."

"No problemo. Maybe things'll quiet down. For a bit."

Karen heard the skepticism and agreed. Crime in such places stopped for no man—or woman. After hanging up, Karen pulled up another contact, this time to a former colleague in Sioux Falls who now worked at the jail. She got the scoop on Lianne—in exchange for a spot at the concert that night.

Judge Rudy frowned down at her. "Sheriff? In your own good time?"

Saying she'd be in touch later, Karen hung up. "Lianne Mehaffey was booked into the Minnehaha County jail last night on charges of possession, soliciting, and resisting arrest. She's not expected to make bail and will likely be held for some considerable time, given her priors."

And just how much of that almost-predictable result was because Karen had slipped Lianne some money? And tacitly let her take the room Marmo had vacated? If she'd brought Lianne back to Reunion, none of it. But she'd live with that guilt if it meant protecting Danielle's future.

Judge Rudy leaned back in his leather chair. "Very well. The petition stated that Lianne Mehaffey was not a suitable candidate for guardianship of her daughter. The state of Nebraska concurs. I also concur."

Well, that was a relief.

The judge turned his attention to Danielle. "Ms. Mehaffey."

Danielle wrinkled her nose, and the diamond nose stud—probably the least likely of her collection of sparkles to offend—glinted. "Yes, sir." Harlan leaned over and whispered in her ear. She reddened. "Your Honor."

Judge Rudy nodded in automatic acknowledgment. Woe be unto anyone who forgot his honors. "Please tell me, in your own words—not those carefully crafted by your... sister-in-law, which seems difficult to believe—as to why you are ready to begin life as an adult at the tender age of sixteen." He paused. "You may rise to address the court."

Danielle froze in her chair, and Karen bit her lip. She should've prepared the girl for this possibility. Judge Rudy was, in his own way, testing the girl's mettle. He'd tested Karen's far too much, and she'd often come up short, so she felt for the girl.

"Buck up, girl," Cookie growled from the gallery in her smoke-cured voice. "You've been through worse."

Nodding, the girl jumped to her feet. "Your Honor, I don't have any big words or accomplishments. I don't even have a diploma, but I'm working on my GED. And I work hard"—the chorus in the gallery silently sang her praises with vigorous head-nodding—"and I support myself. That's important to me."

Judge Rudy pursed his lips. "Yet you may be looking at a large windfall."

"Maybe, maybe not. I won't say I don't care, because that'd be a lie. I'd planned to go into the Army as soon as they'd take me and become a medic, like my brother. Like him, I want to be a doctor." Her chin jutted. "I'm not stupid. I'll work hard. And I'll do it, whatever it takes. Only... now maybe I can go to college after I get my GED, instead of the Army."

Danielle shot Karen an uncertain look, as if afraid that she would disapprove of not following Patrick, or Karen herself, into the Army. "It's a good plan."

The judge shifted some papers before looking back at Danielle with an impassive face. "You have had a difficult life for one so young."

"I guess. Many people have let me down." Danielle didn't look at Karen, but she felt it nonetheless. "I didn't know that I had a single decent relative anywhere... until one of my foster parents got a notice about Patrick's death. I thought he must've known about me, or his wife did, but didn't want me."

"That's not true," Karen protested, risking the wrath of Judge Rudy. "If I'd known you existed, I'd have taken you in, Danielle. I swear that."

For a moment, as Danielle turned to look at her, they were alone in the courtroom. Doubt was clear on her young face. "You gave up Eyre."

"Yes, when I was committed to the Army, scared, and

afraid I'd make my dad lose his job. I wasn't as grown up as I thought—or as grown up as you. But by the time you came around, I had a good job in Sioux Falls, my own place, and a lot of emptiness in my life with Patrick in a coma. I believed he would come out of it. I was wrong. I might have let go sooner if I'd had you to hang on to."

"As touching as that may be," Judge Rudy said in a neutral tone, "the fact is, Ms. Mehaffey, that you had no one but a mother who liked heroin more than you and a foster care system that seems to have also failed you."

The girl seemed surprised that a government official would admit that. She nodded. "Every time I thought it would work out, like the one set of decent fosters who wanted to adopt me? Lianne shows up, all cleaned up, and yanks me back into that yo-yo with Social Services. On and off again."

Now the judge clasped his hands and let his disapproval show. "You ran away. Neither legal nor advisable."

"I was old enough to support myself." Danielle didn't back down. "I had family up here. I *wanted* family, Your Honor. *Real* family. Where they have to take you in. When I found out I had a brother, a dead brother, I thought maybe his wife..." Danielle sent another uncertain look at Karen then back at the judge "... that maybe I could meet her, at least."

His lips twitched. "Only to find she was the law."

"Yes, sir. Your Honor." Chagrin covered her face. "I decided to wait it out until I was old enough to come to court and make my case. But... I got kidnapped."

"And Sheriff Mehaffey and her men—and one remarkable young woman in Deputy Durr—worked tirelessly to free you." His eyes went over her heard. "And your customers and friends at the diner, they searched long into the nights, worrying for you, praying for you."

Her lips trembled, and she nodded.

"In a word, Ms. Mehaffey, *they* are your family." He let that sink in. "But collectively, they can't be your guardian." He paused to consider. "Would you accept either Harlan Pederson or Karen Mehaffey as your guardian?"

Disappointment flooded her face. But Danielle recovered. "Yes, Your Honor."

"Which would you prefer?"

Danielle looked down at the elderly man who had been her champion all along. Then she looked over at Karen and held her gaze for a very, very long moment. "Either."

Judge Rudy pursed his lips. "Petition granted." He pounded his gavel.

"Um... Your Honor?"

His brow lifted. "Yes, Ms. Mehaffey?"

"Which is my guardian?"

"Neither." He paused a beat. "You're a free woman."

Danielle looked blank even as the gallery celebrated with handslaps and backslaps. None of them were brave enough to risk getting thrown out by cheering.

"Oh, but you asked..." Danielle trailed off, obviously still confused.

"You showed remarkable control, Ms. Mehaffey. I like to see that in an adult." The judge gave a pointed look at Karen. "And regrettably, I rarely do."

Great. She'd been put in her place—which was apparently several years of maturity behind a sixteen-year-old girl. So be it.

"As you have also, Sheriff Mehaffey, though belatedly, shown restraint in not pestering me to death over a warrant that I did not see fit to give you, I will now grant that warrant to unseal the codicil of Hal Birchard's... or Patrick Legrande's... will." That did elicit gasps from those who recognized the name, but they subsided under Judge Rudy's hard stare. He turned his gaze back on Karen. "In fact, I already have and obtained same, as I wished to read them before I ruled on the petition at hand. I believe Ms. Mehaffey will also find them of interest."

Judge Rudy handed two faxed papers to the court reporter to deliver. "Court is adjourned."

CHAPTER 36

A S THE FILL-ER-UP GALLERY CLEARED the benches to congratulate the newly minted adult after the judge had left the chambers, Karen went back to the table and perused the two documents. The first was from Legrande and had a somewhat legal air to it.

To Whom It May Concern:

If my will is at any time contested over my identity and my right to bequeath my estate both real and personal under that name or any other, I make the following statement before a notarized official.

My true name is Patrick "Trick" James Legrande, and I have for many years assumed the identity of Harold "Hal" Lucien Birchard, with his full knowledge and consent as the enclosed document attests. While the act itself may have been illegal, I have never shirked any fiduciary responsibility to any government under that name or any other.

I met Hal Birchard at the Dive 'n Dirty in San Juan, Puerto Rico, after he was hit over the head by a drunken fan of mine who didn't like his take on "Washed Up," a signature song of Wild

Abandon, my former band. Hal refused treatment and also refused to press charges, something that impressed me. I bought him a drink and asked him if he often played that song, and he told me it had saved him at a hard time in his life—when he was forced to join the Navy.

In a way I can't explain, we connected immediately, partly based on our shared love of music but also hard beginnings with hard endings. Eventually, I discovered that he was dying. I offered to take him on board my boat for a final tour. When he learned that I didn't intend to publish any new songs because of S&M Records and the hold Saul Merlini had on future work, Hal Birchard offered me an out. Originally, I was reluctant, but I eventually agreed.

Hal Birchard breathed his last as sunset fell over troubled waters. I gave him last rites, as he requested, though I don't know if they are valid. He never pretended to be a saint, but he died with dignity and with a gift I can never repay. But I did promise to seek out any offspring of his half-sister, Lianne Mehaffey, and offer any help that I could if I deemed them worthy. I have been remiss in doing so until a couple years ago, only to discover that I was too late to be of any use to Lianne's son, Patrick Mehaffey. In the last month, I have since learned of Lianne's young daughter, Danielle Mehaffey, who I now make the prime beneficiary of my will, in accordance with that debt. As I have seen the results of too much money without wise guidance, I appoint Patrick Mehaffey's widow and current sheriff, Karen

Okerlund Mehaffey, as trustee—as her family has a reputation for honoring their responsibilities.

If any remain of my birth family in Kansas City, which I doubt, as I have never been contacted by any since I left that city with my bandmates who filled that void of family, I hereby and with full knowledge do expressively bar them from profiting in any way, shape, or form from my estate.

Patrick James Legrande aka Hal Birchard

The codicil was dated exactly a month past. Karen set it aside and looked at the other, which was a copy of a tattered sheet torn from a spiral notebook. Given all the small folds, the sheet must have been carried folded up, likely in a wallet.

I, Harold Lucien Birchard, give to my friend Patrick Legrande all that I have to leave in this world—my name. My only request is that, if he returns stateside, that he find out if there are any children or grandchildren of my half-sister, Lianne Mehaffey, still living. And if he's in a position to do so and thinks they're worthy of it, that he help them pursue a better life than either of us had.

I do know that my sister had at least one child. I visited Lianne soon after her son, Patrick—named after Trick Legrande—was removed from her custody and placed in foster care.

Karen heard a gasp behind her and glanced back. Danielle was reading over her shoulder. "She lied. Lianne. He *did* visit her. She said she'd never seen him again."

Karen almost asked if that surprised her, but she held her tongue and kept reading.

I told her then, that so long as she chose drugs over family, she was none of mine. Of course, I completely ignored young Patrick, the most innocent of all of us. If I had thought about him, I might have decided I wasn't a suitable guardian, and rightly so, but that never even occurred to me.

I've not lived a sainted life. I've drunk too much, smoked too much weed, and generally led the life of a rolling stone. That's one of the reasons I told myself that I had no business trying to contact Patrick or any other kin I might have. My family, if I had any, was music. It sustained me, both body and soul, and gave me faith again—that this wayward son could come home again.

But home is now to be the sea. A fitting end for a washed-up soul.

A shaky hand had signed it with his full name and the date.

"That's so sad," Danielle said. "He sounds like he'd have lots of stories to tell. And music to play. I'll bet he was good, just never had a break. Do you think Patrick would've liked him?"

Karen thought of her red-haired, determined, and relentlessly positive husband. "Yes, I believe he would. I'm sorry Hal never met Patrick." Karen hesitated. "Are you okay, Danielle... about Lianne?" She'd almost said "your mother," but Danielle was officially an adult now, and Lianne was... Lianne. A child full of destructive and unchecked needs in a woman's body. She'd never gone beyond sixteen—or perhaps her terrible twos, given her latest run-ins.

"I'm good." Danielle shrugged with hard-earned

nonchalance. "She is... what she is. Now I know more of *why* she is. But I won't make her mistakes."

That made Karen smile. "No, you'll make others, but that's how you learn. Some never do. Speaking of which, I think we'd better have a talk with a man who's made more than his fair share."

Taking Danielle down to the interview room, Karen had Tammy bring Marmo up from the jail. His rumpled suit was stained with sweat, but he seemed sober, at least. Karen wasn't sure that was a good thing.

"Mr. Marmo, this is Danielle Mehaffey." Karen indicated her young sister-in-law. "We're here to make a deal over the rights to her uncle's music, to avoid an expensive court fight."

That perked him up. He even straightened his tie. "Is that right? Best thing I've heard all week." A gleam appeared in the bloodshot eyes. "What's your offer?"

Trying to look earnest, Karen propped her elbows on the table. "How about a shot at redemption?"

Marmo snorted. "Doesn't pay the bills. No deal. We're talking major rights here." Excitement animated his face, and Karen got an inkling of how and why he'd sold so many the dream—then sold them out. "You need somebody with connections in the business to exploit those rights. I can do that."

Karen dropped the charity angle. "Like you did for all those who complained to the Better Business Bureau? I don't think so."

Obviously unwilling to give up, Marmo turned to Danielle. "Look, you'll be legal soon and can make your own decisions."

Danielle smiled. "I'm already legal."

"All the better." Marmo hitched his chair closer to the girl. "Legrande's rights are golden. Whatever your heart desires, you can have. A house in LA, a yacht, whatever. We're going to hit it rich, you and I."

Danielle just stared at him as if he were off his rocker.

"Leave off the spin, Marmo," Karen told him. "Danielle can't make those decisions, even if she was fool enough to fall for your pitch. Which she's not. I'm the trustee as long as I live or she hits forty."

Marmo turned back to Karen, his eyes bugging out. "How is that legal?"

"Care to challenge it in court?"

His face fell. That took money, which he didn't have. That was her leverage. But then he smiled, no doubt realizing that he could get a lawyer without a retainer, given the potential payoff in visibility if nothing else. Especially if it became a precedent-setting case.

Karen pressed forward. "Here's the deal. If you agree to relinquish all rights—which you'd have to fight me to get anyway—you can take a cool mil to the bank. Take it, Mr. Marmo... Merlini." She wanted him to remember that he'd already crashed and burned once before. "You won't be rich, but if you stash the nest egg with a fiduciary financial advisor and keep your hands off the principal, you'll be set for that retirement you claimed was all you wanted from Legrande."

Before Marmo could spew more about rights and how much they might potentially bring, Karen continued, hardening her voice. "I am not a budding musician on your defunct label that you can exploit, drop, then piss on for future rights. I haven't signed anything with you, nor will I, without my own lawyer." Seeing the gleam return, she clarified. "An *IP* attorney. Perhaps you've heard of him? Daryl Link in Los Angeles." That knocked the gleam off. "He called me, asked if I was interested in his services. For a fee, not a cut. That was Legrande's and his bandmates' mistake. I don't need you, Marmo. You need me. Because there's enough money in the trust to do what I believe Legrande meant to do—to fight you in court for his rights. He'd have won. And I will, if you don't take this deal, here and now. You know it, I know it. Take the mil, up front."

He threw up his hands. "Where can I live on a mere mil?"

"You've been living on less—on credit." She gave him a tight smile. "San Juan, perhaps? You might want to outrun the bad publicity that's going to hit. Again. But at least if you take the deal, you can spin it that you graciously relinquished the rights for a mere pittance."

The gleam reappeared. "What's to seal the deal? A handshake?"

A handshake agreement was sacred in the Dakotas—but not to outsiders. "Oh, no. It'll all be in writing. And reviewed by Link. If nothing else, I've learned that you're absolutely right."

"Am I?"

"Music is a brutal business."

He deflated. "Then I'd better change my name. Again. Because I'll never live it down, that I let some hick... rural... sheriff beat me at the wheel-and-deal."

"A million dollars is rich," Danielle exclaimed, finally letting loose. Maybe she thought Karen was pissing away her inheritance, but lawyers would take more if they went to court. Link had assured her the trust would make up the million lost once they were no longer hamstrung by Marmo's claim.

"Take it from me, kid. It's peanuts." But wearily, Marmo nodded. "Deal."

♪♫♪

After she'd contacted Link to get the ball rolling, she let Marmo go. Danielle lingered at the table. "Can I... suggest stuff? I mean, about the money?"

Surprised and a bit dismayed, but willing to listen, Karen nodded. "Go ahead."

"I'd like to get a gravestone. For Hal, I mean. My uncle."

Karen felt her shoulders relax. "I believe he already has one. In San Juan." The epitaph, predictably, was "Washed Up."

"Under the wrong name. Should we bring him back?"

Karen thought about that. "Your choice, but I'd say no. The real question is, what about Legrande?"

"Maybe they should be together." Danielle frowned. "Or with his bandmates?"

"Or scattered to the winds. We don't have to decide right now." As Danielle hesitated, Karen braced herself. "Okay, what else?"

"I'd like to turn over Hal's... I mean, Legrande's... house and all the instruments and studio equipment in it to the Bolvins, especially Josh."

"All right. We can do that. At least anything not otherwise designated in the will."

"And Josh gets to tour the music first, before anybody else."

"All right."

Danielle's mouth kicked up. "And I want a mansion in LA and a yacht."

Karen opened her mouth on a laugh. "No."

Danielle mock pouted. "You're so strict." Then she shrugged. "All I want is a place of my own, a college education, and..."

"Yes?"

The girl smiled. "A ride."

Karen smiled back. Perfect. She got to her feet. "I think I can accommodate you there—and you don't even need to go through probate."

"Really? You can loan me that much? Cookie's sister's got a Ford Fusion for sale."

Karen looked at the girl in horror. "A Ford? No, not happening. We're a Chevy family." She crooked a finger. "Follow me."

As she'd prearranged with Gotsch, he'd dropped off the vintage red car at the back of the courthouse. No doubt he'd charge her an arm and a leg for it, too.

When Karen walked up to it, Danielle looked flabbergasted. "Is this... do you mean... *this*?!"

Not quite sure if the girl was delighted—or just the opposite, Karen stuck her hands in her back pockets. "I just thought you might like something from family—from Patrick. It was his Corvette. I've taken care of it, but it's not very practical as a backup for me when the Sub dies, as it invariably does. It's not the latest and greatest. And..." A thought struck. "...do you even drive a stick?"

That finally brought the girl's eyes back to her. "Harlan taught me."

Of course he had.

Danielle backtracked. "Just in case. You know, in an emergency, if he had a heart attack at the wheel. Or something."

Karen tucked her tongue in her cheek. "Uh huh." Then she said, "You don't have to take it, Danielle, if it's not your thing. You can get better, the latest and greatest, when things are settled."

Danielle snatched the keys from Karen's hand. "No, no, this is perfect. This is the best day *ever*." She climbed in, ran a hand over the dash, and switched on the radio. The Beach Boys' "Fun, Fun, Fun" blared out, and grinning, the girl took off. Good thing Karen had pulled some strings to get her a driver's permit, or she'd be contributing to the delinquency of a minor. Wait, no. No longer a minor.

Let her cruise into adulthood, Karen thought. If Danielle got pulled over... well, she had connections.

CHAPTER 37

P USHING ASIDE THE PAPERWORK SHE'D just completed, Karen looked up at the two men who sat stiffly on hardwood chairs in front of her desk.

Once again, she had to school her expression. "Gentlemen, I called you here to give you the results of our investigation into the death of... the warbler."

Karen reminded herself that this was deadly serious, to both men, and she needed to get it right.

"Kirtland's," Jack Aspin insisted, his body rigid, perched on the edge of the chair.

"Wilson's," Karl Fike countered, his arms crossed.

She pulled out a fax. "I've already had one case of mistaken identity in this county this week. I don't need another. So I expedited the case. The FBI has made their determination." Thankfully, Sommervold and Wintersgill had come through—for a price. "The bird is... or was..." Would she ever forget now, the power of the sound of silence? "Kirtland's."

For a full minute, no word was said.

"I *told* you so," Aspin said stiffly to a stunned Farmer Fike. "You killed a national treasure."

"Didn't mean to," Fike said, looking scared now, as well he might. Then he lifted his chin and glared at Aspin. "And not my fault. If you hadn't gone over the boundary line—"

"Gentlemen, the deed is done. All that's left is the consequences." Karen pulled on her lip as the two men turned back to her. "Mr. Fike, the maximum penalty for a violation of the Endangered Species Act is a fifty-thousand-dollar fine and a year in prison."

"Prison?" The word barely made it out of a strangled throat.

And was surprisingly echoed by a horrified Aspin. Apparently, while the avid birder felt justice needed to be served, he wasn't willing to go quite that far. Perhaps because of his own experience in the jail below.

"Yes, prison," she said severely. "However..."

"Yes?" Fike asked finally when she dragged it out.

"You are in luck, Mr. Fike. The United States Fish and Wildlife Service recently delisted the Kirtland's warbler from the endangered species list."

"What?" Aspin sputtered.

"It's a success story, apparently. One of few. Be grateful, both of you." Karen rose to her feet, looking down at the two men in varying states of shock—and relief—for different reasons. "I suggest that you two work out the cost of repairing the road and learn to be good neighbors. Mr. Fike, words are far less expensive than dynamite. Use them next time. Mr. Aspin, watch out for artistic license—it might not be viewed kindly by some." She checked her watch. "Whatever you decide to do, whether that's to ignore each other for the rest of your coexistence or have a cookout every Saturday, I hope you will keep me out of it in the future. Now, if you'll excuse me, I have a concert to get to."

She left the men still sitting in their respective corners. And she sang "whee, whee, whee" all the way to the park. Where she found Seoul guarding the gate—a first for the Big Jam. The gate, that is. Even now, an hour before the concert was to begin, the meadow was jam-packed.

Along the perimeter of trees, her men watched, along with a suspiciously large contingent of highway patrol, a Sioux Falls jailer, and The Seasons. Maybe they'd cancel each other out, summer and winter, and they'd all be treated to a perfect night. Scanning the crowd, she picked out Larson, his kids, and Jessica. They'd staked out lawn chairs a couple rows back from the stage. No empty chair awaited her nearby, alas.

"A hard ticket to get," Seoul said with a grin. "I've already had a dozen people try to pass off forgeries." She held out a hand. "Where's yours?"

"My forgery? Sorry, I left it at the office." Karen shook her head as Seoul made a face. "I sprang Rad Wilson and Marmo before I dealt with the warblers. Are they here?"

"Plenty of warblers." At Karen's long stare, Seoul held up her hands in surrender. "Rad's here." Seoul jerked a shoulder over toward the concession stand, where the heavy metal rocker and Marmo were in earnest conversation. "Is Marmo seriously looking to rep her?"

Grudgingly, Seoul said, "Rad wasn't all that bad. If she lost the attitude and hooked up with a good band and kept with it, she could make it."

Per the state's attorney, the girl would get an immunity deal, if not a record deal. Scared straight? Hard to tell. If music was her salvation, perhaps she'd make it, but that was up to her and luck. She doubted Marmo had the connections to do her much good. But at least Marmo would soon be out of Karen's hair and someone else's problem. She'd gladly pay him the million—every theoretical cent of it—to never see him again.

A thought struck her. "Was a winner ever announced for the Jam Off?"

Seoul nodded. "Yeah, the organizers awarded it to Birchard... or Legrande, I should say. The whole thing is dedicated to him—it's all his music, or arranged by him."

"What about you? Disappointed you're not opening?"

Seoul gave a wry smile. "I'm just a Wilson's warbler."

That brought Karen's head around. "Pardon?"

"I'm good but not great. Dime a dozen. Legrande was a Kirtland's. A natural. One of the most gifted musicians of his generation. At least his music will live on."

Karen would make sure of it. She started to move through the gate.

Seoul stopped her. "No ticket." When Karen opened her mouth, Seoul grinned. "You've got a reserved seat as a guest of honor." Seoul waved toward the front row, just off-center, where Marek, Nikki, and Becca sat in their lawn chairs, an unconventional but tight trio. And one solitary chair remained right next to them.

Taking her time, Karen sauntered up to the trio and took in a deep breath of summer air as she sat. "Ah, the smell of summer—bug spray and sunscreen, brats and beer. I'm glad that's all we've got to worry about tonight."

Marek gave her a strangely distracted smile. "Are we squared away?"

"The case? Yes, I've finished the paperwork, and it's in the state's attorney's hands. And Kuhl is in conference with his lawyer." Karen relaxed into the chair. "Instead of at this very pleasant evening's concert." She splayed out her legs. "I'm so ready to chill."

Becca looked up from her perch in her father's lap. She was blowing on her paper cup, making a deep, hollow sound, while on the other side, Em was doing the same while her mother, Penny Bolvin, added a higher pitch. Did they never stop the music in that family?

"Where are the Bolvin men?" Karen asked.

"Singing. Playing."

Karen rolled her eyes. "Forget I asked."

Sunset hit the battalion of white satellite vans that encircled the meadow, turning them into a ring of fire. Karen thought how different the night was compared to that after Legrande, as Hal Birchard, had died. All the world's a stage, she thought, and wondered if Josh Bolvin had any nerves left. And she suddenly felt some of her own. What if he screwed up? Froze? With all the world watching?

But it wasn't Josh Bolvin who opened the concert. Instead, his father walked up to the mic, flanked by his two brothers. Nate cleared his throat, and the crowd silenced.

"As you know, this concert is dedicated to our friend Hal Birchard. You can call him Trick Legrande, if you like, but to us, he was and always will be just Hal, part of the family. Our perfect fourth, our bass, our friend." Nate took out a pitch pipe from his pocket and softly blew into it, giving his brothers the starting note. "We're going to sing an original a cappella number that he wrote for our group, the Quartertones, but we're going to attempt it with just us three. You could call us the Try-Tones, if you like." Nate's smile flickered, caused by either grief or nerves. "The song is 'The Devil in Music.' And we've had a devil of a time with it, so you'll have to forgive any flubs."

Karen exchanged a look with Marek. The devil's interval. Tritones. Triads. Whatever the case, the three Bolvins did it justice. The complicated vocal piece had Nick thumping his own chest like a drum. Becca sat curled up against Marek, and Em against Penny, as the music soared over the meadow.

When they finished, to the roar of the crowd, the sun dipped beyond the horizon, and the rock concert began. Karen's nerves settled, along with the band's, as the music took over, took all.

The music was brilliant and full-throated, with a beat that had many hitting hand to lawn chair arm, or foot to grass. It was music to die for, she thought. But it shouldn't have been.

Trick Legrande should have had the last laugh—the last guitar riff that had the teenyboppers in the crowd squealing. When the band hit their finale, the crowd fell silent. The lyrics of "Plain Sight" washed over the crowd in lush chords and haunting undertones, the words especially poignant.

I'm hiding in plain sight
Doin' what I was meant
I'll never see your slight
So go ahead and rant

Because no matter your lie
I'll never let the music die

You'll take the money
And I'll take the fame
You won't see me
From beyond the grave
But you'll hear me
And the crowds will rave

Because no matter your lie
I'll never let the music die

As the music died, the stage went dark. People looked at each other in the dim light of the satellite vans that shot the music that would never die, around the world. Was it over? Then a voice cut through the night and through the sound of silence, deep and smooth, like butterscotch.

"Hello, darkness..."

A single spotlight, as if in blessing, hit a bowed head. A head of deep, dark color—with a devil's hint of trouble—and red.

Karen let out a silent breath. *Marek, my old friend.* She glanced to her left. Nikki now had Becca in her lap. No Marek. "How...?"

The question carried only as far as Nikki, who leaned over and whispered, "Marek went to pick up Becca, and the Bolvins shanghaied him. Like a little dogie, he said. He was shaking in his Blunnies all the way over."

Turning back, Karen watched another spotlight hit another head. Another note joined the first, and one by one, the four men added layers upon layers as they sang Simon and Garfunkel's "The Sound of Silence," which had to be one of the most haunting tunes ever written.

Karen felt tears well and didn't bother to brush them away as they slipped unashamedly down her face. As the song reached the ending, each head bowed, each spotlight winked off, until only one remained. One long, deep, almost subsonic wash of sound.

"...of silence."

The tension in that note, the deep well of it, made Karen's shoulders hunch as it slowly died into the night. Brilliant but unresolved. Perhaps no death was ever resolved. But one thing was, she thought, as the stage went dark again. For real, this time.

Marek was a natural. The perfect fourth.

AUTHOR'S NOTE

The Hardanger fiddle called "The Devil" in this book is fictitious but based on Helland's "The Troll," whereabouts currently unknown. Fiddle player Halvor Jøren brought it with him to the United States, where it disappeared.

CAST OF CHARACTERS

Aspin, Jack. Manager of the electronic recycling center in Reunion. His residence near the nature preserve adjoins cornfields owned by Karl Fike. Twin Cities native and avid birder.

Bakke, Jessica. Trainee of Dirk Larson at the South Dakota Division of Criminal Investigation (DCI) in Sioux Falls. Has a scar on her face from a violent assault.

Bechtold, Kurt. Senior deputy in the Eda County Sheriff's Office. Unmarried. Lives with his unmarried sister, Eva, who bakes goodies to stave off her many phobias.

Birchard, Harold "Hal" Lucien. Murder victim. Contestant at the Jam Off. Bass singer for the a cappella group Quartertones with the Bolvin brothers.

Bjorkland, Travis "Bork." Swing-shift deputy in the Eda County Sheriff's Office. Unmarried. A native of Minnesota.

Bolvin, Josh. Son of Nate Bolvin and grandson of Patty Bolvin. Teenage budding rock star from Reunion. Worked with Hal Birchard on a video of the song "Plain Sight" that went viral.

Bolvin, Nate. Accountant in Reunion. Father of Josh Bolvin. Member of the a cappella group Quartertones with his brothers and Hal Birchard.

Bolvin, Ned. Works at a feedstore in Reunion and on his family farm. Member of the a cappella group Quartertones with his brothers and Hal Birchard.

Bolvin, Nick. Works on the family farm outside of Reunion. Husband of Penny and father of Emily Bolvin, who is the best friend of Becca Okerlund. Childhood friend of Marek Okerlund. Member of the a cappella group Quartertones with his brothers and Hal Birchard.

Bolvin, Noel. Wrestling coach at Iowa. Former bass singer for the a cappella group Quartertones with his brothers.

Bolvin, Patty. Mother of Ned, Noel, Nate, Nick, and Norm (deceased) Bolvin. Lives with her son Nick on the family farm outside Reunion.

Cantor, Tricia. Pastor of the Congregational Church in Reunion. Former psychology professor from Chicago, Illinois, who lost her family in an accident. Informal profiler and consultant to the Eda County Sheriff's Office.

Connor, Archibald "Chee." Cousin of Laura Connor Russell and caretaker at Grove Park. Husband of Lori Jansen and stepfather of Bobby Jansen. Prefers to go just by the name Connor.

Connor, Lori Jansen. Helps run the trailer park near Grove Park. Mother of Bobby Jansen. Wife of Chee Connor.

Durr, Seoul. Newly hired nightshift deputy from Onawa near the Loess Hills in Iowa. Recent graduate of Briar Cliff in Sioux City with a double major in criminal justice and music. Daughter of Sheriff Kent Durr. Contestant at the Jam Off.

Fike, Jordan. Nightshift dispatcher and jailer for the Eda County Sheriff's Office.

Fike, Karl. Farmer from Fink who owns cornfields adjoining the residence of Jack Aspin near the now-defunct town of Dutch Corners. Uncle of Jordan Fike.

Halvorsen, Blake. Son of Sig and Lynn Halvorsen and fraternal twin of Lance. A mass communications major at the University of South Dakota in Vermillion. Works as a summer intern at a Sioux Falls TV station.

Halvorsen, Sig. Maternal cousin of Arne Okerlund and "uncle" of Karen Okerlund Mehaffey. Owns a butcher shop in Reunion and a small organic meatpacking plant. Husband of photographer Lynn Anders and father of fraternal twins Blake and Lance.

Hudson, Doc. Longtime family doctor who works in Reunion at the only medical clinic in Eda County.

Jansen, Bobby. Son of Lori Jansen and stepson of Chee Connor.

Johnson, Eyre. Archivist for the privately funded Eda County Archives housed in the old Carnegie Library in Reunion. Biological daughter of Karen Okerlund Mehaffey. Adopted by Karen's old basketball coach, Darrin Johnson, and his (now ex-) wife Professor Anne Leggett in Vermillion. After a fire destroyed her apartment, Eyre now lives with Karen at 22 Okerlund Road.

Knutsen, Axel. Eda County musician in his seventies who

sings barbershop, plays the trumpet and fiddle, and is a judge at the Jam Off.

Kuhl, Anton. Owner of Kuhl Records in Los Angeles, California. Owns the rights to the music of Trick Legrande and Wild Abandon. Judge at the Jam Off.

Lanski, Dr. A professor of music at the University of South Dakota in Vermillion. Specifically, he works at the National Music Museum (aka Shrine to Music) on campus and is an expert on traditional music and instruments such as the Hardanger fiddle.

Larson, Brandon. Teenage son of Agent Dirk Larson.

Larson, Dirk. Agent with the South Dakota Division of Criminal Investigation (DCI) in Sioux Falls. Divorced. Father of Madison and Brandon Larson. Formerly a homicide detective in Chicago, Illinois. Once a professional basketball prospect. In a tentative relationship with Karen Okerlund Mehaffey. Currently moving from Sioux Falls to Reunion.

Larson, Eleanor. Widowed mother of Mary Astrid Larson and grandmother of Agent Dirk Larson. Lives in Reunion with her great-grandchildren.

Larson, Madison "Maddie." Teenage daughter of Agent Dirk Larson. Star basketball player.

Legrande, Patrick "Trick" James. Famous songwriter and member of the rock band Wild Abandon. From Kansas City.

Lindstrom, Josephine. A transplant from West River (South Dakota) who married a man from Reunion. He died in Vietnam and she became a secretary for the Eda County Sheriff's Office. After initially retiring, she has returned to work part-time. A champion barrel racer.

Link, Daryl. Intellectual property attorney in Los Angeles, California.

Marek, Lenny. Deceased. A carpenter and abusive alcoholic. Married Vera Kubicek. Father of Jim Marek and Janina Marek and grandfather of Marek Okerlund, who strongly resembles him. Killed two men in bar brawls. Convicted of manslaughter for the first and murder for the second. After being sentenced to life in prison for the latter, he jumped from the third floor of the courthouse, killing himself. Like his grandson, he likely had severe dyslexia.

Marmo, Sal. Manager of musical talent for hire. Judge at the Jam Off. From Califonria.

Martin, Krissy. Daughter of Old Man Martin and Judy Martin. Widow of Dale Hansen. Ex-wife of Troy Ringold and mother of Darcie Ringold. Former bartender at The Shaft and now owner of the same under the new name of Prairie Rose.

Mehaffey, Danielle. Waitress at the Fill-er-Up in Fink in Eda County. A runaway. Daughter of Lianne Mehaffey and half-sister of Patrick Mehaffey.

Mehaffey, Janet Brigid Rose Plunkett. Deceased mother of Lianne Mehaffey.

Mehaffey, Karen Okerlund. Acting sheriff of Eda County. Widow of Patrick Mehaffey, a Bosnian War casualty who lingered in a coma for many years. Daughter of former sheriff, Arne Okerlund, and half-niece of Detective Marek Okerlund, who is four years her junior. Biological mother of Eyre Johnson. Was an outstanding basketball player at the University of South Dakota in Vermillion. Former Army officer in Bosnia and police dispatcher in Sioux Falls. Took over as acting sheriff after her father's stroke. Lives at 22 Okerlund Road in the bungalow where she grew up.

Mehaffey, Lianne. Mother of Patrick Mehaffey and Danielle Mehaffey by different fathers. A drug addict who lives in Omaha, Nebraska.

Mehaffey, Patrick. Deceased husband of Karen Okerlund Mehaffey. An Army medic, he drove over a landmine in Bosnia and was in a coma for many years before his death.

Mock, Mary Hannah. Teenage cousin of Karen Okerlund Mehaffey. Daughter of Elder Sander Mock of the Eder Brethren, an Amish-like sect in Eda County. She is attending high school in Reunion and plans to eventually become a certified midwife. Lives weekdays during the school year with Karen at 22 Okerlund Road.

Nelson, Rusty "Nails." Disabled Vietnam veteran who lives above the old Carnegie Library in Reunion that now houses the county archives. Operates the low-power FM radio station YRUN and reports news from Eda County. Native of Bandit Ridge in Eda County.

Nylander, Tammy. Day-shift dispatcher and jailer for the Eda County Sheriff's Office.

Okerlund, Arne. Former sheriff of Eda County, son of Sheriff Leif Okerlund, father of Karen Okerlund Mehaffey, and half-brother of Marek Okerlund. First married to Hannah Mock and second to Clara Gullick, the widow of his childhood friend. A stroke ended his career as sheriff. He and Clara adopted Clara's grandson and babysit Marek's daughter, Becca. Lived at 22 Okerlund Road until his second marriage. Now lives on Okerlund Road in the old Stan Forsgren house.

Okerlund, Clara Gullick. Widow of Vern Gullick and mother of Deputy Rick Gullick (deceased). Grandmother of Joseph Jaramillo Okerlund. Married to Arne Okerlund after the deaths of her husband and son. Lives on Okerlund Road at the old Stan Forsgren house.

Okerlund, Hannah Mock. Deceased. First wife of Arne Okerlund and mother of Karen Okerlund Mehaffey. Died of ovarian cancer when Karen was in the Army. Raised among the Eder Brethren, she fled as a young woman.

Okerlund, Joseph "Joey" Jaramillo. Toddler son of Rick Gullick (deceased) and Blanca Jaramillo (deceased). Grandson of Vern and Clara Gullick. Adopted by Arne Okerlund when he married the widow Clara Gullick. Becca Okerlund treats him as the brother she lost.

Okerlund, Joseph Leif Manuel. Deceased. Stillborn son of Marek Okerlund and his wife Valencia De Baca. Died with his mother in Albuquerque after their car was hit by a drunk driver.

Okerlund, Leif. Deceased. Former sheriff of Eda County and father of Arne Okerlund by first wife, Kari Halvorsen, and father of Marek Okerlund by second wife, Janina Marek. Grandfather of Karen Okerlund Mehaffey. World War II veteran. His second marriage caused a rift between himself and his elder son (Arne).

Okerlund, (Leif) Marek. Always called by his middle name. Part-time detective for Eda County. Part-time carpenter. Dyslexic. Son of Sheriff Leif Okerlund and second wife, Janina Marek. Half-brother of Arne Okerlund and half-uncle of Karen Okerlund Mehaffey, who is four years his elder. Moved from Reunion to Valeska in Eda County with his mother after his father's death. Left Eda County after high school and ended up in Albuquerque, New Mexico, where he was first a carpenter and then a cop, eventually rising to the rank of homicide detective. Lost his wife, Valencia De Baca, to a drunk driver. Their daughter, Becca, was in the car and survived. Lives at 21 Okerlund Road in the bungalow he spent his childhood in.

Okerlund, Rebecca "Becca" De Baca. Young daughter of Marek Okerlund and Valencia De Baca. A precocious artist, she was mute after losing her mother and unborn brother to a drunk driver but gradually recovered after the move to South Dakota.

Okerlund, Valencia "Val" De Baca. Deceased. Wife of Marek Okerlund. Daughter of Joseph De Baca and New York artist Adrienne Fiat. Killed with her unborn son by a drunk driver in Albuquerque.

Pederson, Harlan. Retired farmer and frequent visitor of the Fill-er-Up diner and gas station in Fink.

Rudibaugh, Judge John Franklin. Also known as "Judge Rudy." Presiding judge at the Eda County courthouse.

Russell, Laura Connor. Childhood friend, basketball teammate, and college roommate of Karen Okerlund Mehaffey. She is the wife of Deputy Walter Russell and mother of three boys. Works as an elementary-school teacher in Reunion.

Russell, Walter "Walrus." Day-shift deputy in the Eda County Sheriff's Office. Originally from Aleford in Eda County and married to Laura Connor. Father of three boys. Pheasant hunter and gun enthusiast.

Solberg, Annika "Nikki" Forsgren. Adopted daughter of Elmer Forsgren, a distant cousin of Karen and Marek. Biological daughter of the Eder Brethren. Made up her surname on leaving for California after high school. Artist and English school teacher in Reunion. Lives off Okerlund

Road in a former one-room schoolhouse. Tutors Becca Okerlund in art. In a relationship with Marek Okerlund.

Sommervold, Agent. Female half of "The Seasons," top guns from the FBI resident agency in Sioux Falls. A native of South Dakota.

Tisher, Norm "Tish." He is the Eda County coroner, with no medical training other than that gleaned as a local mortician. A native of North Dakota.

Two Fingers, Deputy. Swing-shift deputy with the Eda County Sheriff's Office. Mixed maternal heritage of Dakota (Santee), Nakota (Yankton), Mandan, and Arikara. Father (Caucasian) was his mother's rapist. Mother enrolled at Flandreau Reservation in South Dakota but Two Fingers does not meet the blood quantum requirement. Dartmouth graduate and former Air Force pilot.

Van Doren, Andrew. Hal Birchard's estate lawyer in Sioux Falls.

Van Eck, Adam. Reserve deputy on the night shift for the Eda County Sheriff's Office. Former Broadway actor who continues his passion in Sioux Falls.

White, Dr. Oscar Micheaux. Forensic pathologist and native of Sioux Falls. Named for African-American filmmaker Oscar Micheaux, who homesteaded in South Dakota.

Wilson, Radical "Rad." Formerly Jenny Wilson and recently aged out of the foster care system in Sioux Falls. Hard rock fanatic and contestant at the Jam Off.

Wintersgill, Agent. Male half of "The Seasons," top guns from the FBI resident agency in Sioux Falls. A New England native.

ABOUT THE AUTHOR

M.K. Coker grew up on a river bluff in southeastern South Dakota. Part of the Dakota diaspora, the author has lived in half a dozen states, but returns to the prairie at every opportunity. Website: www.mkcoker.com

ACKNOWLEDGEMENTS

I've had this book in mind for some time and it was a pleasure to write. Music was part and parcel of my childhood, given my mother was a choir director. We had no choice but to sing! But I readily admit that my brothers hogged most of the talent.

Much of the plot of this book was inspired by my brother Tim of Vicebox and his synesthete daughter. Brothers Jon and Steve of barbershop (sorry, a cappella!) groups Quartertones and Mellowtones, respectively, were also in the final mix, though they have long since moved on to other musical pursuits. And they've instilled their love of music in their offspring, giving rise to another generation of talented musicians. Bravo, all!

Much applause also goes to the following maestros: my editor Stefanie Spangler Buswell, proofreader Kristina Baker, and beta readers Marjory Coker, Kelli Lapour Cotter, Sheila Molony, and Cherié Weible.